HE WHO IS THE UNIVERSE

Part 1: Paper

A.S. Savi

notionpress.com

INDIA · SINGAPORE · MALAYSIA

To my Nanu, Kuljit Singh Walia

Thank you for everything.

You are the reason this book exists in the first place.

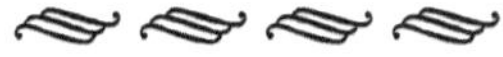

To Anmolbir Singh,

Thanks for being my very first reader.

CONTENTS

Introduction — 1

Prologue One
The Imperfect God — 7

Prologue Two
Into The Freak's Lodge — 15

Chapter One
Asparian — 27

Chapter Two
Files of Fate — 45

Chapter Three
Second Chances — 63

Chapter Four
Bill Blear — 75

Chapter Five
The Span Doorway — 87

Chapter Six
Eternities in Gold — 96

Chapter Seven
Something You Can Die For… — 113

Chapter Eight

Warm Water 135

Chapter Nine

From Books to Bonds 153

Chapter Ten

This Time… I'll Roll the Dice 159

Chapter Eleven

"Hello, Charlie" 179

Chapter Twelve

The Dictator of Destinies 191

Chapter Thirteen

Personal Grudges 204

Chapter Fourteen

Happy Endings 221

Epilogue One

Beyond the Diary 229

Epilogue Two

Strongest Being of the Universe 233

INTRODUCTION
Okay, so everything you're about to read? Completely made up. Characters, triumphs, crazy plot twists – all me, sweating over my keyboard for your amusement. This is my first novel, a world I've built from scratch. Pretty cool, right?
But hold on. Did you hear that? A whisper about breaking the fourth wall? Nah, it must be my imagination. My characters are stuck in this story, like actors on a stage. I control everything… right?
(Suddenly, a loud CRACK echoes through the silence, followed by a faint shimmer along the edge of the page. A tendril of something unseen reaches out, tearing the fabric of the dimension to touch the text.)

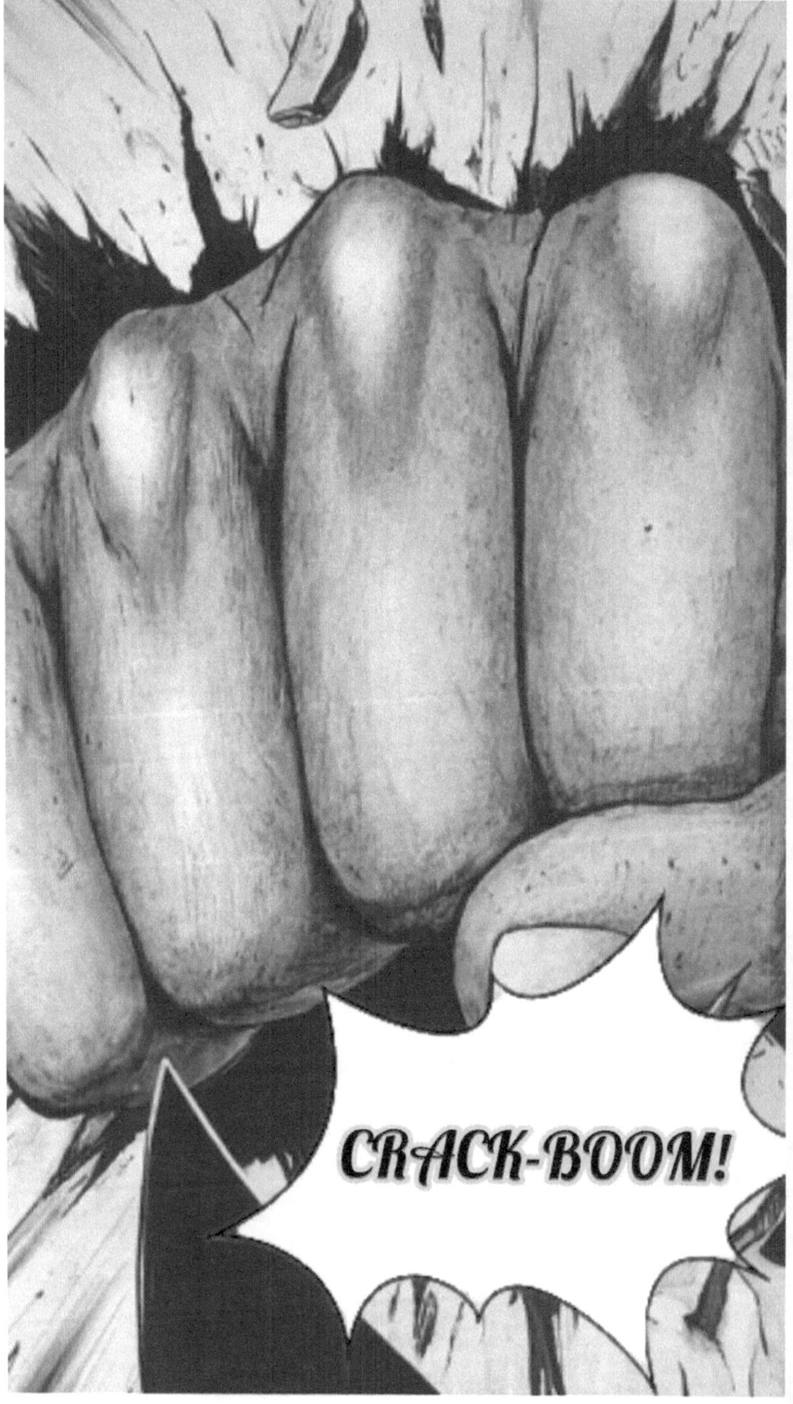
CRACK-BOOM!

Hello Readers!
Alist at your service.

Ah!
Let's
do this

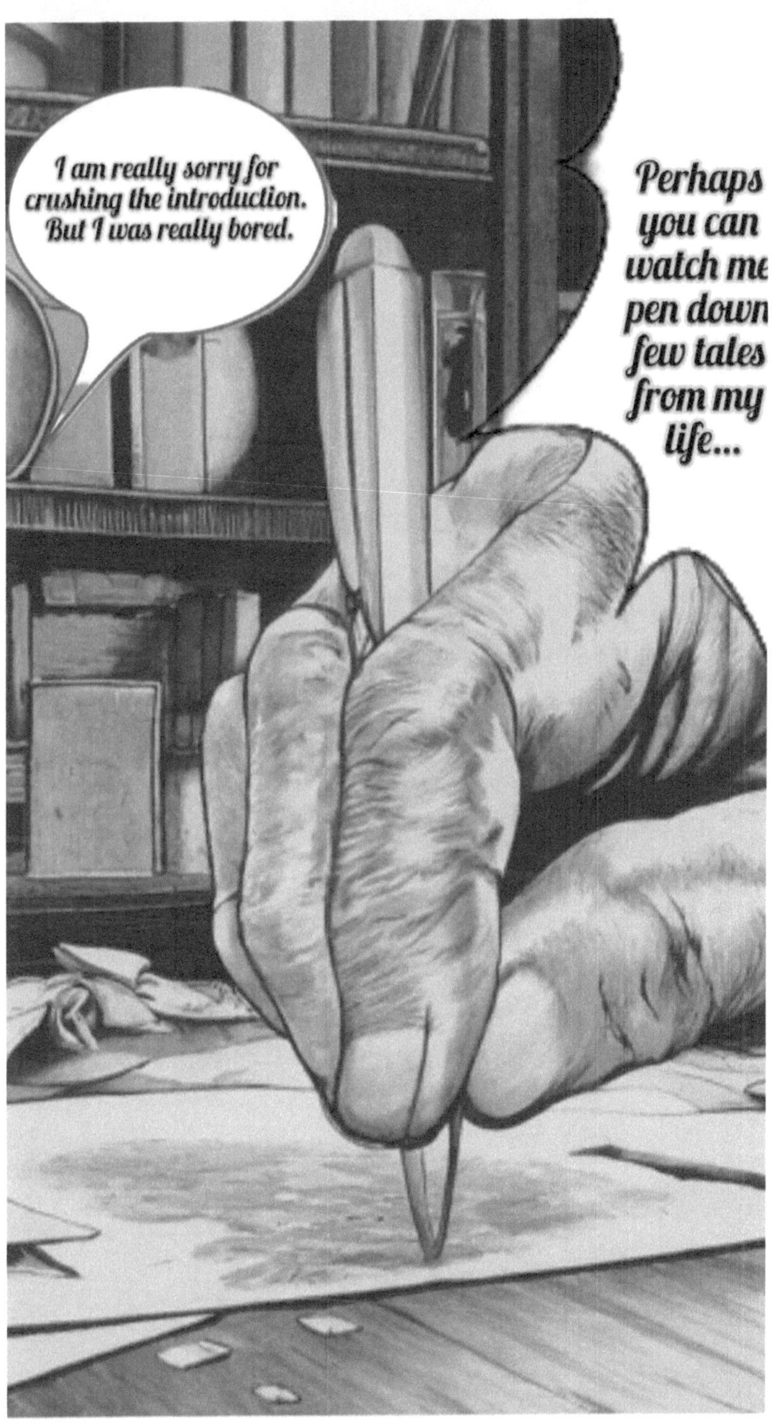

I am really sorry for crushing the introduction. But I was really bored.
Perhaps you can watch me pen down few tales from my life...

THE IMPERFECT GOD

Alist

We all have our theories about God, but what if I told you that I knew Him, that He was my good friend and that I know everything about Him, including His origins? You won't believe me, right? I am still going to tell you.

Yes, I'm talking about the God who sketched the sunset, who colored the cosmos, who drew our destinies. This is no king on a throne, no bearded shepherd in the sky. This is the Weaver, the architect, the very heartbeat of the universe itself.

He who is beyond the universe, yet in the universe, and is the universe. He who has no gender, perhaps even calling Him 'He' won't be grammatically accurate.

He's the only one who could do anything, create anyone, and destroy everything. The only one who cannot be killed, the only one who could control all the realities, all our lives. Though there's just one thing you all might not know: that He wasn't always 'the only one.'

Before there were planets, before there were galaxies, and even before there were stars, the universe was nothing but endless void, darker than the color black itself.

Before the first ember of a star sparked in the infinite black, the cosmos thrummed with life. Countless universal beings, echoes of divinity woven from pure, boundless energy, pulsed within its void.

These weren't gods of gilded thrones and Olympian grandeur, but shapeless beings of pure thought, their forms as fluid as nebulae, and their minds older than time itself.

They could seem like a raven flying in the twilight, a man hovering on the starless night sky, or just a bright white light amidst the eternal darkness.

They conversed in whispers that echoed across eons, sharing knowledge vast as galaxies and forging bonds as intricate as constellations. Yet, harmony, like a star gone supernova, fractured into discord. Disputes, sharp as supernova shards, ignited a war as ancient as existence itself. The war started on a simple question: Who is right? What are the right answers?

There were no superiors or inferiors among the universal beings. Each being, an immortal God, could spawn countless reflections, an army reflected in the void. Victory, however, remained an elusive phantom. None could conquer all; all could conquer none.

Trapped in a mirrored dance, they grappled with an existential truth: **"No one could do anything in a world where everyone could do everything."**

Many wanted to do something, but they didn't know **what**. Many craved to die, but they didn't know **how**. Many wanted to live, but they didn't know **why**.

Hence most, numbed by the futility of choice, retreated into the slumbering depths of the abyss, their echoes fading into the cosmic lullaby.

In the mirrored wasteland of absolute equality, a lone figure stirred. They called him Asparus, a whisper among the slumbering masses, a name that in my native tongue meant: "A God with Belief." Unlike the others, Asparus saw only decay in the reflection of his own unmoored existence. In a world where everyone stood crowned and commoner, where every action birthed its mirrored counterpoint, he saw not freedom, but a stifling paralysis.

No civilization could bloom when all were leaders, no progress when all were builders and none the bricks.

A restless fire simmered in Asparus's eyes, a spark of conviction in a sea of resignation. Asparus wasn't just seeking a solution, but the absolute RIGHT ANSWERS. In his quiet defiance, a silent question crackled: Was this their only reality, or did a path to meaning lay hidden, waiting to be carved out with the chisel of his unwavering belief?

Millenniums passed, or they would have if time existed in his world. Asparus, etched with forgotten hopes, clung to the fringes of existence, a lone ember flickering against the wind. Yet, his will remained unyielding, a beacon in the wasteland.

Then, on a day drowned in silence, he stumbled upon it - a tear in the fabric of reality, a monstrous bruise on the face of the universe. It pulsed with an alien energy, drawing him in with a siren song of secrets and oblivion. The closer he crept, the heavier his form grew, as if the wound itself bled his vital essence.

Was this his ultimate demise, or a terrible gateway to long-sought answers? Fear coiled in his gut, yet a spark of defiance flickered. And Asparus, the God with Belief, stared into its hungry maw.

As he stood before the abyssal wound in reality, a jolt ignited in his mind – a revelation that could rewrite the very fabric of existence.

He remembered the ancient axiom: **"Matter cannot be created nor destroyed."** But the universal beings, he mused, were the exception. They danced with creation, their very bodies being the vessels of infinite energy, shaping and reshaping the cosmos at will.

But destruction of matter was a task that was even beyond the universal beings; hence, death was just a dream for them.

But what if, Asparus thought, his gaze unwavering from the pulsating maw before him, there existed another truth, a hidden corollary to the grand equation? What if, alongside creation's boundless potential, lurked an equal force of destruction, a cosmic predator with jaws hungry for matter itself? **WHAT IF MATTER COULD BE DESTROYED?**

If Asparus had a face, he would have smiled. This gaping wound wasn't just a portal; it was a crucible, a terrifying forge capable of devouring the very essence of things. He had traveled through both the endless end of the universe, yet this revelation was one of a kind.

He spent an eternity - a mere blink in his eye - mastering the abyss's power. Slowly, painstakingly, he shaped it into an instrument of oblivion. A tool named 'The Crux,' if wielded with precision, could unmake what the universal beings had made and were made from.

Was it a blade, honed to a molecular edge, a spear, thrumming with the hunger of the void? Or perhaps a chilling scythe, reaping the stars themselves? Legends differ, whispers lost in the eons. All that remains is the echo of its terrible song.

News of Asparus' weapon, a harbinger of unmaking, spread through the mirrored wasteland like wildfire. Asparus wasn't evil; he just sought answers. He didn't know how he would find them, but he absolutely knew what he had to do first. **A complete annihilation of his kind to finally establish a… SUPREME!**

The other universal beings saw it as the solution to their problem, as a key to their freedom, as a cure to their disease.

But not all embraced the allure of nothingness. Some saw the weapon for what it truly was - a harbinger of tyranny, a means for one to rule over all by wielding the power to unmake existence itself.

These dissenters, these whispers of rebellion, were met with Asparus' wrath. They were born of infinite energy, yes, but even deities weren't immune to the finality of absolute annihilation. One by one, they fell, all infinite of them. **Finally, THERE WAS JUST ONE GOD IN THE SKY!**

The tapestry of night shimmered with the cold fire of fallen gods. Each pinprick of light, they say, was a star forged from the ashes of an immortal being, consumed in Asparus' relentless purge. The massacre yielded to a grim waltz of oblivion, leaving the universe littered with celestial debris.

He walked among the wreckage, a titan in a graveyard of giants. Galaxies, accidentally formed from the remnants of the dead, appeared as cosmic pebbles kicked aside in his quest for nothingness. Solar systems were miniature gems. Yet, amidst this rubble, something unexpected caught his eye—a flicker of defiant life.

Amidst the desolate expanse, there it was — a spark of defiance, a defiant bloom in the wasteland. Life, fragile and fleeting, had taken root on a wayward planet, a testament to the universe's inherent resilience.

Asparus could have snuffed it out with a mere thought, another speck of ash on his broom. But as he gazed upon this tapestry of writhing forms, a flicker of doubt ignited within him. The imperfect form of the mess he created gave him an idea.

If Asparus had eyes, he would have cried with tears of joy. For what he saw in that life was a hope, a chance, a purpose. Not to obliterate but to mend became Asparus' new creed.

He wielded the same energy that once devoured stars, now to sculpt celestial nurseries, coaxing forth swirling light to cradle nascent suns. In his hands, galaxies pirouetted, their orbits tweaked to cradle planets humming with the nascent song of life. He scattered cosmic dust like stardust, birthing continents upon barren rocks, weaving rivers of molten gold into veins pulsing with lifeblood.

And that is how, my friends, the universe we know was formed!

None of Asparus's kind ever thought about creating creatures like us. **Creatures that were so weak had limited skills, were bound by time, and had an end. Nothing seemed more beautiful to him.**

Creatures that actually needed him, whose lives he could alter, whose stories he could watch. Who knew that the world created by mistake would have given his world a home?

Asparus hoped that the answers he didn't find in his immortal world would be found in the world of mortals.

Perhaps we've all encountered Asparus at least once in our lives, although we never recognize him as he could disguise himself as anything.

He could be a frog who hops in the rain, a lion trapped in a cage, or even a friend who attends school with us. He had lived innumerable lives in every corner of the universe where life subsisted. He is at some places once at a time and sometimes everywhere all at once.

Miracles, as we call them, these unexpected brushstrokes upon the tapestry of our lives. It was always Asparus who intervened to change our script.

Asparus is everything we imagine in the Almighty God. He is the echo of our dreams of the Divine, the one who transcends time, the one who can rewrite destiny with a flicker of his will. **But beneath the tapestry of omnipotence—despite everything I've told you about him—there's just one thing that he's not—perfect.**

INTO THE FREAK'S LODGE

Aamira

Let's just say my neighbor, Mr. Alist, is quite the fiction writer. Unlike the divine pronouncements found in dusty religious texts, his portrayal of God reads more like a whimsical fever dream. The man even claims to be on a first-name basis with the Almighty himself. Now, that's what I call a healthy dose of delusion, served with a side of questionable sanity.

Now, you might be wondering how I, Aamira Khan, resident magnifying glass enthusiast and self-proclaimed mistress of mystery (though some might scoff and say "nosy parker"), ended up privy to Mr. Alist's theological fanfiction. Well, buckle up, buttercup, because this is where things get interesting.

Let's just say my penchant for investigating literally anything that holds still, including flower beds and couch cushions, has earned me a colorful reputation. My college buddies see me as a real-life Sherlock, albeit one with a penchant for poking around in people's trash.

Yes, you read that right. Trash. Don't ask. It's a dark corner of my personality I'd rather not explore.

Anyway, while on a recent spelunking expedition through Mr. Alist's garbage (hey, a detective's gotta do what a detective's gotta do), I stumbled upon a treasure trove – 4 crumpled pages, stapled together like a deranged ransom note. It was filled with Mr. Alist's fantastical scribblings about a character named Asparus.

But before we delve into that existential rabbit hole, let me properly introduce myself. I'm a whirlwind of curiosity encased in a brown-eyed body. My IQ? Well, let's just say it's so high it would make Stephen Hawking look like a toddler with a rattle. (Though, to be fair, the man was a genius, and toddlers are adorable, so maybe that analogy needs work.)

My idol? My sister, Rumi, a superstar detective who nabs bad guys like they're going out of style. Well, she used to nab bad guys. Now, thanks to a pesky hit list with her name scrawled across it in bold, we're hiding out in a Mexican ghost town that makes dust storms look exciting.

Let me tell you, this place is the definition of backwater. We're talking Stone Age with a side of cacti and tumbleweeds. The only thing more deserted than this town is my social life. And don't even get me started on the losing streak I'm on against Rumi.

Sudoku? Obliterated. Monopoly? Bankrupted. Checkers? You guessed it, pummeled. Even a simple coin toss – you know, the game where it's literally fifty-fifty to lose – somehow ends in defeat 8 times in a row. It's like the universe itself is conspiring against me.

As if that wasn't enough, the only neighbors we have are this sweet but perpetually clueless couple with a gaggle of gremlin children who seem to exist for the sole purpose of driving me insane.

Just the other day, I found a lovely message scrawled on my wall in what looked like crayon dipped in drool: *"Here Lives the Cranky Mean Girl."* Now, while the description could technically apply to either Rumi – who, by the way, is about as mean as a kitten with a belly full of cream – or myself, the whole ordeal left me feeling a tad triggered.

So, here I was, stuck in this technological wasteland, with nothing to keep me company but my trusty magnifying glass, a never-ending inner monologue, and the occasional existential crisis.

But hey, at least there's Mr. Alist. The man may be equal parts odd and off-putting, but there's no denying he's shrouded in an aura of peculiarity. Plus, the mysterious goings-on around him are the closest thing I have to entertainment these days.

So, stay tuned, dear reader, as I, Aamira Khan, amateur sleuth extraordinaire, unravel the mysteries of Mr. Alist, his God-infused fiction, and maybe, just maybe, find a way to get those infernal children to lay off the permanent marker.

Let's just start with Mr. Alist's appearance. Imagine a man sculpted from granite, framed by a majestic beard that would make a Viking jealous. His long hair, once a wild mane, is now tamed into a topknot, a concession to practicality perhaps.

Adorning his upper lip, a meticulously groomed handlebar mustache stands as a testament to his pride and attention to detail. Towering at a respectable 6 feet 3 inches, his age lingers somewhere between 45 and a touch of "seen-it-all." But the most arresting sight is definitely the cybernetic eye that he wears occasionally.

Now about his residence…

Spanning thousands of desolate meters, this barren wasteland is home to just 3 structures: 2 modest houses and Mr. Alist's grand mansion. Calling it a mansion is an insult to actual mansions; it's more like a crumbling monument, perhaps misplaced from the sixteenth century.

Faded murals adorn the weathered stone walls, while the grand entrance door boasts a healthy dose of rust at the bottom.

Most windows resemble spiderweb showcases, and the entire structure leans precariously, like a weary giant.

Yet, according to our chatty neighbors, Mr. Noah and Mrs. Emily, this architectural disaster is brand new. One wonders, why build a house that looks like it was cobbled together from yesterday's leftovers?

Mr. Alist, a man of few words and, it seems, even fewer social graces, keeps to himself. Apparently, he wasn't a huge fan of their son, Drake (bless his adventurous soul), who may or may not have received a well-deserved knuckle sandwich for attempting a midnight mansion infiltration. Sneaking around someone's property is a no-no, but come on, Drake called me mean! The nerve!

My own foray into Mr. Alist's world involved 2 awkward encounters. The first, a meet-and-greet with yours truly and my ever-so-charming sister, Rumi. Eager to befriend our fellow residents, we approached the mansion with hopeful smiles.

Initially hesitant, Mr. Alist seemed inexplicably swayed by Rumi's undeniable beauty and dulcet tones. There was a brief, frankly creepy phase where he flirted with her (and to my horror, she seemed to enjoy it!). The pièce de résistance?

He whisked Rumi inside after a particularly bad pick-up line, leaving me staring at the closed door like a rejected puppy. It was as rude as it was bizarre. My own sister, abandoning me in the cold embrace of social exclusion!

Rumi spent what could only be described as a date-like eternity within the mansion's dusty halls. Upon her return, she practically glowed. It was like a ray of sunshine had pierced the dreary wasteland of her existence.

She couldn't stop raving about Mr. Alist's dulcet tones (apparently, they sang duets?), their profound conversations, and how he reminded her of the good ol' days in Boston – you know, the ones with mom, Dad, and a fulfilling job. This one meeting apparently reignited the spark of joy in her life, and she couldn't wait to see Mr. Alist again.

The next morning, however, wasn't quite as rosy. Brimming with topics for their second rendezvous, Rumi approached the mansion with a shy smile. Before she could even utter a greeting, Mr. Alist slammed the door shut with the emotional range of a brick wall.

Poor Rumi. One minute she's singing love songs, the next she's facing the social equivalent of a door in the face.

Needless to say, she wasn't best pleased. "Jerry?" She mumbled his name like a mantra, her eyes welling up as she kicked a nearby pebble. There was a heartbreaking cocktail of confusion, anger, and a touch of "seriously, dude?" swirling on her face.

It was clear Rumi had developed a bit of a crush on him, which, considering the age gap, was slightly unsettling from my perspective. Mr. Alist's callous behavior added another name, "Rumi" to his ever-growing list of Alist-haters, joining the ranks of Mr. Noah, Mrs. Emily, and their children, Drake, Liza, Lilly, and Marshall.

Now, the burning question: did I, the future detective extraordinaire, join the ranks of the Alist-haters? The answer, my dear reader, is both simple and utterly complex. On one hand, logic dictated that I despise him for crushing my sister's fragile heart. On the other hand, a true detective never jumps to conclusions. Thus began "Operation: Expose Alist."

Phase one involved a thorough interrogation of Rumi. Though understandably glum and resistant to Alist-related discussions, I managed to glean a few nuggets of information.

Apparently, the man was a vault of secrets, revealing nothing about himself except his peculiar nickname, "Jerry."

He was a great listener, but whenever Rumi inquired about the curious mansion, he'd skillfully dodge the topic and distract her with music and lame jokes. No wonder she liked him – funny nature, talent to sing, and patience to listen to the jibber-jabber of a girl – all the qualities of an ideal man.

Fueled by an investigator's insatiable curiosity (and perhaps a touch of sibling rivalry), I graduated from interrogation to infiltration.

Phase 2: Peeping Through Rumi's Binoculars commenced, transforming my room into a makeshift spy central. My vantage point offered a prime view of Mr. Alist's bedroom, but let's just say the intel I gathered wasn't exactly Earth-shattering.

Here's the scoop: Alist seemed to be a man of routine. A large chunk of his day was spent hunched over a hefty notebook on his desk, scribbling away like a man possessed. In between these literary marathons, he'd take breaks to sprawl on his bed – though I never witnessed any actual sleep happening, not even during the nighttime hours (in his bedroom, at least).

The only other sounds emanating from the creepy mansion were a daily two-hour lunchtime serenade courtesy of Mr. Alist himself. Apparently, the man possessed a set of pipes and a penchant for lovelorn ballads. Maybe it was a reflection of his past, or perhaps he just had a thing for the genre. Who knew?

Despite my valiant efforts with the binoculars, Phases One and Two left me no closer to unraveling the enigma that was Mr. Alist. Hence, it was time to unleash my ultimate weapon – Phase Three. But first, a minor obstacle.

Christmas Eve found me trudging through knee-deep snow, a determined glint in my eye, and a rapidly diminishing sense of hope.

As I approached the imposing structure, I couldn't help but notice the handiwork of a particularly "gifted" soul (read: Drake, the neighborhood nuisance) scrawled across the door in all its artistic glory: "The Freak's Lodge." Charming.

The usual entrance, I knew from my intel gathering, was a dead end – Mr. Alist favored a more clandestine backdoor strategy.

Taking a deep breath, I knocked – politely, of course. Silence. Twenty minutes later, the same story. My inner zen master remained remarkably calm (for the first 10 minutes), prompting a repeat performance. After another 30 minutes of fruitless knocking (and the zen master's fiery demise), I resorted to a more forceful approach.

Basically, I turned into a banshee, pounding on the door with numb fingers and hollering like a woman possessed, "Mr. Alist! Open up!" for all the world to hear.

An hour later, the torture ended. The door creaked open, revealing Mr. Alist in all his glory. Compared to me, bundled in 5 layers like a Michelin Man, he sported a sleeveless t-shirt and shorts.

Clearly, his internal furnace ran on a different fuel source. He scowled, "Ah, what do you want?" His question hung in the air as thick as the snowflakes swirling around us.

"Rumi lost her necklace," I blurted, channeling my inner damsel in distress. "The one from her mom, you know? She thinks she might have left it here. Would you mind awfully if I took a quick peek?"

He pondered this weighty request for a few seconds before grunting out an unenthusiastic, "Okay," in a voice that strangely resembled Johnny Cash.

This Mr. Alist seemed a far cry from the charmer Rumi described. He shuffled past me, favoring one leg as if harboring a hidden injury, and plopped down at the dining table, his eyes glued to a DVD player. The man barely acknowledged my existence.

Stepping inside the mansion for the first time was like entering a museum of oddities. Dustbins overflowed with trophies and medals, while a mountain of broken crockery occupied the opposite corner. The bedroom walls were adorned with a gallery of empty picture frames – 40 of them, to be exact.

Mr. Alist's personal quarters resembled a hoarder's paradise – flickering tube lights, decrepit furniture, and half-melted candles creating a delightfully creepy ambiance.

The pièce de résistance, however, was a brand new, hundred-inch monstrosity of a television dominating the kitchen – a space that could easily house a small family reunion. Even more peculiar, the kitchen was devoid of any food, utensils, or cookware. Just a lonely coffee maker, a few mugs, sugar containers, and enough cappuccino mix to fuel a small army.

My locket quest turned up drier than a desert tumbleweed. Emerging from the kitchen empty-handed, I found Mr. Alist still glued to the DVD player, a statue lost in contemplation. The man hadn't even blinked. Finally, I shattered the silence.

"No luck on the necklace front, Mr. Alist," I ventured.

His head swiveled slowly in my direction, a flicker of life returning to his eyes. He drained the last of his coffee with a sigh, then grunted another unenthusiastic, "Okay. Maybe you should head out then."

With that, he shuffled toward his bedroom, a limp barely noticeable in his gait. Halfway there, he stopped abruptly, his gaze falling on the empty coffee mug clutched in his hand. In a move that defied his sluggish demeanor, he hurled the mug with surprising force against the wall. It shattered spectacularly, adding its porcelain shrapnel to the ever-growing mountain of broken crockery in the corner. Well, that explained the debris, but it opened a whole new can of questions about Mr. Alist's temperament.

By the time the clock chimed 20 to midnight, I was back home. Rumi, mid-scramble in the kitchen, shrieked my name. "Aamira! Where have you been? Visiting Jerry?"

"Just retrieving your missing locket," I replied with a sly grin.

"Locket? What locket?" Her confusion quickly morphed into suspicion. "And what on Earth are you doing with Jerry's diary?"

A smug silence was my only response. I ascended the stairs, a mischievous glint in my eye. The real mission, you see, had only just begun the moment I crossed the threshold of that peculiar mansion. Phase Three: Into the Freak's Lodge was afoot.

You see, gaining entry was paramount to unraveling the enigma of Mr. Alist. The fabricated locket story was merely my Trojan horse. During my interrogation (ahem, friendly conversation) with Rumi, I gleaned the existence of a book titled *"He Who Is the Universe,"* Mr. Alist's supposed autobiography.

What better way to crack a man's secrets than to delve into his own words? Thus, pilfering his diary became the centerpiece of my operation.

Now, some might question my relentless pursuit of a man who, for all I knew, was just another rich eccentric with a social aversion. But amidst the bizarre happenings surrounding Mr. Alist, one detail defied all logic. According to Noah, on their return from a month-long vacation, they found a fully constructed mansion where none had stood before. And mansion wasn't quite the word for Mr. Alist's peculiar abode. It was a skyscraper, a fifty-six-floor behemoth that scraped the clouds and yet counting.

With the stolen diary cradled in my hands, I brushed away the dust from its cover and cracked it open at midnight. With a silent prayer that its pages held the key to Mr. Alist's mysteries, I began my Christmas reading...

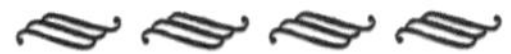

*Perhaps we have reached a million miles
from where we started, yet have never moved on.*

~ Alist

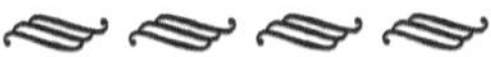

CHAPTER ONE

ASPARIAN

Alist (Diary)

The dust motes danced in the shaft of light filtering through the grimy mansion window, landing on a faded scrap of paper clutched in my hand. Bloodstains dotted the edges. **It was a fragment of my childhood, an essay from a time when dreams were simpler, smaller.**

"Little dreams are too underrated," the scrawled handwriting declared. **"Why strive for godlike heights when happiness whispers from cozy corners? Scaling impossible tasks isn't the only path; sometimes, joy blooms in the quietest gardens."**

A smile tugged at my lips. **"I yearn for a haven of laughter and melody, where shadows of loved ones dance on the walls, and every note I sing becomes a bridge, drawing us closer, erasing the ache of absence and filling the void with harmony – a small, perfect home."**

My gaze then swept across my cavernous, empty mansion. Trophies and medals lay abandoned in a dustbin, while a classical lament drifted from the forgotten DVD player. A bitter chuckle escaped my lips. **"Hell! How did I end up here?"**

The faded paper, a portal to the past, transformed into a pristine sheet. My body shrank, mirroring the transformation.

I was 8 again, ecstatic over a perfect score on my essay, **"Where do I see myself in the end?"** The pristine white sheet proclaimed an A+, and I envisioned my parents' faces alight with pride. The joy bubbled in my chest.

Three years had passed since my brother, Sane, disappeared. His absence loomed, a specter over my parents' anniversary celebrations. Determined to bring a flicker of happiness back to our home, I insisted on celebrating. Dwelling in the past, I reasoned, wouldn't bring him back. Also, this time I had a perfect gift for them: a test sheet with a perfect score.

Everything was normal in my life apart from a peculiar girl who followed my every step. She peered through my window, materialized at every park visit, even enrolled in my school despite the distance. Stranger still, she'd been our neighbor 2 years prior, inexplicably moving when we did.

As for friends, the soldiers residing in the army quarters were the only ones I had apart from school. Man, they were an extraordinary bunch – brave, cool, and always up for a good time.

Army Quarter building, 1:15 P.M.

News of Captain Demy's return with his squad after a successful mission sent a thrill through me. I raced to their quarters, greeted warmly by Mr. Manny, the vice-captain, "Well, well, look who's here – our friendly neighborhood singer!"

The soldiers buzzed with celebratory energy. "Come on, Jerry, sing with us!" they called out, beverages in hand. Mr. Manny, wielding a slice of cake and a frosting-coated plastic knife, approached. "Looking for Captain Demy?"

"Good afternoon, sir," I piped, eyes wide. With a nod, Mr. Manny led me to the rooftop.

Captain Demy and his right hand man, Mr. George, were engrossed in birdwatching, a friendly competition to identify birds perched hundreds of meters away.

The new recruit, Mr. Henry, gaped as Mr. George relied on binoculars while Captain Demy effortlessly observed with just his piercing blue eyes.

"Captain Demy, can you truly see that far without binoculars?" Henry exclaimed, utterly bewildered. "I can hardly make out anything from here. Frankly, from such a distance, I doubt if anyone could see clearly, if at all."

Curiosity bubbling, I blurted out before Captain Demy could answer, "He's no normie. He's an Asparian."

"Asparian?" Henry echoed, utterly lost.

"They're descendants of the first humans," I said, the explanation tumbling out of me, fueled by curiosity. "Masters of the 5 senses. Legend tells of the God, Asparus, who encountered the first human, Surapsa, on this planet. It was a sight that awed even the omnipotent being. Petroglyphs found there speak of Asparus living among them for a year, sharing his wisdom and elevating their way of life. Before leaving, the stories say, he blessed Surapsa with unique abilities, making him superior to any other creature in the universe. Surapsa's descendants inherited these gifts and became known as the Asparians, the blessed race. Their home country was Asparia, named after God, himself."

Mr. Henry stood speechless; his brow furrowed as he tried to grapple with the avalanche of information I'd unleashed in response to his simple two-word question.

"The strongest creatures possess the greatest instincts," Mr. Manny chimed in, elaborating on their prowess. "Moreover, the eyes of an Asparian hold the remarkable ability to see a hundred times farther than the average human eye. They can sense danger, move faster, and even boast lifespans exceeding 3 centuries."

Mr. Henry was astonished to learn about such superior beings, finding it hard to believe most of it. He cast a different gaze at Captain Demy, looking at him as if he were an entirely new person.

Standing out amidst the soldiers in their modern fatigues, Captain Demy was a stark contrast. He wore medieval iron armor and a flowing blue cape, resembling a prince from a bygone era. Mr. Henry, overwhelmed, bombarded him with questions. "Why the archaic attire? Why a bow and arrows when everyone else carried firearms?"

"The armor I wear is to carry my ancestors with me into battle," Captain Demy replied with pride. "The bow connects me to my culture and reminds me of the traditional fighting methods of my people. It's also about testing my skill, not holding anything back, and embracing the struggle for the fun of it."

Mr. Manny, ever the showman, corroborated Demy's claims. "He could disarm the entire squad with that bow if he wanted to. He's one of the strongest soldiers I've ever seen."

Army Quarter building, 1:41 P.M.

Captain Demy ushered Mr. Henry toward his quarters, the camaraderie between them evident. "Let's get you settled in," he said with a reassuring smile. "Tomorrow, I'll personally brief you on your duties and how we operate as a squad."

Captain Demy wasn't just cool; he **radiated** coolness. It emanated from him like sunshine, effortless and contagious. He never seemed to break a sweat, even under pressure, and his smile could light up a room. Skinny and peace-loving as I was, Captain Demy was my ultimate role model.

He turned to me, his gaze softening as we all descended down the stairs. "How's your father doing these days, kid?"

I eagerly shared the details of my surprise for him, mentioning a slight improvement in his condition compared to previous

years. Demy commended my thoughtfulness, acknowledging the maturity it took for someone my age to understand the complexities of a parent's struggles.

Reaching Mr. Henry's room, they discovered it locked. Mr. Manny, ever the forgetful one, had misplaced the key. Unfazed, Demy calmly requested, "May I borrow that for a moment?"

He took the plastic knife Manny held and, in a single, swift motion, severed the padlock clean in 2. Manny offered a nonchalant smirk, as if this feat were commonplace, while both Mr. Henry and I gaped in astonishment.

"How on Earth...?" Mr. Henry stammered, bewildered. **"Steel with a plastic cake knife?"**

"It's all about blows," Captain Demy replied. **"Once you understand the right amount of pressure, speed, and technique, you can cut steel with plastic, wood with rubber, stone with glass. Water, a mere liquid, when propelled with enough pressure and speed through a water jet, can even cut diamond."**

Army Quarter building, 7:02 P.M.

The clock tower chimed 7, casting a warm glow into Mr. Henry's room as he peered out the window. The soldiers celebrated their victory with boisterous laughter and lively dancing around a crackling bonfire in the heart of the nearby community park. Just then, Captain Demy materialized in the doorway with his characteristic quiet presence.

"Not joining the festivities?" he inquired, leaning casually against the doorframe.

Mr. Henry rose from his bed, his gaze lingering on the joyous scene outside. "I wasn't part of their victory today," he responded thoughtfully. "Perhaps next time, after I've proven myself on a mission, I'll deserve to celebrate alongside them."

Captain Demy's eyes reflected understanding and a hint of respect for the new recruit's sincerity. "Care to join me for a walk, Mr. Henry? It's a beautiful evening, and I'd appreciate the company."

Grateful for the offer and eager to bond with the esteemed captain, Mr. Henry readily accepted. As they ventured out into the twilight, the distant echoes of the soldiers' merriment still lingered in the air. Curious about his new environment, Demy inquired about the other soldiers.

Mr. Henry spoke with genuine admiration, detailing each man's unique personality. He described Mr. Manny as a constant source of amusement and positive energy, while Mr. George, though initially stern, possessed a wellspring of compassion beneath the surface. Finally, he turned to Captain Demy, his voice filled with awe.

"You, Captain Demy, are unlike anyone I've ever met. A true leader, a man of remarkable ability."

A flicker of humility crossed Demy's face as he countered gently, "The most remarkable? Compared to the people of Asparia, I am but a shadow."

Intrigued by this revelation, Mr. Henry pressed on, barely daring to believe his ears. "People even more extraordinary than you, sir? And speaking of Asparia, that young fellow, Jerry, seems quite knowledgeable about the subject."

"Of course, Jerry is." A deep chuckle rumbled from Demy's chest. "He is an Asparian himself."

Mr. Henry's curiosity flared. "There's another Asparian here?" he exclaimed.

Captain Demy began a reply, "Well, that's—" but his words were cut short.

In a heartbeat, he shifted into a defensive stance, his eyes fixed on a hidden threat. Two five-inch iron nails, propelled with deadly force, hurtled toward them.

With lightning reflexes, Captain Demy snatched them both mid-air, inches from Mr. Henry's head. A cold sweat prickled Mr. Henry's skin as he realized how close he had come to a gruesome demise.

"Run!" Captain Demy barked, hurling the nails back with astonishing power in the direction they came from. Still reeling from the shock, Mr. Henry hesitated for a moment.

Captain Demy wasted no time, grabbing his arm and leading him into the narrow alley between 2 houses, seeking refuge from the unseen attackers.

Hidden in the shadows, Mr. Henry tried to make sense of the sudden chaos. Moments ago, they were engaged in a casual conversation. Now, here they were, unarmed and clad in sleepwear, facing a brutal assault.

"Ambush!" Captain Demy explained in a hushed, serious tone. "Five attackers were lurking behind that house. They're using high-powered nail guns, likely aiming for a silent kill to avoid alerting the residents."

"Two down, I believe," Captain Demy continued, scaling the house with surprising agility. "My aim with those nails was true. A single hit from these poison-coated projectiles is enough to bring a man down."

"Poison?" Mr. Henry gasped, scrambling after Captain Demy. A wave of terror washed over him, tempered by a flicker of relief. The enemy numbers had been reduced, but fear remained a constant companion. He found a sliver of solace in Captain Demy's unwavering confidence, a sense that even without weapons, the captain could handle the situation.

Reaching the rooftop, Captain Demy helped Mr. Henry up and offered a reassuring pat on the shoulder. "Don't worry," he said, his keen eyes scanning the surrounding area.

His enhanced Asparian vision pierced the darkness, allowing him to see clearly despite the night. He spotted their comrades, still celebrating safely in the park, roughly 4 hundred meters away. A new concern furrowed his brow as he noticed another group of heavily armed, unidentified men approaching the park.

"Three attackers here, but they're not the ones who initiated the assault," Captain Demy muttered, his voice laced with growing concern. He turned to Mr. Henry, his expression grim. "We have more company on the way."

Five figures emerged from the shadows onto the rooftop with an unsettling grace. Cloaked in the sleek, obsidian uniforms of Casa, the most technologically advanced nation on the planet, they were a chilling vision of futuristic warfare. Centuries ahead of the rest of the world, Casa boasted unimaginable weaponry.

The intruders bristled with an arsenal of deadly tools – nail guns, pistols, ammunition belts, and stun batons. Their menacing appearance was accentuated by strange, mechanical bands encircling their necks, arms, and knees.

Captain Demy couldn't mask his surprise. All 5 attackers stood unharmed, defying his calculations. Two should have succumbed to the poisoned nails he launched. This unexpected development cast a heavy shadow over the situation.

Mr. Henry, a complete novice in this life-or-death struggle, felt a surge of panic. Though possessing decent combat skills, his lack of weaponry left him utterly vulnerable. The odds were stacked overwhelmingly against them.

Casa's military hierarchy was evident in the ranking system displayed on their uniforms. Stars, ranging from one to 5, signified an individual's strength and experience.

Leading the group was a five-star officer, an imposing figure with a shaved head, bulging muscles, and a dominating presence. His malevolent grin left no room for doubt about his murderous intent. With a curt nod, he signaled his subordinates to commence the attack.

A relentless barrage of nails erupted from the 4 Casa assailants' guns. Captain Demy displayed a breathtaking display of agility, effortlessly dodging the incoming projectiles.

His movements were not only self-preserving but also protective. He continuously repositioned Mr. Henry away from the hail of nails, catching them with his bare hands and even deflecting them mid-air in a desperate attempt to thwart the attackers.

Captain Demy formulated a two-pronged attack. He planned to disable one attacker with a powerful punch and send a well-aimed nail hurtling toward the other. However, his strategy encountered an unforeseen obstacle.

As his fist connected with the first assailant's jaw, a searing pain erupted from his hand. It burned with an intensity that threatened to consume him.

Simultaneously, the nail he hurled at the second attacker inexplicably veered off course, as if an invisible barrier deflected it.

This unexpected development threw Captain Demy off balance, both literally and figuratively. The searing pain in his burned hand hampered his usually exceptional agility.

Spotting a deadly nail hurtling toward Mr. Henry, fired by one of the attackers on the right, Captain Demy reacted with lightning speed. Pushing his physical limits, he lunged forward in a desperate attempt to intercept the projectile.

With a remarkable display of reflexes, he managed to stop the nail with his foot, albeit at a cost. The nail pierced his shoe, but with a skillful maneuver of his toes, he narrowly avoided contact with the poisoned tip.

Meanwhile, thrust into the heart of a battle he never anticipated, Mr. Henry found himself paralyzed with fear. He slumped to the ground, his head bowed in a gesture of surrender.

Captain Demy, ever the protector, echoed the words he had spoken earlier, his voice laced with unwavering conviction, "Everything will be fine." Mr. Henry lifted his head, a sliver of hope flickering within him.

Seizing the opportunity presented by Captain Demy's act of protecting Mr. Henry, the leader of the attackers closed the distance with stealthy movements. He wielded a stun baton, a weapon capable of discharging a staggering 10 thousand volts of electricity upon contact. With a swift strike, he delivered a brutal blow to Captain Demy's neck.

The impact sent Captain Demy crumpling to the ground, his consciousness teetering on the brink. As he lay there, vulnerable, and defenseless, another volley of deadly nails rained down upon him and Mr. Henry.

In a display of selfless heroism, Captain Demy ignored the nail targeting him and mustered every ounce of remaining strength to crawl toward Mr. Henry, shielding him with his own body.

He was mere inches away from his comrade when a nail struck his left shoulder. Another found its mark, plunging deep into Mr. Henry's abdomen.

The poison coursing through Mr. Henry's veins inflicted excruciating pain. His complexion rapidly transformed into a ghastly shade of purple.

Clutching at his wound, he drew a final, shallow breath. As his voice faded, he managed to utter a single word in Captain Demy's direction, "You were…" Tragically, the poor soul couldn't complete his sentence.

"Any ordinary human would have succumbed to the poison within moments, let alone endure the 10 thousand volts you received," the leader remarked, approaching Captain Demy, who struggled to stay conscious and maintain any semblance of composure. "But you are no ordinary human, are you? Perhaps this poison is not meant to kill an Asparian."

Witnessing Captain Demy's precarious state, the leader revealed a chilling truth. He explained that regardless of Captain Demy's exceptional speed, his efforts were futile as he couldn't make physical contact with the attackers.

The strange, mechanized bands encircling their bodies – a basic device from the technologically advanced nation of Casa – generated an electromagnetic shield that enveloped their bodies.

This impenetrable defense system could withstand even grenades and rocket launchers. In fact, nothing in the world had ever breached these seemingly invincible shields.

"What is your purpose?" Captain Demy rasped, his voice barely audible, his hands trembling from the after-effects of the electric shock.

"What was that?" the leader inquired, feigning ignorance as he cupped his ear and let out a condescending chuckle. "I can't quite hear you."

Mustering remaining strength, Captain Demy roared, locking eyes with the leader, "I SAID, WHAT'S YOUR PURPOSE?" The raw pain coursing through his body did little to diminish the fire in his eyes.

"Our purpose, you ask?" the leader replied, a cruel smile twisting his lips. "Well, we were sent here all the way from Casa to assassinate Mr. Mouse."

"Mr. Mouse? That's Jerry's father!" Captain Demy muttered in his mind, a new wave of worry washing over him.

"Considering the lengthy journey we undertook," the leader continued, his voice dripping with sadistic amusement, "simply eliminating one person wouldn't satisfy our sense of honor. Hence, we've decided to make a game of it and exterminate anyone else we stumble upon. All for our own amusement, of course."

"I'll slit your throat!" Captain Demy roared, his vision blurring at the edges. His heart hammered against his ribs, a frantic drumbeat against the backdrop of his throbbing shoulder wound.

The leader's amusement morphed into a chilling sneer. His soldiers, emboldened, joined in with a chorus of jeering laughter. "Kill me?" he scoffed. "You can't even touch me. This shield is practically diamond-hard, maybe even stronger."

A spark ignited in Captain Demy's mind. His own words echoed in his head: **"It's all about blows. Once you understand the right amount of pressure, speed, and technique, you can cut steel with plastic, wood with rubber, stone with glass."** But could he push the principle to its very limits?

He assessed the scene in a split second – the attackers relishing his agony, the leader basking in his perceived victory. With a surge of raw Asparian instinct, Captain Demy summoned every last shred of his remaining energy. His normally light blue eyes deepened into an inky indigo, a telltale sign of an Asparian channeling their stored power.

Taking a deep, steadying breath, Captain Demy launched himself off the ground in a defiance that belied his near-death state. The leader, caught off guard by this sudden burst of speed from a seemingly broken man, lunged forward with his stun baton.

With a blur of movement, Captain Demy dodged both the baton and the volley of 4 nails his attackers unleashed. Ignoring the searing pain in his shoulder, he ripped out the lodged nail and, in the fastest throw he'd ever executed, hurled it at the leader's neck. His aim was true, intended to pierce the shield and silence his tormentor.

The world seemed to slow down. The other attackers watched in stunned disbelief as a hairline crack snaked across the leader's electromagnetic shield. But just as hope flared in Captain Demy's chest, the unthinkable happened.

The iron nail, imbued with his last desperate surge of power, inexplicably snapped in half, the broken tip clattering harmlessly to the ground. The crack on the leader's shield, a testament to Captain Demy's near-breach, flickered for a mere 10 seconds before seamlessly repairing itself.

Defeated, Captain Demy slumped back, clutching the useless half-nail in his hand. His body, drained of its last reserves, screamed in protest.

The leader, his initial fear replaced by a surge of triumphant rage, reached for his throat – the closest anyone had ever come to breaching his supposedly invincible defense.

With a feral roar, he unleashed a bone-crunching punch to Captain Demy's face, plunging him into a dizzying spiral of darkness.

The last shred of Captain Demy's consciousness clung desperately to the leader's final words, "...You'll need someone far more formidable, far more seasoned. You can only..." The sentence hung unfinished, echoing in the vast emptiness of his fading mind.

Mouse Residence, 11:50 P.M.

At home, the clock ticked relentlessly toward the celebratory family gathering. Ten minutes remained until the joyful ritual of cutting the anniversary cake.

My eyes were glued to the clock, a silent plea for time to slow its relentless march. My fingers nervously traced the folded test paper in my lap, a talisman of hope against the unknown future.

The doorbell chimed, shattering the peaceful anticipation. Mom, adorned in the emerald green dress Dad had gifted her earlier that day, hurried to answer the door.

A wave of dread washed over her as she saw 8 armed figures, the leader at their head, crowding the entrance.

Rooftop, 12:02 A.M.

Captain Demy stirred, dragged back from the precipice of oblivion by a symphony of pain that pulsed through every fiber of his being. He struggled to sit up, his mind a tangled mess as he pieced together the events.

Why had the Casa soldiers spared him? Had they taken something more precious than his life?

An unsettling silence hung heavy over the park, a stark contrast to the usual raucous celebration that marked his squad's victories. This unnatural quietude gnawed at him, for his comrades were known for their marathon revelry after triumphs.

With a leaden dread pulling at his heart, he knew he had to face the truth, no matter how horrifying. He steeled himself and turned his gaze toward the park. Tears welled up unbidden, blurring his vision as he took in the scene before him.

The once vibrant bonfire lay cold and extinguished in the center of the park. **His squad mates, their faces forever frozen in expressions of surprise and horror, lay lifeless in the garden.**

Mr. Manny's body slumped in a chair, his celebratory meal scattered around him, a testament to the abruptness of the attack. The 3 figures who had approached the park earlier had exacted a ruthless toll.

Fearing the worst for my family, Captain Demy braced himself for another wave of crushing grief. He stumbled toward my house, willing himself not to look at my mom lying motionless by the entrance.

He pushed forward, each step fueled by a desperate need for closure. In my father's room, another lifeless body lay sprawled on the bed.

With a heavy heart, he entered the kitchen, expecting to find yet another victim and steeling himself for the inevitable sorrow. **But what greeted him defied all expectations.**

A jarring dissonance ripped through Captain Demy's fading consciousness. The sterile silence of his near-death state was replaced by a thrumming, intense soundtrack that seemed to pulse in his very veins. He wrestled his eyelids open, the world blurring into a horrific tableau.

Across the kitchen floor, the 8 Casa soldiers lay sprawled in a grotesque parody of their former arrogance. Their once-proud uniforms were now mere tattered rags, mute testament to the violence that had unfolded.

The leader, a grotesque reminder of their cruelty, was missing a hand, his fingers scattered like grotesque confetti across the kitchen counter. Their vaunted nail guns, once instruments of terror, were now twisted metal wreckage.

One unifying wound marked each soldier – a clean, precise severing at the neck, a violation that bypassed their supposedly impregnable shields. It defied logic, a scene ripped straight from a nightmare.

In the center of this horrific display sat me. Shock held me in its icy grip, tears yet to form despite the welling of grief.

The only stains marring the otherwise pristine floor were the crimson trails marking the soldiers' throats and the blood seeping from the half-torn test paper clenched tightly in my hand.

Slowly, I lifted my head, meeting Captain Demy's gaze. My normally light blue irises, the color of a summer sky, began a chilling transformation.

They darkened, deepening into a shade of cerulean so intense it seemed to emit an inner light. My eyeball turned blue as if it emitted immense energy, as blood from the test paper poured on my hand.

Captain Demy, a pillar of stoicism shattered, stood rooted to the spot. His jaw hung slack, a mask of pure astonishment etched on his face.

The room vibrated with an unseen power, and his body trembled uncontrollably, not from pain but from the overwhelming aura radiating from me.

His brow furrowed in concentration as he pieced together the fragments of information, desperately searching for a coherent picture. His gaze darted between the crimson stain spreading on the sheet and the innocuous paper clutched in my hand.

The only words he could manage, a desperate plea escaping his lips, were, **"WHAT'S THE POWER TO CUT... DIAMOND WITH PAPER!"**

CHAPTER TWO

FILES OF FATE

Alist (Diary)

Eight years old, and the world was a symphony of voices. Every conversation, no matter how fleeting, held the promise of connection.

In a society dominated by the rigid rhythm of marching boots, where children were a rare melody, school was my sanctuary – each classmate, a unique instrument in life's grand orchestra. We shared whispered secrets, the joy of shared laughter, the pure, untarnished music of friendship.

Then, the music died – a single, horrific note that shattered the harmony forever. That day when the 8 Casa soldiers, their arrival a discordant chord that ripped through the delicate melody of my childhood. Imagine the world going silent, the vibrant symphony replaced by the chilling emptiness of an eight-year-old's grief. My world fractured by the cruelty of strangers who found pleasure in inflicting pain.

Captain Demy became the anchor in my storm, my lighthouse in the encroaching darkness. He shouldered the responsibility of my education, reshaping my understanding of the world.

Under his tutelage, a harsh truth resonated within me – not everyone sings the song of friendship. Darkness lurks within hearts, capable of twisting even the most innocent melody into a dirge of suffering. Even those who appear benevolent may harbor discordant notes within their souls.

Captain Demy preached the gospel of solitude, claiming social connection was a relentless cycle of attachment, heartbreak, and the arduous reconstruction of self.

This revelation felt like a jarring note in our own, tentative duet. His gift for conversation, a tapestry woven with heartfelt words, could bridge the gap with any stranger, creating instant bonds.

As a child, I grappled with the dissonance in his teachings. But with each passing year, the melody of his past shifted. He became a different composition, a melancholic tune replacing the former vibrancy.

For 5 years, I accepted his sheltered symphony, a melody of obedience that masked a growing curiosity about the world beyond our walls. Perhaps he had his reasons, a silent chorus of past events that justified his isolation. It was a respect that kept the questions locked within, a silent harmony waiting to be played.

Toronto (Replica), 8:07 A.M.

Sixteen found me a changed young man. My stature had commanded more respect, a faint mustache now claiming its territory above my lip. My once-boyish hair had sprouted into a rebellious man bun, a towering monument tied at the back of my head.

My signature style – vibrant blue aviators – had become an extension of myself, turning heads as I navigated the bustling city streets. Today, my usual black tracksuit served as a comfortable cloak for my morning walk.

A crowd had gathered around a newly erected giant. Towering at 8 meters, the stone statue depicted a turbaned man with a distinguished salt-and-pepper beard, a figure instantly recognizable as Sikh. Statues of this prominent figure, the supposed architect of the city and the entire nation of Casa, were popping up all over the city like mushrooms after a warm rain.

The throng, armed with smartphones, eagerly captured the scene, their animated conversations buzzing about the greatness of the turbaned man. The rising din spurred me to quicken my pace, seeking refuge from the commotion.

The eight-year-old me would have thrived in this lively atmosphere, striking up conversations, snapping photos, forging connections with strangers with effortless ease.

But the past years had reshaped me. My focus had narrowed, my interactions governed by a set of self-imposed rules.

My social circle revolved around the 2 close friends I'd managed to make in the city during my three-year stay. My new approach dictated that I only engage with 3 categories of people: established friends, potential friends, and those forced upon me by circumstance, like roommates.

As I neared my apartment building, I found myself waiting beside a stranger for the elevator. He towered over me slightly, radiating an air of someone in his twenties.

We stood in companionable silence, both our gazes fixed on the impending elevator door. Breaking the silence, the man beside me initiated a conversation, a friendly, "Hey there, buddy, what's your name?"

Glancing at him briefly, I chose to ignore him, fixing my attention back on the lift door.

A tad rude, perhaps, but he didn't fall under any of the 3 categories I deemed worthy of conversation. Plus, I harbored a personal grudge against people taller than me – a peculiar quirk, you might say.

Sensing the awkwardness, the man raised his eyebrows and persisted, "Look dude, I'm new in town. Any chance you could point me toward apartment 4H?"

Swiftly, I turned toward him, a warm smile replacing my earlier indifference. "Well, hello there! How are you doing today, friend?"

His confusion was written all over his face. A moment ago, I'd given him the cold shoulder, and now I was radiating sunshine. To an outsider, I must have looked like a total weirdo based on this first impression, but I had my reasons.

Apartment 4H was my residence, and today marked the arrival of a new roommate – most likely this very gentleman inquiring about the same unit. Roommates, as mentioned earlier, fell under category 3 – "forced upon me by circumstance" – hence the sudden shift in demeanor.

Extending his hand, the man introduced himself, "I'm Bill Blear."

I reciprocated with a handshake, "Alist."

"Alist what?" Bill inquired, a hint of amusement in his voice.

"Oh, it's just Alist. But you can call me by my nickname, Jerry Mouse," I replied, our handshake lingering a touch awkwardly.

"Isn't it weird, your real name does not have a last name but your nickname does?" Bill remarked, his curiosity piqued.

"Well, that's... complicated," I responded with a perplexed expression. The elevator door whooshed open, and I gestured toward it. "Let's head up. We'll have plenty of time to chat – right roomie?"

The cramped apartment buzzed with nervous anticipation as I ushered Bill through the door. There, I introduced him to my city's social circle – Charlie and Tanya.

Charlie, my roommate, and closest confidante, mirrored a wilted sunflower on the couch. Tanned skin, usually crinkled with laughter lines, was pulled taut with worry. His usual contact lenses were abandoned today, replaced by the vulnerability of bare glasses.

Across from him, Tanya, my unofficial older sister, and Charlie's girlfriend, held court. Two years our senior, her dark eyes, usually warm with empathy, sparkled with amusement. Originally from India, she was a familiar face from the building next-door, practically an extension of our own little household thanks to her constant visits.

Bill, initially formal, quickly adopted a "make yourself at home" attitude. Introductions barely over, he raided the pantry, consuming 3 bananas in record time. He then shed his black coat with the flourish of a magician, folding it meticulously before placing it on the couch next to Charlie.

Bill continued peeling off layers until he settled on a sleeveless vest, perfectly suited for his impromptu push-up routine that followed. His dedication to fitness was impressive, even if his discarded clothing resembled a haphazard battlefield.

Charlie, sitting on the couch, looked as if the weight of the world was on his shoulders. Tanya, ever perceptive, noticed his distress.

"Alright, Charlie-boy," she teased, amusement in her eyes. "Up and at 'em! Whatever's got you looking like a kicked puppy, we can't be late. Remember, this is all for the greater good... or something like that."

Tanya's urgency stemmed from the looming specter of the Casa citizenship test, the holy grail for anyone seeking residency in this supposedly utopian land of gleaming technology and unparalleled quality of life.

Casa, however, wasn't in the business of handing out welcome mats. Oh no, to even be considered worthy, one had to navigate the labyrinthine citizenship test, a bureaucratic beast guarded by the ever-watchful Casa immigration board.

The test itself was preceded by mandatory classes held in the heart of the city, designed to equip hopeful residents with the knowledge needed to conquer this administrative leviathan.

Today marked the first of these classes. Charlie and Tanya, starry-eyed with dreams of a brighter future, were all for embracing this Casa citizenship quest. I, on the other hand – let's just say I was applying for the test under peer pressure.

The truth is that Captain Demy, my ex-soldier guardian who hung up his fatigues for retirement, had immigrated to Casa about 3 years ago. He'd also helpfully "suggested" I take the citizenship test and join him once I came of age.

So, here I was, facing the prospect of uprooting myself and moving to Casa, all because of a reunion with a slightly overbearing ex-military man. Talk about a gilded cage.

Apartment 4H, 10:00 A.M.

The cramped apartment thrummed with anxious tension, the air thick with unspoken worry. In this sea of muted tones, I couldn't help but stand out.

My electric blue fur jacket, a personal declaration against conformity, blazed against Charlie's usual drab gray jeans and Tanya's comforting brown sweater. Their clothes mirrored their moods – Charlie, a storm cloud threatening rain, and Tanya, a warm cup of tea offering solace.

As I adjusted my trusty blue aviator glasses, Tanya, ever the picture of meticulousness, finished applying a final coat of crimson lipstick, her reflection radiating determination from the cracked mirror above the fridge.

Charlie, eyeing the Casa citizenship application form peeking out of Bill's bag, inquired about Bill's class attendance.

Bill, unfazed, flashed a dazzling smile that could rival a toothpaste commercial. "Bingo!" he declared, taking a hearty swig of his protein concoction. "But hey, knowledge is like a protein shake – got to get it fresh, you know? Besides, the first days are for rookies. I already know what they're going to cover. Besides, the gym has this killer core workout at the same time. Priorities, my friend, priorities!"

Charlie's jaw dropped faster than a poorly balanced Jenga tower. "Wait, you mean... you've already been to these classes?" he stammered, his voice bordering on bewildered.

Bill, completely missing the bewildered undertones, grinned. "Actually," he admitted, downing the rest of his shake in one impressive gulp, "I was recently... deported from Casa itself."

The revelation hung in the air thicker than the dust bunnies under the fridge. Before Charlie could launch into a full-blown interrogation, Tanya's voice, laced with a hint of desperation, echoed from the hallway, "People! We're going to be late! Chop, chop!"

Charlie, momentarily forgetting his Casa citizenship crisis, scrambled to throw on his blazer, the action as graceful as a baby giraffe learning to walk. Out in the hallway, a familiar sight awaited us.

Charlie, clutching his learner's permit like a security blanket, opted to occupy the passenger seat, leaving the driving duties (as always) to Tanya. He was, after all, the kind of guy who'd hop in a cab even in the virtual world of GTA 5 – a fact that never failed to elicit a playful eye roll from Tanya.

As Tanya expertly navigated the bustling city streets, Charlie, gazing out the window at the snow-covered houses lining the sidewalks, muttered, "Looks just like Canada, doesn't it?" His voice held a hint of longing, a wistful yearning for a home that perhaps no longer felt like home.

"It is Canada, silly," I replied, unable to contain a stifled giggle.

Charlie's eyes, momentarily flickering with confusion, betrayed a touch of melancholy. "Is it, though?" he murmured, the question hanging in the air like an unanswered riddle.

Casa Institute, Prep Class C, 10:20 A.M.

We skidded into the institute with 10 minutes to spare, yours truly fashionably late thanks to a detour at the canteen to snag water bottles for the hydration trio (me, Charlie, and Tanya, of course).

The classroom buzzed with a unique brand of nervous energy, a hodgepodge of hopeful residents-to-be – teenagers like us, seasoned adults, and even a couple of folks with faces that whispered tales of decades past.

My plan for seating arrangements was a two-pronged attack. Option A: Snag a spot next to Charlie, my fellow Casa citizenship test soldier. Option B: Sit alone.

Unfortunately, option A went belly-up faster than a week-old soufflé. Tanya, the strategic mastermind, had already claimed the prime real estate beside Charlie on the third row.

I shot her a look that could curdle milk, but she just rewarded me with a mischievous giggle. "First come, first served," she chirped, clearly enjoying my misfortune.

With option A reduced to ashes, I scanned the room, my gaze landing on a lone figure in the back – **What the hell, it was the very girl who'd haunted my childhood like a particularly persistent shadow.**

Yep, it was her. The same girl who'd followed me through the schoolyard gates like a puppy, the same girl who'd mysteriously materialized as my next-door neighbor back in the Captain Demy days.

Despite her impressive stalkerish dedication – window-peeping, park-trailing, and roof-observing – she'd never uttered a peep to me. Annoying as I found her back then, puberty had replaced that annoyance with a spark of… curiosity.

Maybe it was the air of mystery that clung to her like yesterday's perfume, or maybe it was just the sheer audacity of her silent following.

This was the first time our paths had crossed in 3 years. Her green eyes, wide with surprise, landed on me as I approached. Encased in a comfy hoodie, she looked oddly cute – definitely someone who fell under the second category, "Potential friends."

Everyone has a bucket list, right? Some dream of exotic vacations, others crave career conquests. Me? My sole ambition in life, fueled by years of silent observation, was to witness this girl's teeth before I die.

Reaching her bench, I contemplated a gentle shoulder nudge to grab her attention. Unfortunately, my social skills, honed by the grand total of 2 friendships in 8 years, were about as sharp as a butter knife.

In a move that could only be described as hilariously awkward, I ended up accidentally palm-checking her cheek with the greeting, "Hey."

She jumped out of her skin, eyes wide as a startled owl's. Nervousness radiated off her like heat waves in July, causing a barely-there tremor to run through her frame. Ignoring the social faux pas of epic proportions, I forged on. "Can I, uh… sit with you?"

Her cheeks turned the color of a ripe tomato, and eye contact became her sworn enemy as she buried her head in a desk-based faceplant. Perhaps, like me, she too adhered to certain social interaction rules.

Two girls from the next row, sensing the awkwardness that hung in the air like thick London fog, called out, "Hey dear! Come sit with us!"

Mortified by the whole debacle, I stammered, "N-no thanks," and chose the route of social exile. Settling on the floor with crossed legs and a healthy dose of self-loathing, I leaned against the wall, contemplating the wisdom of ever leaving my apartment again.

A hush fell over the classroom as the door swung open, heralding the entrance of a man who could have walked straight out of a Bollywood awards ceremony. His polished suit pants gleamed under the harsh classroom lights, and a single red rose bloomed elegantly from the pocket of his tailored coat.

A distinguished green turban crowned his head, mirroring the one I'd seen earlier on the statue outside. The resemblance between the 2 was uncanny, though surely not a case of the statue coming to life (although, judging by the day's events so far, I wouldn't completely rule it out).

He strode purposefully toward the front of the room, his presence commanding immediate attention. Taking center stage at the podium, he adjusted his beard and with a voice that boomed like a well-amplified foghorn, declared, "General Anmolbir Singh at your service!"

A hefty stack of yellow files rested in his arms, and as he began distributing them among the students, a prickle of unease settled over me.

Only the mysterious girl and I remained conspicuously file-less. General Singh, with a flourish that could rival a magician pulling a rabbit from a hat, launched into his address, his enthusiasm bordering on manic.

"Alright, class," he boomed, his voice bouncing off the walls, "let's dispel a few obvious things, shall we? This planet you're all so comfortably settled on? Not Earth. That bustling metropolis outside your window? Not your beloved Canada. Nope, folks, buckle up, because it's time for a reality check! This whole place is a REPLICA! But you all already know that. It is all a meticulously crafted copy of a world you once knew, built by the very first human who ever set foot on this far-flung corner of the Andromeda galaxy. And guess who gets to call this place home? The UNFORTUNATE ones! You lot!"

"You there, brown sweater!" He punctuated his last statement by jabbing a finger toward a random student – it turned out to be Tanya, her face as pale as a sheet. "Open your file and share the juicy details with your classmates!"

Tanya rose obediently, her hands trembling as she unfolded the contents of her file for all to hear. The details within painted a brief of her existence:

Name: Tanya Malhotra

Date of Birth: 6-4-2044

Place of Birth: New Delhi, India

Date of Death: 28-12-2067

Place of Death: Mumbai, India

Cause of Death: Speeding

Details: "On the ill-fated day of April 25, 2064, Tanya Malhotra, driven by an insatiable need for speed, took the wheel, playfully mocking her friend for driving at a sluggish pace. Their destination was a girls' party, and they set out from their hotel in high spirits. However, destiny had a cruel turn in store for them as their path intersected with a speeding truck.

The collision left Tanya's friend relatively unharmed, escaping the clutches of serious injury. Tanya, on the other hand, bore the brunt of the impact. The aftermath of the accident rendered her face disfigured, legs severed, fingers amputated, and her jaw shattered, leaving her robbed of the ability to speak.

Her resilience was tested as she grappled with the profound challenges posed by her altered condition over the ensuing years."

Despite her struggles, the weight of despair eventually overpowered Tanya's spirit. In a tragic culmination, she succumbed to the depths of hopelessness. The year 2067 witnessed her tragic demise as she chose to end her own life, a gunshot echoing the silence of her shattered existence.

Tanya's voice, a mere tremor escaping her lips, cracked as she finished reciting the horrific details from her file. Her eyes, glistening with unshed tears, darted around the room, searching for solace that wasn't there.

The weight of the revelation pressed down on the classroom like a physical entity, stifling the air and constricting breaths. In a voice thick with raw emotion, Tanya finally found the courage to confront General Anmolbir Singh, the embodiment of this unsettling new reality.

"What in God's name is this supposed to mean?" she cried, her voice cracking with a mixture of disbelief and terror.

General Anmolbir, his polished façade momentarily flickering with something akin to empathy, sighed deeply.

"This, my dear Tanya," he began, his voice solemn, "is a glimpse of the life that awaited you on Earth, a life we deemed unfit for someone like yourself." He pushed himself away from the podium, his movements measured as he began to pace the room.

"Life on Earth," he continued, his voice laced with a hint of disdain, "is a cruel mistress. It metes out hardship with a far heavier hand than fortune. A staggering two-thirds of the global population find themselves drowning in a sea of adversity – victims of horrific accidents, prisoners of poverty, slaves to circumstance, or condemned to a slow demise by an unforgiving disease. Casa," he declared, his voice ringing with a newfound conviction, "was envisioned as a sanctuary, a haven where weary souls, plucked from various points in time, could find solace and forge a new beginning."

He strode purposefully toward the whiteboard, a flourish in his every step. Seizing a marker with the practiced ease of a seasoned lecturer, he began to sketch a diagram.

"Fate, as we have traditionally understood it," he explained, his voice dropping to a professorial tone, "implies a predetermined script, a narrative already written from the cradle to the grave."

With a swift stroke, he drew a line across the board, illustrating the linear flow of time. "The Casa board," he continued, his voice laced with a hint of pride, "possesses the unique ability to not only comprehend the individual destinies of each of you, the grand narrative from 'A' to 'B,' but also to exert a measure of influence upon it."

Charlie, unable to contain his burgeoning anxiety, shot up from his seat. "But wouldn't tampering with the past create a ripple effect, a chaotic disturbance in the delicate fabric of time? Changes in the past can lead to changes in the future."

General Anmolbir nodded sagely, acknowledging the validity of Charlie's concern. "Indeed, young man," he replied, a hint of amusement dancing in his eyes. "Tampering with time is a precarious endeavor, fraught with the potential for unforeseen paradoxes. For instance, bringing back a person from the Stone Age who discovered fire could reshape history dramatically. The discovery of fire was a cornerstone of human civilization, leading to numerous inventions. Altering this could plunge the timeline into chaos and also lead to complete destruction."

The General's steely gaze raked across the classroom, silencing the room with its intensity. Students leaned forward, rapt with attention. "But," he persisted, his voice dropping to a conspiratorial whisper, "what if we, as humans, could play God, not in the capricious, all-powerful sense, but with a surgeon's precision? The founder of Casa, a visionary far ahead of his time, devised a theory he called the *Theory of Influence.*"

He paused dramatically, allowing the weight of his words to sink in. "This theory posits that our present reality is the culmination of countless choices and influences, monumental and minute, made by individuals throughout history – a tapestry woven from a billion tiny threads. If we opt not to bring back the person who discovered fire but instead bring back his close friend, the course of history still changes. Events leading to the discovery were influenced by his friend, be it through shared ideas or protection from dangers. We can't even retrieve a person without influence, as even seemingly insignificant individuals may have descendants destined for remarkable deeds."

Charlie probed further, "How does this align with us being brought back? Wouldn't that alter history?"

General Anmolbir clarified, "According to the *Theory of Influence*, approximately 0.00074% of every 8 billion people are those without any discernible impact – no influence on others, no significant deed done, and even no future generations affecting the future. Removing and bringing back such individuals wouldn't disturb the course of anyone's future. These are often people who live solitary lives, have no children, or meet an early demise."

"So basically, we don't matter!" Charlie murmured, a mix of anger and gloom.

"You didn't; that's a fact, but now you do." General Anmolbir approached Charlie, shaking his hair with his hand. "Despite the people listed above, our second approach is to bring back individuals seconds before their deaths and fix them, thanks to Casa's superior technology. Bringing those seconds before their death does not affect the future; of course, they can't influence anyone after they die."

Just as Tanya aimed to snatch the water bottle teetering on Charlie's desk, the General swooped in like a thirsty hawk, gulping down all the contents in a single, greedy swallow. Tanya's face mirrored the emptiness of the bottle, while the General, smug with his ill-gotten hydration, continued his pompous pronouncements.

"Currently," he declared, his voice booming like a malfunctioning foghorn, "we repatriate individuals from across the annals of history, but not directly to Casa. We've meticulously crafted replica countries to serve as acclimation zones for these... ahem... chronologically challenged individuals. For instance, folks yanked from the years 2000 to 2256 are deposited in Canada and stuck in a permanent 2030 time warp. Those unfortunate souls ripped from 1865 to 1999 get to experience the delights of England circa 1919. Once they've successfully acclimated to these technological theme parks, they can then apply for Casa citizenship and take the oh-so-important Casa Citizenship Test. Here, they learn all about the wonders of Casa and the delightful menagerie of creatures lurking just beyond our borders."

With a pointed look in my direction, General Singh added, with a hint of something that suspiciously resembled mischief in his eyes, "There might even be a few such creatures among you already."

He then marched toward the center of the room, his every step a seismic event. With a flourish worthy of a magician about to produce a rabbit from a hat (though, in this case, the trick involved cracking a wooden desk with a single mighty blow), he bellowed, "Open those files and feast your eyes on the fates that could have been yours! But remember, dearies, after you've finished your light reading, **TEAR THOSE PAGES TO SHREDS!** Because that's not who you are anymore! Tomorrow's a brand new day, and Casa welcomes you with open arms…"

The classroom transformed into a tomb of rustling paper and choked gasps. Each student, eyes glued to their files, relived the horrors (or, perhaps, dodged the bullets) of their averted destinies.

Some faces contorted in raw terror, reliving a near brush with death or misfortune. Others, a flicker of relief dancing in their eyes, skimmed the pages, the weight of a life unlived lifting from their shoulders.

Charlie, however, couldn't tear his gaze away from his file. His hands, usually steady, trembled like leaves caught in a whirlwind as he devoured the contents.

As students shuffled out, a flurry of torn paper swirled in the air, settling like a confetti graveyard on the classroom floor. We were all dismissed with a promise of "real classes" starting tomorrow, a phrase that hung heavy with unspoken questions.

Apartment 4H, 2:08 P.M.

Bill nudged Charlie, "Still holding onto that memento? Didn't they tell you to tear it along with that 'new beginning' crap?"

"What's wrong, Charlie?" I asked.

Charlie finally looked up, his eyes shadowed with a turmoil that mirrored the shredded remnants of his file. In a voice barely above a whisper, he choked out, **"I... I want to go back home."**

CHAPTER THREE

SECOND CHANCES

Alist (Diary)

Casas Institute, Cafeteria, 2:05 P.M.

"You know, Captain Demy?" Intrigued, I leaned toward General Anmolbir in the near-empty cafeteria. Charlie sat across from us, quietly absorbing our exchange.

"Know him? Hired the man myself. We dueled back in the day, blades singing secrets only steel understands," General Anmolbir replied, his mind wandering back to old memories as he savored his lasagna.

My eyebrows shot up. "You dueled? Against an Asparian? Captain Demy's instincts and strength are legendary. Were you able to hold your own?"

The General's eyes snapped back to the present, a glint of challenge replacing the wistful haze. "Hold my own? He was the one chasing my shadow."

Charlie's attention fixed on our conversation; he absorbed every word. Though it was past 2, most patrons had already left, yet we lingered with our instructor. One might wonder why.

Following Bill's advice, we were here for the Casa board's bi-monthly hearing. Every other Saturday, they granted applicants a platform to voice their concerns. Charlie, yearning for a return to Earth, had secured a hearing. Unfortunately, our military-minded yet tardy instructor detained us for nearly half an hour.

Oblivious to our growing anxiety, General Anmolbir sauntered between abandoned tables, collecting stray butter knives like a whimsical conqueror.

"Eyes front, rookies!" he boomed, a showman taking center stage. With a flourish, he balanced the 5 precarious blades on his outstretched fingers, a testament to his supposed dominance over Captain Demy.

The knives remained perfectly still as he exited the cafeteria, each a testament to his claimed prowess. Charlie, mesmerized by the General's display, trailed after him into the hallway adorned with sports-themed wallpaper – baseball bats, soccer balls, tennis rackets, and archery targets competing for attention.

"Asparian, you are too, Jerry?" General Anmolbir boomed, his eyes twinkling with a competitive glint. In a blur, he snatched all the knives from his right hand and slammed them into my palm. "Show me what you can do."

A bead of sweat trickled down Charlie's temple as he watched my fingers dance around the blades. I could have stopped there, simply mimicking the General's parlor trick. But this wasn't about mere imitation; it was about dismantling his dominance.

A wider grin stretched across my face as I spun the knives between handle and tip, their razor-sharp edges impossibly still against my skin. Charlie swallowed audibly, a mix of fear and exhilaration flickering in his eyes.

With practiced ease, I transferred the knives from my right hand to my left, holding them inches from the General's face. I rotated my fingers in a mesmerizing display – the knives remained impossibly balanced.

Up, down, side-to-side – not a single blade wavered. Charlie watched in astonishment, convinced the knives were magically glued to my hand. He'd never witnessed such a display of control and precision.

A challenge gleamed in the General's eyes as a smile mirrored mine. With lightning speed exceeding human limitations, he snatched a knife from my index finger. The duel was on.

The stale air in the hallway, thick with dust motes, crackled with sudden tension. The blade lunged toward me. A momentary flicker of surprise crossed my face, but I reacted instantly, halting it with my pinkie finger and applying pressure against the flat of the blade before it reached my chest.

Simultaneously, I manipulated the remaining knives in a blur of motion, wedging 3 between my other fingers and sending the fourth into a mesmerizing spin before the General's face.

The atmosphere in the hallway shifted as the duel intensified. General Anmolbir reveled in the challenge, adjusting his mustache confidently, sensing the competitive gaze burning through my blue-framed glasses, a silent dare that ignited the fire in my veins.

Charlie's mind raced. Why was I competing with the General? Was it to prove myself? Defend Captain Demy's honor? Or simply push my own limits?

The battle unfolded in a whirlwind of motion. The General relinquished the blocked blade, his eyes fixed on the one spinning in mid-air.

To create confusion, I sent the 3 wedged knives flying in a synchronized roll, the lone circling blade continuing its hypnotic dance. As he lunged for any of the airborne weapons, I expertly deflected them all with lightning strikes, sending them clattering in opposite directions.

Just as he switched to retrieve the falling knife instead (the one he dropped), I executed a precise move. With inhuman speed,

I not only slipped my foot out of my shoe but also snagged the falling knife with my toes.

I raised my leg; the captured knife pointed directly at his neck. His beard bristled with the force of my movement, and for a fleeting moment, astonishment flickered in his eyes. Defeat was etched on his face.

Charlie, stunned by the rapid exchange, struggled to piece together the events that transpired in a mere 10 seconds.

I broke the silence, placing my feet back on the ground, addressing General Anmolbir, **"For a mere human, you're just a hundred times weaker than me. That's pretty strong!"**

"Well, I'll take that as a compliment," General Anmolbir retorted with a hint of sarcasm.

Casa Institute, Hallway, 2:08 P.M.

I walked back to the car where Bill and Tanya awaited, leaving General Anmolbir to instruct Charlie to proceed to the hall for the scheduled hearing.

As General Anmolbir stretched before leading Charlie away, his gaze fell upon something unexpected. **The knives I'd sent flying were embedded in the archery board wallpaper, 2 on either side, all hitting the bull's eye with pinpoint precision.**

"Remarkable, even for an Asparian," he muttered to himself, a newfound respect for my abilities flickering in his eyes.

Casa Institute, Parking Lot, 2:10 P.M.

A prickle of unease snaked down my spine as I approached the parking lot, responding to Tanya's exuberant wave. My instincts flared, alerting me to a shadow clinging to my steps. A casual glance over my shoulder confirmed my suspicions – a tail.

Any guesses who the stalker was? Of course, it was the mysterious girl who had been a constant but silent observer, attempting to conceal herself behind a nearby pillar. Her hiding skills were really pathetic.

Her persistence had grown tiresome, and I decided it was time to end this cat-and-mouse game. Implementing a strategic approach, I devised a technique I called "Reverse Following."

The idea was simple but effective — by abruptly switching roles and following the person who had been following me, I aimed to confuse her and prompt her to retreat to her own space.

It was a calculated move to turn the tables and confront the elusive observer once and for all, making the hunter the prey.

"Here, here!" Tanya's voice echoed from a distance, beckoning me to join her in the parking lot. Instead, I diverted my path toward the mysterious girl who had persistently trailed me.

Tanya, puzzled and frustrated, watched my unexpected change of direction, muttering to herself about my seemingly erratic behavior, "Where in the world is he going?"

Alma's Caravan, 2:22 P.M.

I followed the mysterious girl, implementing my strategy, and surprisingly, my gambit worked. Her trails led me to a surprisingly spacious caravan within walking distance of the institute.

Inside, the two-person bed, bunk above it, and compact kitchen painted a picture of a life lived on the fringes.

Having successfully cornered the mysterious girl in her own abode, she had no choice but to provide a reasonable explanation for her decade-long surveillance of me.

An awkward silence hung heavy in the air as we faced each other at the round kitchen table. The girl, years of solitude etched on her face, trembled under the weight of potential conversation. Her averted gaze and trembling hands confirmed my suspicion – genuine human interaction was unfamiliar territory.

"Let's start with the basics," I offered gently, sensing her anxiety. "Your name?"

A faint blush colored her cheeks as I reached out, momentarily leaving my chair. I smoothly turned the back of hers, intending to create a less confrontational environment. The unexpected touch of my fingers against her shoulder elicited a reaction I hadn't anticipated.

I returned to my seat, mirroring the change in orientation, and spoke, "An extrovert understands what people say; an introvert senses what they hide. Having been both, I know that sometimes, after not talking to anyone or hiding something for an extended period, communication becomes challenging. Maybe if we're not facing each other, it might be easier for you to talk."

I acknowledged the sacrifice I was making by suggesting this arrangement. **It meant I wouldn't be able to see her when she spoke, shattering my goal of catching a glimpse of her teeth— a dream that, sadly, would have to wait.**

A tentative voice broke the silence. "My name," she began, "is Alma." Each word emerged with a shaky breath, betraying her lingering nerves.

"Alma, perhaps it's been so long since you last talked to someone that you've forgotten how to speak," I offered gently.

As she raised her head, her clenched fists betraying an inner struggle, I realized my words had struck a chord.

Alma extended a letter toward me, and its sender was a man named Griffin Wander. "These letters started arriving when I was 6," she confessed, her voice barely a whisper. "Alone, with no family or home, they offered a lifeline. Griffin Wander promised to provide for my needs in exchange for complete obedience. My life became a series of instructions – following you, completing tasks, maintaining a watchful presence. It wasn't espionage; he never requested reports. He provided a house near yours, enrolled me in your school, and deposited weekly rations. This isolated existence has been my reality ever since. I've never met Griffin, nor do I understand his motives."

Listening carefully, I absorbed the revelations before offering my own. "I didn't receive a fate file in the first class because I haven't been brought back from time. You see, I am from a race of beings native to this planet itself." My words hung in the air, waiting for Alma's response. "But why didn't YOU receive a file? ARE YOU A HUMAN?" I probed further, my tone solemn.

"Kind of," Alma murmured, hinting at a complexity she was hesitant to unveil.

"Can you elaborate?" I pressed, sensing the walls she'd built around her past.

Fear and uncertainty colored her reply. "I can't tell you."

The questions persisted as I sought to unravel the layers of her mysterious existence. "What was your life like before the age of 6?" I pressed on, hoping for a glimpse into the enigma that was Alma.

"I can't tell you that," she repeated, her voice now trembling even more, the weight of untold stories evident in her tone.

Undeterred, I continued my quest for understanding. "What task did Griffin Wander instruct you to do?" The relentless interrogation hung in the air.

"I CAN'T TELL YOU!" Alma's voice erupted in frustration, tears welling up in her eyes as she started crying out loud. The barrage of questions had unearthed emotions long kept hidden.

Suddenly, she reached toward my head. Though my gaze remained fixed forward, I instinctively intercepted her arm.

"The way you moved, it wasn't like you were trying to hit me or mess with my hair," I remarked, my grip firm. "What were you attempting?"

Panic laced her voice. "I can erase memories with a touch," she confessed between sobs.

"Hold on," I interrupted, releasing her arm, and turning to face her. I took a deep breath, realizing that so far, I was doing it all wrong. "You don't have to explain anything now – not your abilities, not the missing file, or anything else. Trust takes time to build. **Perhaps all these years, you extended your hand to people to wipe their memories of you,**" I suggested, moving my hand toward her. "**Now, I want to extend my hand to you, for creating memories with you.**"

Her tears subsided as she grasped my hand, her shimmering green eyes filled with innocence. I encouraged her to meet Charlie, Tanya, and Bill, socialize with them, and embrace this new chapter.

As I prepared to leave, her voice rang out, "Thank you!"

Curiosity piqued, I turned back, a chuckle escaping my lips. "What for?"

A nostalgic smile touched her lips. "Back when you lived with Mr. Demy, I spent hours staring at the ceiling, utterly alone. But you... you played guitar in your room every day at noon. I could clearly hear your voice in my house, and... I loved it. Those 2 hours were the best moments of my day!"

Her words filled me with joy, realizing that I had unknowingly brought happiness to someone's life.

However, this positive moment was soon overshadowed by a nagging memory. The realization struck me that I might have inadvertently irritated someone, and that person could be harboring resentment not too far away.

Casa Institute, Parking Lot, 2:29 P.M.

"If I spot Jerry anywhere, I swear I'll end him!" Tanya exclaimed from the backseat of the car, her impatience evident after waiting for me at the institution for an hour.

Meanwhile, Bill, seated in the driver's seat, began rummaging through Charlie's bag, which had been left on the front seat.

Noticing Bill's actions, Tanya questioned, "Why are you going through Charlie's personal belongings?"

"I'm just really bored," Bill replied casually, pulling out Charlie's fate file from the bag. "Might as well read it now."

"But that's not right," Tanya protested, her moral compass unwavering. "Charlie explicitly told us not to read his file."

Bill, seemingly unfazed, looked at Tanya and said, "I'll read it aloud for you too."

"Oh well, go ahead then," Tanya uttered, her morals dying faster than a flame in a storm.

Bill began reading aloud:

Name: *Charlie Green*

Date of Birth: *26-8-2216*

Place of Birth: *Winnipeg, Canada*

A Brief of Life: *"Born in the twenty-third century, Charlie Green aspired to become a great physicist, aiming to bring about positive change* *for humanity. However, at the age of 18, he faced a setback as he failed to secure admission to his desired college, attributed to his average performance in school. Tragedy struck when both of his parents perished in a riot when Charlie turned 19. Despite diligent efforts to study and sacrifices made in socializing, Charlie's dreams remained elusive. He passed away at the age of 40 with no friends, having achieved none of his aspirations and living an unsatisfactory life."*

Date of Death: *25-4-2256*

Place of Death: *Cape Town, South Africa*

Cause of Death: *Murder*

Details: *Not to be disclosed!*

Casa Institute, Hearing Hall, 2:30 P.M.

A sterile aura clung to the hearing hall's metallic walls, a stark contrast to the warmth Charlie vaguely recalled from Earth's courtrooms. General Anmolbir, cloaked in a judge's robe that dwarfed his lean frame, perched on the elevated bench. His eyes glinted with a curious mix of regret and resolve.

The air crackled with nervous energy; murmurs from the Casa board members and instructors, a fifty-strong audience, rippled like dry leaves through the room.

Charlie, confined to a witness box tilted at a defiant angle, drew a deep breath. "I stand before you," his voice echoing in the hushed hall, "to accept my fate. But fate, I believe, can offer redemption. I humbly request a return to Earth, to 2232, the life I abruptly abandoned."

Anmolbir's face softened for a fleeting moment before a mask of stoicism settled back in place. "I understand your yearning, kiddo," he spoke, his voice low and gravelly. "But the threads of time, once woven, cannot be unraveled. Three years you've spent here, and altering your course now would ripple through history like a dropped stone, distorting the tapestry of destiny."

Charlie's eyes welled up, his longing threatening to overflow. "Then grant me a glimpse," he pleaded, voice thick with emotion. "My parents. They're fated to die when I'm 19. Let me spend their remaining days by their side. Or," his voice cracked, "bring them here. Snatch them from the precipice of their demise."

General Anmolbir's expression hardened. "Regrettably, that's not an option," he replied solemnly. "The last retrieval mission occurred 6 months ago. We face a century-long wait before restarting the process."

Rage flickered in Charlie's eyes. "This is kidnapping! I never consented to the Casa board's intervention!"

General Anmolbir retorted to Charlie's accusations with a touch of anger. "So, you propose we go back in time, a task that requires substantial resources and people, and first ask individuals whether they want to come or not? Convince them by revealing their destiny and informing them about a place on another planet? Well, that's not practical."

General clenched his fist and continued, "Here's the paradox: if you inform people about their future, that future no longer holds as they can change it, deviating from the steps they took that led to their original fate. Consequently, we can't even leave them on Earth, even if they choose to stay after learning their fate. So, what's the point of seeking consent?"

"Unjust and wrong!" Charlie exclaimed, forcing down a surge of anger. "You manipulate destinies, dictating fates from your sterile ivory tower! You meddle with the divine plan!"

General Anmolbir slammed his fist on the desk, the impact echoing through the room. "The divine plan, you say?" Anger contorted his features. **"Perhaps this world is the Devil's**

plaything, a cruel puppeteer who scripts our suffering for his amusement. The world we left behind was hell on Earth. We, humanity, rose up to play God, to build this haven."

A flicker of pain crossed his face, his voice softening. **"Charlie, I've witnessed centuries of bloodshed, the scars etched onto innocent souls. I, too, lived in that hell until redemption brought me here. Not everyone gets a second chance, Charlie. But when offered, clinging to the past is folly. It stunts growth, cripples the spirit."**

Charlie opened his mouth to protest, but Anmolbir silenced him with a raised hand, the gavel in his grip pulsing with power.

"I, General Anmolbir Singh, hereby declare," his voice boomed, **"your request for a return to Earth is..."** The gavel crashed down, shattering the soundbar into a million glittering fragments. **"DENIED!"**

CHAPTER FOUR

BILL BLEAR

Alist (Diary)

Apartment 4H, Balcony, 11:33 P.M.

"Forty years... sounds like a long time to live, doesn't it?" Charlie mused, leaning against the railing of our apartment balcony on the fourth floor.

"Over there, you see that house? The one just behind the hotel, next to the second house? That's an exact replica of my family's house on Earth. Built by my great-grandparents, and even in the 23rd century, after a bit of renovation, my parents chose to live there." Charlie pointed at the house with a nostalgic smile, connecting the threads of his past to the present.

Bill stood beside Charlie, a calm and attentive presence as he listened to Charlie's reflections. Despite our relatively short acquaintance of just 2 weeks, Bill had seamlessly woven himself into the fabric of our group. Since Tanya developed a fear of driving, Bill effortlessly took on the wheel, becoming an indispensable part of our daily routines. In short, he became our driver.

Having attended Casa classes before, Bill proved to be a valuable resource, sharing insights about tests and helping us navigate the complexities of the institution.

His five-year stint as a resident of Casa came to an end due to rule violations, an aspect of his past that added an air of mystery to his persona.

He claimed a mix of British and Indian heritage, but interestingly, he didn't fit the visual stereotype of either and carried an unmistakable American accent. Standing tall at 1.84 meters, Bill boasted a remarkably fit physique, a testament to his dedication to the gym.

There was a time when his commitment to fitness led him to miss a week of classes, a clash of priorities that underlined his passion.

Eventually, with some persistent advice from Charlie, Tanya, and myself, Bill not only resumed attending classes but also switched his gym -- although I suspect the fines imposed by the institution might have played a major role in steering him toward this decision.

Charlie's voice, heavy with the weight of unlived years, sought solace in Bill's wisdom. "Bill, 3 more years with parents or a lifetime with friends? What would you choose?"

Bill's response was a deep exhale, a journey inward. **"Parents. Always. Friends come and go, but parents... 2 precious souls, better than a million friendships. Even instead of 3 years, if I was given a chance to spend just a day more with them, my answer still would have been the same."**

Charlie's smile was a bittersweet echo. "You're so sure. I never was. I love my folks, but Jerry, Tanya... leaving them behind was like ripping a part of myself away. Even Jerry's support couldn't erase the fear, the doubt. I can sense the hurt deep inside Jerry. I always had second thoughts about returning back to Earth. There was a fear within me, a fear of whether I could endure my fate even after accepting its awful reality. Strangely, since my plea to return got denied, a significant burden of decision-making has been lifted from my shoulders, although my heart still grapples with dissatisfaction."

"Ever since the Casa board brought me here, I harbored the same desire to return. My plea, much like yours, was met with denial. Over the passing years, I concocted an elaborate escape plan, though I must admit, it was somewhat fantastical, as it hinged on a crucial missing element." Bill disclosed to Charlie in a solemn tone.

"My roots trace back to India, born in 1896, during an era when India was under the grip of the British Empire. My father, a British officer, defied the norms of his regiment and fell in love with an Indian woman who suffered under the oppression of his own regime. In a radical move, my father married her, renounced his position in the British army, and dedicated himself to the cause of Indian freedom. Unfortunately, I had little time with my parents, as British soldiers took their lives when I was only 6 years old. At 7, I found myself transported to this alien planet, Alistia. Upon reading my fate file, a surge of anger enveloped me. The narrative painted a picture of a life filled with strife as I valiantly fought the British for the rights of my people. It predicted that my destiny was to hang at the age of 20, a martyr in the cause of freedom. While this sacrifice of mine might have remained known to only a few, I couldn't shake off my resentment toward the Casa board for tampering with the course of my life," Bill fixed Charlie with an intense gaze, excitement coursing through his words. **"Imagine, Charlie, WOULDN'T THAT HAVE BEEN... A DAZZLING WAY TO DIE!"**

Charlie stood stunned, absorbing the intensity of Bill's narrative and the fire in his eyes – The weight of his back-story lingered in the air.

Suddenly, their attention was drawn inside by an unexpected noise—the unmistakable sound of teeth chattering, a symphony of shivers resonating through the apartment. It was me, emerging from a hot water bath, clad in a sleeveless vest, and underwear, my wet hair wrapped in a turban towel.

Apartment 4H, Bedroom, 11:40 P.M.

The icy bite of the balcony air sent shivers down my spine despite my best efforts to appear unaffected. Bill, oblivious to my discomfort, shut the door with a final thud.

"Isn't that a bit dramatic?" he scoffed. "It's not that cold."

"Actually," Charlie interjected smoothly, "Jerry's kind comes from a perpetually warm climate. They feel the cold a lot more than humans do."

My chattering teeth corroborated his point. Winters were my nemesis, a relentless enemy that seeped into my bones no matter how many layers I bundled myself in. Tonight, I'd clearly underestimated the chill.

Bill's gaze flicked over me, surprise flickering in his eyes. "For someone who doesn't hit the gym, you're in pretty great shape," he conceded.

"Th-th -Thanks," I replied, blowing hot air onto my hands to combat the cold.

"Well, of course you can't be born with such a nice body, and also you would have to maintain it. Care to share your secret?" Bill inquired with me.

"There's no secret; it's just how Asparian bodies are normally made," Charlie interjected instead as I struggled to survive, finding some clothes in my suitcase.

"The internal structure of Asparian bodies is quite similar to humans, except for their hearts. Their hearts not only pump blood but also generate a kind of energy that flows through their bodies – making Asparians way more durable, helping them to recover fast and immunizing them to various ailments, except from cold for some reason. The residual energy left after normal functioning is automatically used up to keep the body in its best possible state — perfectly balanced to maintain both speed and strength."

Bill's expression transitioned from admiration to a hint of concern. Perhaps he worried I missed out on the satisfaction of hard-earned muscle.

As I finally unearthed my sleepwear, a glint of curiosity sparked in Bill's eyes. He fixated on a peculiar band I strapped to my arm, its surface dotted with needles.

"What's that contraption?" Bill blurted.

"It's a bit complicated," I stammered, but Charlie, ever the translator, took over.

"That's a device specially built for Jerry to suck up excessive energy from his body."

He retrieved a book titled *A Brief Guide to Asparians* and flipped it open to a diagram of an Asparian body. "Jerry's different," he explained. "His heart produces an abnormal amount of energy."

Bill's posture shifted, a newfound attentiveness radiating from him. With Charlie laying the groundwork, I felt ready to share my story.

"Back with Captain Demy," I began, a wave of nostalgia washing over me, "every month, my body would overload. I could sense everything at once – every sound, every movement. It was overwhelming. My reflexes were hyper-sensitive, and time seemed to crawl. My eyes even glowed blue as they tried to expel the excess energy. I couldn't even cry during those days."

Bill, now wearing a look of someone who pieced together parts of the puzzle, ventured a guess, "That Demy guy might have trained you to normalize living with that energy."

I shook my head. "Quite the opposite. He told me never to resort to violence and never to rely on my power. He insisted that I must suppress it. Hence, the device on my arm, called 'The Pack,' was ordered from Casa. I only need a fraction of my energy to live, so this device extracts all the excess energy, channelizing it through tubes and storing it inside a capsule embedded in it. Since this device was quite expensive, the Casa board made a deal to send the energy stored in the capsule to them on a quarterly basis in exchange for it."

We settled into a comfortable conversation, roommates sharing a glimpse into each other's worlds. As I packed away my clothes, a flash of blue fabric caught Bill's eye.

Bill was an aficionado of clothes, but only branded ones. His most cherished possession was the black coat he wore on almost all occasions, even sometimes during workouts. He cleaned it with his own hands and never let anyone touch it.

"What brand is that?" he asked, reaching for the suitcase

"Whoa there," I laughed, snatching the cloth before his fingers grazed it.

"It's a very precious thing to me—it's the very reason I am taking the Casa citizenship test. It's Captain Demy's cape, the one he adorned with his military outfit. When he left for Casa, I found it in a dustbin, and ever since, I have taken it in order to return it to him someday."

"I'm really sorry if you think my hands are too filthy to touch this majestic cape," Bill said in a sarcastic tone. "Anyway, it looks really expensive. I can tell just from its shine and the fabric it is made from."

"More than gold and rubies," I agreed. "It's made of Asparian metal."

Bill's eyebrows shot up. "Metal? It feels like cloth."

Intrigued, I unfolded the cape and invited him to hit it lightly. The soft fabric produced a dull thud. I instructed him to try again, this time with me holding it a little tighter. The sound transformed into a metallic clang.

"Asparian metal is condensed energy," I explained. "Our blacksmiths can manipulate it with their bare hands, shaping it into weapons and armor. It's virtually indestructible."

To demonstrate, I ripped a piece of the cloth. As it tore, a faint hum of energy emanated from the rip. Bill watched, mesmerized.

"Only the most skilled Asparians can convert energy into metal and back again," I continued, clenching the torn fabric in my fist. I opened my hand to reveal the cloth transformed into a ball of swirling blue energy.

"Beautiful!" Bill breathed, captivated by the sight.

Casa Institute, Prep Class C, 10:25 A.M.

The morning sun found me by Charlie's bench, 5 minutes pre-class. A vacant seat beside him sparked a mischievous grin.

Tanya, bless her bladder, was stuck in the restroom. Perfect timing to snag the spot and maybe even prank her by claiming it. Got to take revenge for the first day.

Just as I was about to take my seat, a gentle push on my cheek from behind startled me. It was Alma, attempting to catch my attention. She let out an innocent laugh, reminiscent of our first encounter in class.

It's not that I didn't notice her; I could have easily prevented her hand from reaching me, but "We're even now," I declared to Alma with a happy smile.

She gestured toward her usual seat at the back, a mix of authority and undeniable charm in her eyes.

"Perhaps you should make your way to the back," Charlie, privy to my recent Alma revelations, chuckled. He knew she preferred my company, and their last conversation hadn't exactly transformed her into a social butterfly.

Forgetting about Tanya's misfortune, I joined Alma. The back bench offered a decent view, but missing the chance to mess with Tanya left a slight pang of regret.

As fate would have it, karma swooped in just as Tanya approached the now-empty seat beside Charlie. Bill, entering a beat behind her, playfully shoved her aside and plopped himself down.

From my corner, Tanya's expression was a masterpiece. Itching for popcorn, I relished the verbal tirade she unleashed on Bill. "Misogynistic brute! How dare you take a girl's seat? Get your muscular, mannerless bulk out of my sight!"

Bill, a firm believer in avoiding angry women, simply ignored her. He turned to Charlie, his earlier seriousness returning amidst Tanya's ongoing rant. "Something important, buddy. We'll talk after class, but first, a whiteboard and marker. Stat."

Charlie, bewildered by the sudden shift in Bill's demeanor, could only manage an awkward "Sure."

Casa Institute, Prep Class C, 10:30 A.M. (Onwards)

The day unfolded in its routine fashion, with lectures progressing through the usual subjects. The initial class delved into the intricacies of Casa's political system, providing us with a foundational understanding.

Following that, the second period widened our perspective on the technological marvels that defined life in Casa.

The third period shifted focus to the diverse lifestyles within Casa and the myriad professions its inhabitants pursued.

However, the fourth one, a distinctive feature of our daily schedule, was dedicated to a different realm. Led by our class in-charge, General Anmolbir Singh, this period was a departure from Casa-centric topics. Instead, General Anmolbir enlightened us about the planet we found ourselves on (Alistia), delving into the intricacies of its ecosystems.

He vividly described creatures that existed beyond the secure boundaries of Casa—entities bearing resemblances to humans but diverging significantly in terms of abilities, intelligence, and evolutionary progress -- quite like Asparians.

General Anmolbir, owing to his role in the Casa exploration squad, shared firsthand encounters with these creatures. He recounted instances where these entities, sometimes ferocious, posed a threat, necessitating a display of the weaponry employed by the squad. The weapons, products of advanced Casa technology, were diverse and formidable.

Among the array of cutting-edge weaponry, one stood out to me—the 'Bolt Pen.' This ingenious device, cleverly disguised as an ordinary ballpoint pen, served a dual purpose: to deceive intelligent adversaries and function as a last line of defense. The pen is electric enough to generate 3 potent bolts of lightning, each capable of dispatching even the most massive of creatures, akin to an entire elephant, with a single strike.

General Anmolbir's demonstration of these fascinating and formidable weapons had only scratched the surface when the bell signaling recess interrupted our enlightening session.

Casa Institute, Common Garden, 1:02 P.M.

A daily ritual, as sweet as the treats themselves, unfolded beneath the benevolent shade of the institute's tallest tree.

Every forty-minute recess, I couldn't resist the siren song of the canteen, drawn by the promise of my eternal weakness – ice cream. The icy delight was a betrayal to my Asparian core, but its allure, a first love, was impossible to deny.

Today, as usual, I secured my raspberry-flavored treasure with practiced ease. But amidst the bustling crowd vying for their own treats, I spotted Alma. At a petite 5'6", she struggled to see over the heads of the throng, her brow furrowed in concentration. Determined, she took a small jump, a valiant effort to glimpse the colorful offerings. It wasn't enough.

Undeterred, she mustered her courage for another leap. This time, her mission was intel – the price of the delectable ice, like the one clutched in my hand.

With a burst of effort, she resurfaced a triumphant glint in her eye reflecting the menu she'd finally seen. Reaching into her pocket, she retrieved a crisp hundred-dollar bill, ready to conquer the ice cream counter.

"Hey, Alma!" I called, waving with a grin. "I'll be under the big tree. Care to join me?"

A subtle nod was her only reply, but it held volumes.

As I settled beneath the sprawling branches, eager to tear into my icy prize, a wave of unease washed over me. It took Alma a full 4 minutes to appear, her hand clutching only the lonely hundred-dollar bill. Disappointment clouded her features, and I knew exactly why.

The boisterous crowd would have been a formidable opponent for Alma's quiet nature. Even navigating the throng was likely a feat, let alone speaking up to order. Her voice, barely a whisper on most days, would be drowned out in the cacophony.

And then there was the issue of change. The ice cream was a mere 5 dollars, but with only a hundred in hand, getting the correct change required a specific request – something easily overlooked by the harried canteen lady.

A simple ice cream purchase had morphed into an insurmountable challenge. Alma stared at the fallen leaves; her shoulders slumped in defeat. My heart ached for her. The raspberry ice cream in my hand, succumbing to the warmth, mirrored the disappointment melting in her eyes.

With a sudden impulse, I turned to Alma and extended the ice cream toward her. Misinterpreting my gesture, she opened her mouth wide, taking a surprised bite right off the end I held.

I couldn't believe it—I finally caught a glimpse of her teeth -- a dream come true.

Instead of correcting the misunderstanding, a playful warmth bloomed in my chest. After her initial, innocent bite, I took one myself, a smile tugging at my lips.

We continued this unexpected exchange, serenaded by the rustling leaves and the playful dance of the cold wind, sharing the ice cream bite by bite.

Unbeknownst to us, Charlie observed from afar a smirk playing on his lips. "Well, he never shares his food with me, or with anyone." He muttered to himself, his eyes gleaming with curiosity at this unforeseen turn of events.

At the same time, Bill approached Charlie from behind, giving a gentle slap that Charlie, unfortunately, felt quite keenly.

With barely an explanation, Bill thrust a half-day leave application for both of them under Charlie's nose and hustled him out of the institute. Charlie grumbled protests about missing class, but Bill cut him off with a cryptic, "We have bigger fish to fry."

Apartment 4H, 2:00 P.M.

Back in their apartment, Charlie slumped onto his bed – Bill, meanwhile, was positively giddy. He ran his fingers over the smooth surface of his newly acquired whiteboard, a strange glint in his eyes. The air crackled with a nervous energy as Bill's usually jovial demeanor morphed into a manic intensity.

He gripped the marker like a general wielding a sword and attacked the whiteboard, the marker screeching in protest as he drew a forceful circle. "Remember my escape plan?" Bill's voice rumbled deeper than Charlie had ever heard it.

"Uh, yeah," Charlie stammered, a sliver of unease creeping up his spine under Bill's intense gaze. "So?"

Bill's response was a dramatic flourish of his arm as he filled the circle with continents. Then, with a force that sent shivers down Charlie's spine, he plunged the marker through the center of the makeshift planet, the tip emerging from the other side of the board.

"LET'S JUST GET YOU BACK TO EARTH!" Bill roared, his voice echoing in the small room.

CHAPTER FIVE

THE SPAN DOORWAY

Alist (Diary)

Apartment 4H, 2:40 P.M.

"Time travel had always been a whispered rumor, a tantalizing illusion woven by the enigmatic Casa board. But how do they do it? What secrets did they glean from their glimpses into the past and future, like voyeurs peering through a celestial keyhole?" Bill began to explain his plan to Charlie, starting with a serious question.

My knuckles pounded against the doorframe, echoing Bill's frantic call. Twenty minutes had passed since he'd ordered me to drop everything and join them, urgency crackling in his voice. I burst into the apartment, taking a seat on Charlie's desk, the air thick with withheld information.

Bill, eyes narrowed in irritation, glared at me. Not only was I late, but I'd dared to interrupt his grand pronouncements.

"The Green Sphere," he declared, his voice tight with barely contained excitement. "Think of it as a cosmic peephole, a device or a resource letting them see any event, on any planet, at any time. Except..." He leaned closer, his voice dropping to a conspiratorial whisper, "Except for here. Alistia, the very planet we are currently on, remains a blind spot, shrouded in an impenetrable fog; no one can see through the events of this planet, not even the Green Sphere."

Bill snatched Charlie's numbered glasses from the desk and wore them himself to look even more serious, the lenses glinting like predatory eyes.

"But that's just the tip of the iceberg. The Green Sphere might offer a glimpse, but it's the Channel, the hidden conduit connected to it, that grants them access. The channel allows them to pluck people from specific moments, from various periods, without disrupting the tapestry of time itself at precise moments when they won't influence anyone or anything. But here's the rub," Bill added, a wry smile twisting his lips, "the sphere needs a guiding hand, a needle threading through the fabric of existence. Without the Channel, they're disabled, only capable of seeing the events without having the ability to influence them."

Charlie's eyes gleamed with understanding, processing Bill's monologue like a seasoned code-breaker. "So, the Green Sphere's a time tunnel, but the Casa board needs a Space Channel to bridge the gap?"'

I, meanwhile, was wrestling with a different kind of gap - the one between my limited sci-fi knowledge and Bill's technobabble. With a hesitant raised hand, I confessed, "Can you, uh, dumb it down a bit?"

Bill chuckled, the gears in his mind turning. "Sure, Jerry. Think of it like magic. Imagine a crystal ball that lets you waltz through time. Use it in your house, and you'll hop across centuries, but the house itself stays put. A hundred years back, it might be a jungle, but your location stays the same."

I nodded, a flicker of comprehension lighting my eyes. "Okay…"

"Now, picture a magical door that whisks you anywhere instantly. Open it in your house, and you'll pop up a hundred miles away, at the same time, in a different place. See? Swap the crystal ball for the Green Sphere and the door for the Space Channel. Combine them, and you've got a cosmic taxi to anywhere, anytime!"

"Okay, I get it a bit," I said, nibbling on the cap of my pen. "But how does this all tie back to sending Charlie home? And does he even want to go? I thought he was set on staying here." My voice cracked on the last part, trying to hide a pang of sadness twisting in my gut. The thought of Charlie leaving was something I didn't want deep down.

Bill chuckled, raising a placating hand. "Patience, Jerry. I was just getting there. See, to bring a single person back from a specific point in time; the Casa board needs a special kind of Space Channel - they call it a 'Span Doorway.' Imagine it like a tunnel, a portal connecting 2 points even light-years apart. It's a one-way trip, though, and building it requires a boatload of energy. Enough to power an entire country for a year, in fact."

Charlie's jaw dropped. **"A whole nation's worth of energy to bring back one person? Even for the Casa board, that seems extreme."**

Bill shrugged. "Strangely, yes. Prioritizing people, their motto," he muttered, then leaned forward, eyes gleaming. "But that's not the point. The Green Sphere, the most precious item of Casa, their crown jewel, is untouchable. But the Span Doorways are not that unique. They're mass-produced, readily available but illegally. I can help you get your hands on one, and Charlie is free to go home."

Jerry's brows furrowed. "Hold on, I don't understand much scientific stuff, but that's a gaping hole in your plan. Without the Green Sphere, how do we pinpoint the right time? The Span Doorway just jumps places, not years."

Bill smirked. "Exactly." He replied to me and turned toward Charlie. "So, tell me, if we use the doorway without the sphere, what year do you think we'd land on Earth? Any guesses Charlie."

Charlie's eyes widened. "The exact year that's going on Earth in comparison to this planet? Time flows differently on different planets."

"Precisely!" Bill snapped his fingers, a mischievous glint in his eyes. "As we speak, Earth's clock ticks in the year 2007. So, if Charlie used the doorway today, he'd land smack dab in 2007. But remember, he needs to land in the year 2232. The good news? Every month here equals 15 Earth years. Mathematically, he spent a year and a quarter on this planet before using the doorway, and 2 hundred 25 years have whizzed by on Earth, landing Charlie exactly where he should."

Our jaws hung slack. Bill's audacity, his intricate knowledge of Casa's secrets, and the sheer audacity of his plan left us speechless. Five years living in Casa, was that the wellspring of his expertise? But beneath the awe, a cold knot of dread twisted in my gut. If Bill's plan worked, I might lose my best friend.

"I've seen the Casa board's power firsthand," Charlie whispered, his voice heavy with gloom. "And getting a Span Doorway is illegal. They denied my return for a reason. Reading my fate, seeing this place... going back now would ripple through time, affecting countless lives, including yours. The Casa board would notice, and we'd all be in trouble." He looked at Bill, a flicker of gratitude battling his fear. "Thank you for trying, Bill, but it's all in vain. After all, there's no such thing as a perfect plan."

A strange glint sparked in Bill's eyes. The villainous laugh that erupted from him sent chills down our spines. "Not finished yet," he declared, his voice laced with manic glee. "This is a **perfect plan.**"

"The only flaw," he continued, leaning closer, **"was the memories. The memories of my fate file, of this place. They threatened to unravel everything, the reason I couldn't**

escape this place. **But what if we could erase them?"** Bill questioned, looking at me with a serious smirk.

My heart jolted. I remembered that I told Bill about someone who could manipulate memories. "Alma! You want to use her on Charlie," I gasped, realization dawning. "Without those memories, it'll be like he never left Earth! He can easily resume his life on Earth without changing the course of time."

Bill grinned. "Not just erase them, Jerry. Enhance them. Here's the summary of my plan: We get the Span Doorway, use it after 15 months, erase Charlie's memories, and send him back to 2232. But then, 6 days later - 3 Earth years - we bring him back using another doorway, memories restored. So, he'll be back with us after roughly a week, and hence, the Casa board wouldn't even notice, though he'll be 19 now."

"Wow! **That's some God-level planning**." I uttered in awe.

Bill's eyes sparkled with manic glee as he leaned toward the speechless Charlie, his grin stretched wide. **"So, what do you say, mate? Three years with your family, escaping your grim Earthly fate, and a lifetime with us at the end? Not too shabby for a masterstroke, eh?"**

Charlie, still reeling from the mind-bending possibilities, stared back at Bill. His eyes, though, spoke volumes, silently expressing gratitude and a flicker of hesitant hope. "Alright, Bill," he rasped, his voice thick with emotion. "I'm in. But where the hell do we find a Span Doorway? Those things aren't exactly lying around in supermarkets."

Bill snorted; the sound was oddly cheerful, considering the gravity of the situation. "Oh, I know just the fella," he winked, eyes gleaming with mischief. "But for his... expertise, we'll need to provide a little, shall we say, incentive -- The amount of energy that is capable of lighting an entire nation for a year."

Charlie's face crumpled in frustration. "What are you talking about? We don't have that kind of energy! Nobody does!"

Bill's grin widened, a sly, conspiratorial glint sparkling in his eyes. "I know we don't have that kind of energy", he purred, his voice dripping with cryptic promise. "But we have its eternal source."

My breath hitched, and "What?" escaped my lips before I could stop it. Charlie echoed my question; his brow furrowed in confusion.

But Bill remained silent, his finger pointed accusingly at me with a playful glint in his eye.

(Three weeks later)

Alma's Caravan, 4:05 P.M.

The wind howled like a restless animal outside Alma's metal haven, clawing at the caravan's thin walls. Alma lay tucked in her black leaf-patterned blanket, the chill seeping through despite its woolen warmth.

Another cold evening, another half-eaten cup of noodles mocking her from the tiny table. Her Caravan, always meticulously tidy, felt suffocatingly empty this time, the silence a living thing pressing down on her.

Introverts come in 3 shades, each with its unique relationship to social interactions. The first category comprises those who not only prefer solitude and also find it challenging to engage in conversations. Despite their contentment with a quieter existence, a subtle nervousness colors their interactions with the external world.

The second category encompasses introverts who possess the ability to engage in dialogue but consciously choose silence.

Much like myself, these individuals find solace in their quietude, embracing it with a sense of contentment and boldness.

Then, there's the third kind – those introverts who harbor a deep desire for connection but struggle to bridge the gap. Alma fell into this category, a yearning soul restrained by an invisible barrier.

Her heart longed for meaningful interactions, and the inability to do so left her with a pervasive sense of nervousness and melancholy. In the quiet corners of her life, she carried a persistent feeling of missing out on something profound and significant, an elusive connection that seemed just beyond her grasp.

She traced the swirling leaf veins on the blanket, her mind swirling in chaotic currents of its own. Thoughts eddied and crashed, a relentless tide of what-ifs and maybes inside the deep ocean of overthinking.

Then, abruptly, a knock shattered the silence, startling her with its unexpectedness. Alma rarely had visitors; in fact, she never did. Heart pounding, fearing some ill intention, she hesitantly opened the door.

Standing on the threshold, framed by the cold winter sunset, was Tanya, a familiar face wrapped in a thick green sweater and 2 overflowing suitcases her companions dropped by her taxi on the ground.

The sight stole Alma's breath, replacing fear with a bewildered surprise. Tanya, in her caravan? Why all of a sudden? It was too fantastical, surely a figment of her overactive imagination.

Grasping for reality, Alma reached for her phone, a familiar shield against the overwhelming world.

She started texting Tanya, even with her standing right in front of her, "Hello, good evening. What brings you to my small abode? How can I help you?"

"Seriously?" Tanya exclaimed, snatching the phone with a playful exasperation. "I'm going to live with you from today, remember? Can't hide behind texts anymore."

Suddenly speechless, Alma's face became a canvas of unspoken questions, "What? Why? How? Her eyes are wide with a confusion that mirrored the chaotic storm within.

"Don't worry," Tanya chuckled, stacking the suitcases against the wall, "Jerry wouldn't shut up about needing a roommate for you. Finally, I agreed with him yesterday, and voila, here I am. Looking at your face, it seems like he forgot to mention it, though."

Alma's tongue felt thick and clumsy. "J-Jerry asked you?" she stammered, gaze fixed on the floorboards. "What... what did he say?"

Tanya's smile softened. "He was worried about you, Alma. He is on a mission to turn you into a social butterfly, as he put it. Said that opening up in public starts at home. He thought maybe a roommate would give you the company you crave, bring a little sunshine into your quiet world."

A nervous giggle bubbled up from Alma's chest, then spilled over into a full-blown laugh. The enormity of it all hit her like a rogue wave.

Fear mingled with an unexpected warmth, a dawning realization that Jerry, in his clumsy, well-meaning way, might have given her something she hadn't even dared to dream of. Her haven, her solitude, was about to be breached, not by an unwelcome storm but by the possibility of sunshine, laughter, and maybe, just maybe, by a true connection.

"Where's Jerry, by the way?" Alma asked, her soft voice surprisingly steady.

Tanya's grin widened, "Don't you know? Today's the big day. Jerry and Charlie are out there on the mission to fetch the…" Her voice trailed off, replaced by a deeper tone. "SPAN DOORWAY."

CHAPTER SIX

ETERNITIES IN GOLD

Alist (Diary)

Magus Train, Wagon 26, 12:53 P.M.

And there we were, Charlie and I, aboard a train bound for Asparia – the very land of my origin, a realm extending far beyond the confines of Casa and its replica countries.

Seated in the cozy three-seater train coupe, I couldn't help but feel 'The Pack' discreetly hidden beneath the sleeves of my royal blue suit. This ingenious device, designed to absorb excess energy from my body, stored an astounding power within it.

Reflecting on the sheer magnitude of energy held within 'The Pack,' I marveled at the unforeseen potential it possessed. "Who knew I could be a walking power plant?" I mused to myself.

Bill's revelation had cast me as an eternal source of energy – a fount of power so potent that, when accumulated over 6 months, it could serve as the building blocks for a Span Doorway. This realization formed the cornerstone of Bill's intricate plan.

The first phase of the plan involved our journey to Asparia, where we aimed to rendezvous with a certain individual named Albert. His role was pivotal; he was the link between my Asparian energy and the construction of the Span Doorway.

The mechanics of the plan dictated that once we reached Asparia, I would provide Albert with a sample of my unique energy. If the deal was struck, Albert would then proceed to channel this energy over the next few months – culminating in the construction of the elusive Span Doorway that would pave the way for Charlie's liberation.

The intricate dance of fate had begun, weaving together the threads of energy, trust, and escape in a clandestine ballet of inter-dimensional proportions.

"Twenty-six spacious wagons and scarcely any passengers—this train is certainly giving me the creeps," Charlie expressed, perturbed by the eerie quietude enveloping the train.

He had approached me after a brief exploration of the seemingly antiquated and desolate wagon we occupied. The windows were opaque and firmly locked, and the cushions on the seats betrayed signs of wear and tear.

"We have some time until we reach; perhaps we can explore the other wagons," I suggested to Charlie, observing as my breath materialized into a mist in the chilly air, dissipating like ethereal clouds.

"It's alright, I can check them out myself," Charlie replied, noticing my slight shiver in the cold. "Here, take this," he continued, removing his black blazer, and offering it to me. "It's chilly, but given Asparian genes, you certainly need it more than I do."

Gratefully accepting the blazer, I draped it over myself like a makeshift blanket. Charlie proceeded to investigate the other wagons, leaving in his gray vest. He kept his light blue fedora hat atop my head, providing a bit of warmth and concealment.

He moved like a wraith through the silent carriages, each click of the train echoing his unease. As he proceeded to the second-to-last wagon, he couldn't help but regret offering me his blazer.

The temperature in that wagon seemed noticeably colder than the last. Unlike the previous wagon where I sat, the coupes' windows here were transparent, allowing Charlie to easily witness the snowfall on the dark roads outside.

Upon entering the third-to-last wagon, Charlie was taken aback by the unexpected warmth, a stark contrast to the freezing cold of the wagon before.

However, his disbelief reached its peak when he gazed out through the window. The scenery had undergone a complete transformation – the once snow-covered, dark roads had given way to radiant grasslands illuminated by the warm light of the sun.

In a state of disbelief, Charlie retraced his steps to double-check, only to find that both wagons displayed distinct sceneries and existed in different time slots. Tension crept across his face as he pinched himself, half-expecting to awaken from what he believed to be a hallucination.

The rusted brakes screeched as the train lumbered into a bustling station, momentarily jolting Charlie from his introspection. Glancing out the grimy window, a flicker of recognition sparked in his eyes.

The sunbaked platform, the cacophony of hawkers and vendors, the worn paint peeling from the station clock – it was eerily familiar.

He slid the window open, leaning out to soak in the scene. Then, amidst the throng of passengers, a flash of cerulean caught his eye. It was 'The Canadian,' the very train that used to link the major cities of Canada during the twenty-first century.

Meanwhile, inside the dimly lit coupe, my own slumber was shattered by the jarring clang of the train door. A woman, cloaked in mystery like a brown trench coat and round reflective sunglasses, glided past rows of empty seats and settled with disconcerting grace directly beside me – in Charlie's reserved spot.

A knot of apprehension tightened in my gut, her presence as unnatural as a snow leopard amidst cacti. Her gaze, shielded by those dark lenses, remained fixed forward, the silence pregnant with unspoken secrets. Then, in a voice laced with both ice and amusement, she broke the silence.

"I actually came here to kill you… Alist," she announced, the words slicing through the air like a thrown blade.

My body reacted before my mind could catch up. Years of honed instinct propelled me into a defensive crouch, aviator glasses slipping down my nose to reveal blue eyes ablaze with a cocktail of anger and bewilderment.

My gloved hands clenched into fists, the leather splitting into tatters under the sheer force of my grip. The woman, however, remained unfazed by my reaction, a chilling smirk playing on her lips.

"But that was the initial plan," she added, her voice dropping to a conspiratorial whisper.

Silence descended once more, heavy and suffocating. Anyone in my shoes would be stunned, to say the least. A stranger materializing on a random train, uttering murderous threats in a silky tone, while addressing you by your real name.

With a predatory swiftness that was almost breathtaking, she was upon me, her hand poised at the center of my chest. Time seemed to warp again, my mind grappling with the suddenness of it all. Should I defend myself? Strike back? Or remain still, a deer caught in the headlights?

"Oh, you poor-poor boy." Her touch, when it came, was surprisingly gentle, a stark contrast to the glint of malice in her eyes. She lingered for a moment, her fingers tracing a fleeting pattern on my chest, before withdrawing with a predatory smile.

"It's when I saw your heart, truly saw it," she purred, a touch of madness lacing her voice. **"That I realized leaving you alive would be a far greater... torment."**

Confusion clouded my mind. What words were these? What game was she playing? Before I could even form a question, she turned, sauntering toward the other carriage, her voice trailing back like a wisp of smoke.

"I'm Amber Astound," she said, the name an enigma in itself. And with a final, mocking wink, she added, "Pay my regards to Mr. Ion when you reach your destination, Alist."

Her departure left me reeling, the silence of the train punctuated only by the frantic hammering of my own heart. Who was Amber Astound? And what did she mean by her cryptic message?

The silence was shattered by a shriek so sudden it made me jerk upright. In the doorway stood Charlie, eyes wide and breath ragged.

"This train is wicked!" he declared, practically throwing himself into the seat beside me.

My thoughts, still tangled in the enigma of Amber Astound, snagged on his words. "Well... so are the passengers," I echoed, brows furrowed.

He launched into a breathless account of his exploration. Each carriage, he swore, pulsated with its own bizarre reality: swirling snowstorms, sun-drenched meadows, even a glimpse of a train from another time - the Canadian, he gasped.

I, too, exchanged my bewildering experience with Amber Astound. Our discussion only deepened the confusion, and we found ourselves grappling with more questions than answers.

We pondered whether Bill was aware of the strange occurrences on the train. Despite Bill providing a detailed plan, there were gaps in our understanding.

How did Bill know someone in Asparia? Who informed him about this clandestine train that illegally transported people out of the replica countries? Why didn't he accompany us? And how did he possess such advanced scientific knowledge, given his origin in the year 1896?

Considering the rules of the replica countries, individuals brought back from different times were prohibited from traveling beyond their boundaries until they became citizens of Casa.

However, Bill had devised a way to orchestrate our journey by securing tickets on this peculiar train. He deliberately reserved our seats in the last carriage and emphasized that, upon reaching the destination, only I should open the door, not Charlie. Bill cryptically warned of dire consequences if this protocol was not followed.

???, 1:30 A.M.

The rhythmic rattle of the train ceased as a hush fell, thick and expectant. We braced ourselves, united by the weight of the unknown. Following Bill's precise instructions, I opened the door, and both Charlie and I disembarked.

"Is this Asparia?" Charlie asked in awe; our eyes widened in unison. The ground beneath our feet, the buildings that scraped the sky, and the very air we breathed shimmered with the golden sheen of pure, unadulterated gold. "You never told me Asparia was made of gold."

"It isn't," I replied, perplexed by the sight of an entire city constructed from gold. "I've never actually been to Asparia, but I'm sure that the buildings, trees, and fountains are not made of gold."

The surreal scene took an even stranger turn when our gaze snagged on a figure approaching us – a man, or something resembling one, crafted entirely from burnished gold, his eyes like glinting amber chips.

"Well, also, people in Asparia are certainly not made of gold," I added in disbelief.

"Well, that settles it," Charlie said, his voice barely a whisper. "Wrong station."

"So, let's return to tr-," I turned around, suggesting we return to the train when I was met with an unsettling sight—nothingness. Not a whisper of steam, not a groan of metal remained. **And the train is gone.**"

"Even the train tracks are gone, or were they ever there to begin with? How was the train even running?" Charlie's voice held a note of worry, mirroring the confusion that now enveloped us.

Charlie glanced at the golden man, then back at me, his eyes wide with dawning horror. "What the hell is this day?" he whispered, his voice cracking.

The golden man marched on, his metallic footsteps a clanging counterpoint to the unsettling stillness. Every inch of him gleamed in gold – his kingly robe, his shoulder-length hair, his flowing beard, even the ornate patterns on the sandals strapped to his golden feet. Only the diamond ring on his index finger dared disrupt the monotony of gold.

Despite the unsettling scene, his wide grin, surprisingly benevolent under his gilded features, disarmed me momentarily.

With a hint of apprehension, I raised my hands in greeting. "Hello there."

My gaze locked on his, a mental chess game playing out behind my eyes. Friend or foe? Shake his hand or shatter him to dust, or brace for attack?

Neither.

He tucked his hand behind his back, the smile strained. "I… can't do that," he rumbled, his voice a hollow echo in the gilded expanse. His face, devoid of wrinkles yet looked old in its stoicism, confirmed the weight of his words. "But I'm truly glad to see real people. Come, travelers, let's talk. Just… Please, don't touch me."

The invitation hung heavy in the air; a riddle wrapped in an enigma. With the rejection of my handshake, I relegated the gold man to a category of beings with which I could not interact, leaving Charlie to navigate this peculiar encounter.

I walked a bit away from Charlie and the gold man, my gaze fixed on the ten-foot gray metal door set within a sixty-meter-tall golden circular wall encircling the town. My gaze wandered from the colossal door at the city's edge to the whimsical sky above, where cotton candy clouds shimmered with a golden sheen.

Meanwhile, the gold man effortlessly hoisted a throne crafted from a single block of gleaming metal – easily 15 hundred pounds. He placed it before Charlie with a sigh that could have cracked mountains. He then settled on the cold ground himself.

"Is this golden paradise your kingdom?" Charlie asked, sitting on the throne, his voice laced with awe and respect.

"My prison, actually," the gold man chuckled, a sound like wind chimes in a forgotten temple, carrying both amusement and sorrow.

"What are you exactly, sir?" Charlie inquired, puzzled by the unexpected answer.

"Have you heard the tale," the gold man began, his voice gravelly, "of the greedy fool who bargained with a God for everything he touched to turn to gold? And how he ended up turning his own daughter, his love, into a gilded statue?"

Charlie nodded, the story familiar from childhood bedtime whispers.

"That fool," the gold man continued, a flicker of guilt flickering in his golden eyes, "is me. The name's Midas."

"The Midas?" Charlie exclaimed, his voice bouncing off the gleaming walls. " But why aren't you flesh and bone? How did you end up... this?" He gestured at the golden figure, a mix of awe and amusement dancing in his eyes.

"Well… I touched myself," Midas replied with a wry smile.

"Fair enough," Charlie responded, his reply tinged with an awkward undertone.

Midas, however, pressed on, "But there's a part of the story untold. I was betrayed and fought to undo the curse, only to find myself confined in this town, left to wither away alone. Withering away alone would have been a mercy. I've lost count of the centuries spent imprisoned here. As a man turned into a golden anomaly, I no longer hunger, nor do I require air to breathe. I can't die, and every time I am shattered into pieces, I just feel the agony, only to reassemble again. I don't even know how my body's still moving."

"And here I thought I had a tough break," Charlie mused silently, absorbing Midas's tragic tale.

"ALL I EVER WANTED WAS TO LIVE ETERNITIES IN THE CASTLES OF GOLD," Midas roared with a sense of regret, his voice echoing through the golden expanse. He looked around the golden town, **"never did I imagine it would come to this."**

Standing near the colossal metal door, my senses hummed with the unique pulse of Asparia. Beckoning Midas and Charlie closer, I leaned against the imposing barrier.

"This," I explained, my voice echoing in the stillness, "is Asparian steel forged from the very essence of that land. Peering through the small window of the door, I can see newly blossomed flowers unique to Asparia. Our destination lies beyond, but the door stands locked.

"Jerry, being Asparian, can't you just cut it open?" Charlie inquired.

"No can do, Charlie; that's where Asparian steel gets tricky. " I responded, clanking the door's body. Untouched by brute force, it just bends to an Asparian's skill of converting it into energy and reshaping it."

"Then why not convert it into energy, turn it into a passage and then change it back into a door? I saw you tearing Captain Demy's cape," Charlie suggested.

"Not possible at the moment, especially when I'm just operating at an ounce of my power. 'The Pack' absorbs 99 percent of my energy. With only one percent left, I can just convert small amounts of Asparian metal. Captain Demy's flimsy cape is one thing, but we're dealing with a thousand-pound door here. One option is to remove 'The Pack' and wait for a month until I'm back at my full strength."

"So, we're stuck here until you recharge? But what about food and drink for a month?" Charlie asked seriously. "Also, instead of breaking the Asparian metal door, shouldn't we break the golden wall that encircles this town and escape?"

Midas, towering beside us, intervened in our conversation. "Months, years, eternities," he rumbled, his voice tinged with ancient pain. "I've tried numerous things to escape," Midas uttered, landing 2 straight blows with his metal hands on the wall, creating a hole. The only thing visible through that hole was a bright white light. "You can't escape through the walls; beyond it is just never-ending white light with nothing, not ever air. Even if you try to climb over the walls, you still end up in the void of nothingness."

Midas then pointed to the large door, saying, "Only this door is a way to escape. It's a door locked without a keyhole, reminding me of my everlasting cage."

Showing us his primal longing for freedom, Midas lashed out at the door, his fists raining blows like hailstones. Each impact sent tremors through the air, but the steel held firm. "I've tried for forever now, as hard as I could," he roared in frustration and pain as his metal hands cracked from banging on the door. "But this damn door won't break," he cried, his arms shattered into pieces.

"Easy, Mr. Midas," Charlie interjected, sensing the raw anguish radiating from the golden figure. "Why not turn the door to gold? It might break easier then."

Midas's reply was grim, "It's not so simple, kid. I've spent enough time learning the limits of my curse, turning everything within reach to gold, except a few.

I've learned that I can't turn things that are more valuable than gold—diamond, platinum, palladium, and the metal this door is made of.

As I observed Midas, his metallic form shimmering under the dim lights, I noticed a glint in his eyes that seemed suspiciously like tears. "Are you crying, Mr. Midas?" I asked softly.

He scoffed, "Cry? I haven't shed a tear since this golden body claimed me."

"Perhaps not from your eyes," I countered, my gaze sweeping over his gilded form. "But your sorrow weeps inside you, a constant ache beneath the gleaming surface. Maybe it leaks in your smiles, the way you welcome strangers into your hellhole with a façade of cheer."

Without hesitation, I stepped forward and embraced his cold, unyielding form, offering a tangible warmth amidst the suffocating isolation. "Don't worry, Midas," I promised in a soothing tone. "You won't be trapped forever. You have a friend now, and together, we'll find a way."

Midas pushed me gently, a mix of fear and concern in his voice, "You could have turned to gold by touching me."

"I knew I wouldn't," I interrupted, a gentle smile softening my features.

"How?" he breathed, disbelief tingling his voice. "I am cursed to gild all I touch."

"You said yourself," I reminded him, my voice carrying a quiet confidence. **"You can't turn things more valuable than gold. And surely, a friend... a good friend... is worth far more than any precious metal."**

Midas stood speechless, my words sinking in like liquid gold, melting away the hardened shell of despair. His eyes, which had mirrored the cold glint of his prison, began to shine with a spark of newfound hope. "But what if..." he started, his voice trembling between grief and gratitude.

"Well then," I chuckled, a light tinkling sound that broke the heavy silence, **"becoming a golden statue doesn't sound so bad."**

Gold Town, 3:34 A.M.

"We have a big problem here." Charlie's voice suddenly resonated from behind as he pressed his nose against the frosted glass of the door, a grimace twisting his features. "The once vibrant flowers outside have withered, and the climate appears to have undergone a drastic change."

"But those things last for 7 weeks, I responded, a perplexed furrow creasing my brow.

"Perhaps this town exists in another dimension connected to Asparia through this massive door," Charlie suggested in a somber tone. "Time might flow differently here. It's been only 2 hours since we arrived, but it seems like weeks have passed in Asparia. So, if we stay here for a month, mathematically, about 60 years would elapse in the outside world. That implies—"

"When you finally leave this place, everyone you know or love will be either old or dead," Midas finished the sentence with a grave intonation, his golden eyes reflecting the weight of the revelation.

I gazed at Charlie's worried expression and sensed Midas's concern about our predicament. Inhaling deeply, with only one viable course of action ahead, I declared, "Well, it's settled then." With a flair for the dramatic, I continued, **"It's time to give my heart a workout!"**

Undoing my royal blue blazer, I loosened my tie and addressed Midas, "Will you hold that for me?"

Concern etched across Charlie's face as he questioned my change in behavior. "What are you going to do, Jerry?" he asked, worry evident in his tone.

"Asparian metal is essentially energy manipulated and solidified," I explained, moving closer to the ten-foot door.

"Being an Asparian, I can manipulate it to some extent, but the large door is too much to handle, given that I'm at an ounce of my power. Hence, instead of manipulating the energy of the metal, I'm going to absorb it inside me. The energy will pass through my heart and be absorbed by 'The Pack.' This way, not only will the door become lighter, but I'll also gain additional power to absorb more."

"ARE YOU NUTS?" Charlie screamed at me. "Captain Demy's book clearly states that a pound of Asparian metal contains 437 million kWh of energy, and this door clearly weighs over 2000 pounds."

"I'm aware of it," I replied, grabbing the doorknob with both hands. "Best case, we all escape."

"YOU REALLY ARE GOING TO ABSORB EIGHT HUNDRED SEVENTY-FOUR BILLION KILOWATTS OF ENERGY?" Charlie continued to scream. "And what's the worst case scenario?"

"Worst case, the power is too much for me to handle, and it solidifies from inside of my veins, exploding them along with all my internal organs," I admitted, maintaining a smile. "But!" I declared, thinking of all the people dear to me, and rotated the doorknob to initiate the process.

The colossal Asparian metal door transformed into pure energy, flowing within the door frame like radiating electricity as I tightened my grip on the knob. The energy's intensity was palpable to everyone present.

I redirected the flow of energy toward me, feeling its force surge through every ounce of my body. I screamed in agony as my arteries and veins felt like they were on the verge of exploding. The sleeves of my white shirt tore into pieces, and my back and arms developed several cuts, with blood streaming down.

"What power!" Midas exclaimed, watching the force from afar in awe.

The power overflowed, and unexpectedly, 'The Pack' on my left arm exploded, causing severe burns and adding to my agony. The explosion of 'The Pack' disrupted my plan, as now my heart had to bear the full load. The force intensified tenfold on my body, making me feel like I was engulfed in flames.

My blue aviator glasses slipped on my nose, and my blue irises darkened, eventually emitting a radiant blue light. My face contorted in pain, my nerves visibly straining.

Twenty seconds seemed like a century... I had completely absorbed the massive metal barrier and collapsed to the ground. My burned and wounded hands trembled as I breathed heavily. It felt as if I had experienced death countless times in that moment.

The only view before my hazy eyes was a pink sky with golden clouds on the left and a blue sky with white clouds on the right. **My body lay precisely between the golden ground of Midas's prison and the green grass of Asparia.**

CHAPTER SEVEN

SOMETHING YOU CAN DIE FOR...

Alist (Diary)

Asparia, Thick Fog, 8:00 A.M.

Leaning against Charlie's sturdy shoulder, I stumbled across the uneven terrain of Asparia. My body throbbed with the dull ache of severe injuries. The oppressive fog, thick as pea soup, swallowed the world around us, reducing visibility to a scant few feet.

"Heads down," Charlie muttered, his voice a reassuring rumble despite the disorientation. With a calloused finger tracing the faded lines on a well-worn map, he navigated us deeper into the swirling mist.

Our destination: Albert's factory. Midas, recently liberated from his cramped cage, trailed behind us. Confined for too long, he had nowhere else to turn.

The Asparian fog snaked through the skeletal landscape, clinging to my torn clothes like a shroud. Each ragged breath sent puffs of white swirling into the icy air, my lungs burning with the effort. I'd come so far to help a friend go back home; my mind lost deep in some old memories along the way.

Kindergarten, 11:08 A.M. (9 years ago)

What is a man without a purpose? What is he without a goal? Some drift like soulless machines, devoid of direction, while others consciously evade purpose, seeking refuge in the comforting embrace of routine.

Yet, can mere indolence be hailed as a profound purpose? Certainly not, for no one would willingly lay down their life for laziness nor find pride in a retrospective glance at a purposeless journey.

Now, ponder another question: What defines a true purpose? Is every purpose inherently right? A true purpose, I posit, is one that empowers a person to face the imminent shadow of death with an unwavering smile, embracing it with a sense of honor.

It is an objective that, once attained, allows an individual to confront mortality with either a triumphant smile or a reflective acknowledgment of a journey enriched with profound meaning and significance.

In the classroom of my youth, a moment crystallized these musings. "Children, what's your purpose in life?" inquired Ms. Aniston, our kindergarten teacher.

Seven-year-old me, a whirlwind of boundless curiosity, shot his hand up with the force of a miniature rocket.

Ms. Aniston smiled, anticipating the vibrancy my eager response would bring to the room. "Yes, Jerry! Tell us, what lights your fire?"

A grin reminiscent of a summer sunrise spread across my face. "I want to love!" I declared, my voice bubbling with unbridled enthusiasm.

A ripple of surprised giggles danced through the classroom, and Ms. Aniston chuckled, her eyes twinkling with warmth. "Love? As if romantic love?"

"Loving people, in general," I added innocently. "For me, love isn't a secret shared behind cupped hands. It's a cluster of connections, waiting to be splashed across the canvas of life. I want to love everyone."

"Everyone, you say? Even the shy ones whispering in corners, the boisterous ones overflowing with laughter, and even the grumpy ones hiding behind frowns?" The teacher asked with warmth.

I, oblivious to the subtle undertones, bounced on my toes, my excitement crackling in the air. **"Every single one!"** I exclaimed. **"I want to be their friend, understand their stories, fill their days with silly jokes and shared laughter, and weave memories that shimmer like constellations in the night. That's what I plan to live for because I know when I'll be at the end of my life, I'll be surrounded by a plethora of people and millions of moments."**

Back to my sixteen-year-old self—Do I still have the same purpose? Yes! Is my purpose entirely the same? No!

A lot happened during my journey from a kid to an adolescent. Though my goal is still to love, it is no longer to love everyone. Only a few selected people—a small circle that I want to surround myself with—Charlie, Tanya, Bill, Alma, and a newly added member, Midas.

Asparia, a few miles to Albert's factory, 8:35 P.M.

"Okay, now I can manage on my own," I declared; the jolt of newfound strength ripped me from my reverie. With a resolute yank, I withdrew my hand from Charlie's shoulder, my numb fingers instinctively clasping together to ward off the biting cold.

Charlie's gaze flickered to my arms, visible through the tattered sleeves. Surprise flickered across his face. "Jerry," he breathed, astonishment lacing his voice. "Just an hour ago, you could barely move, burns crawling across your body. Fifteen minutes ago, you needed my arm for support. Now you're talking about walking on your own?"

"Yeah, the pain's mostly gone," I admitted, shivering as the chill seeped through my threadbare clothes. "Just this damn cold that won't quit." I shot a glance at Midas, trailing behind us. "Heck, even Midas had his arms shattered, yet look at him now - good as new."

"Well, being made of gold has its perks," Midas chimed in, his voice metallic. "Break me, and I just put myself back together."

"Midas's self-repair is a curse," Charlie countered, a few factory buildings looming into view. "But your recovery is a different story altogether. Maybe it's the absorbed energy, the excess mending your body."

I struggled to focus on Charlie's explanation, consumed by the primal urge for warmth. "Midas," I rasped, "remember that blazer I lent you back in the golden town?"

Midas fumbled, producing the garment. Its once familiar fabric had solidified into a block of gleaming gold under his touch. Disappointment washed over me, a cocktail of grief, lost hope, and sheer awkwardness. "Nah, that's alright," I muttered, staring at the once-cozy fabric, now a useless, cold metal slab.

A note of regret tinged Midas's deep voice. "Sorry, I'm a freak. I can never belong."

I chuckled, turning to face him. "Freakish abilities make for good company, Midas – At least in our group. We've got Charlie and Tanya, pulled from the clutches of time itself. Bill, the enigmatic oddball. And Alma, the memory-eater extraordinaire."

"And don't forget," Charlie chimed in, a hint of amusement in his voice, "you're standing next to a walking power surge, someone who just absorbed the annual equivalent energy output of 2 entire nations."

Midas's golden eyes, if they could have welled up, would have done so now. With playful roughhousing, I grabbed Charlie and Midas by the neck. "To the freaks!" I declared, a grin spreading across my face.

A genuine, non-metallic glint shone in Midas's eyes. "Maybe this truly is a new beginning!"

"Of course it is!" I enthused. "Second Chances, remember? That's the motto of Casa. Once we nail down the deal with Albert for the Span Doorway, we'll all be heading home. You'll get to meet Bill and Tanya. Well, maybe not Alma so much; she's not big on socializing. But hey, I have an idea! How about we all chip in, buy a small apartment in the replica city, and call it *The Freaks' Lodge*?"

Asparia, Albert's Hometown, 9:04 A.M.

The fog cleared a bit, only a bit, revealing a town dotted with imposing factories, eerily silent. "Albert's factory isn't far away; keep your eyes open," Charlie ordered. "The plan was to give a sample of your Asparian energy to Albert, but with The Pack being destroyed, a visit could prove futile."

"Hope for the best," I consoled Charlie. "Maybe he can build a substitute or find some other way to extract energy from my body."

I sprinted ahead as my Asparian eyes caught the glimpse of the address Bill mentioned, a few miles away.

"And now he's running," Charlie murmured in awe. "For a man who was close to death a few hours ago, he's in pretty good shape. I wish I was an Asparian."

It took a while for both of them to keep up with my speed, especially Midas — it was hard for him to move, given his metal body. Not to mention, I wasn't even running at my full potential.

We 3 stood dwarfed by the looming behemoth, a factory sculpted from cold, gray stone. Medieval echoes whispered in its design, 3 stories of shadowed windows peering down like watchful eyes.

The fog conspired to shroud its secrets, yet whispers of unseen stories bled through the swirling white, beckoning us closer to the mysteries it held within.

An unsettling shift in the atmosphere seized me. My skin prickled, a whisper growing into a cold hiss as I counted, eyes darting like trapped birds, "5, eight, 11, 15." I murmured, turning, the grim tally painting the other side. "Twenty-, 37..." My head whipped back, my breath catching in my throat. "Forty-... 51!"

Midas, his gilded face etched with confusion, echoed, "Fifty-one what?"

Suddenly, as if summoned by my count, 51 armed men materialized through the fog. They surrounded us in a menacing ring, their uniforms stirring unwelcome memories of Casa soldiers and the horrors of the incident that took place 8 years ago. My breath hitched in my throat.

Midas, eternally unfazed by such threats, observed the scene with detached surprise. Charlie, however, wasn't so stoic. Faced with a bristling arsenal of automatic weapons and stun batons, a sheen of nervous sweat slicked his brow.

A figure emerged from the throng, a paradox in a crisp suit amidst the chaos. Tall and impeccably dressed, his midnight hair framed eyes that shifted between cerulean and emerald. His mutton chops exuded an undeniable charisma, defying logic itself.

A crackling walkie-talkie amplified his voice as he addressed us. "Two children and a gilded monstrosity. Quite the delightful gathering."

His gaze swept over us, his authority undeniable. A muscular build and a badge emblazoned with the words "Aryan Aracari" completed his imposing presence, captivating us even as dread coiled in our guts.

"Intruders," Aryan boomed. "We've been watching you since you set foot in this country. Hands behind your backs!"

Midas, his voice a rumbling undercurrent, stepped forward. A gauntlet of guns tracked his every move, their sights trained on his heart.

"We mean no harm," Midas rumbled deeply. "These children merely seek an audience with one called Albert. We'll vanish like smoke once our meeting is concluded."

Aryan's jaw clenched. "Albert? Dead for years now." His fingers twisted into white-knuckled knots. "*The Hovershell* rules these wastelands. I, for the last and only time, warn you, step back, Golden Freak. Hands. Behind. Your. Backs."

The news of Albert's demise slammed into us like a physical blow. Before we could fully comprehend it, Midas, fueled by raw emotion, lunged forward. His intention was to seize Aryan's arm, transmuting him into a golden statue.

But fate, as always, had other plans.

Aryan, like his soldiers, wore a formidable force field belt – a Casa invention standard issue for their troops. This belt enveloped the wearer in a diamond-hard electromagnetic shield, impervious even to a nuclear blast.

The telltale red light on the belt indicated the shield was active. As Midas made contact, a jolt of shock surged through his hand, forcing him to recoil.

Without hesitation, Aryan retaliated, thrusting his outstretched hand toward Midas in a blaze of rage. The metallic glove he wore concealed mini flamethrowers. The flames, unleashed with a deafening roar, devoured Midas's golden form, shattering it into a thousand glittering shards.

His head, untouched by the inferno, rolled to the ground, a silent testament to the deadly ballet that had just unfolded -- a gruesome testament to the deadly technology at Aryan's disposal.

Charlie's scream, a raw shard of grief, pierced the tense silence. "MR. MIDAS!" he shrieked, ignoring Aryan's warnings, his eyes fixated on the fallen head lying near a soldier's boot.

Aryan, cold and calculating, met defiance with force. True to his word, he signaled his men to open fire, spitting a metallic hurricane in Charlie's direction.

Anticipating his demise, Charlie squeezed his eyes shut, bracing for the inevitable impact.

The world warped into a deafening symphony of gunfire, each shot a hammer blow against time. Fifty seconds stretched into an unbearable eternity, yet amidst the chaos, an unexpected silence bloomed.

Charlie, to his bewilderment, felt no pain. He wondered if he had reached the afterlife; his vision was dark as his arms wrapped around his head.

Hesitantly, Charlie unfurled his arms, expecting the cold kiss of death. Instead, his vision met a scene both perplexing and horrifying. Despite the showering rain of bullets, not a single one struck him.

A ripple of terror washed over the soldiers. One choked out, his voice cracking, "What in the world just happened?" His question echoed off the 47 fallen comrades who now littered the ground, silent testaments to the carnage.

The bullets, instead of finding their mark on Charlie, were being deflected with incredible force, finding their deadly targets – the soldiers themselves.

The deflected bullets wreaked havoc on their own ranks, each one striking with lethal precision through the soldiers' heads, bypassing their supposedly impenetrable shields. Panic erupted, blood blossoming on the ground where each soldier fell.

"Is this sorcery? Is he a sorcerer?" another soldier stammered, paralyzed by fear. Another, trembling, questioned the capabilities of the scene that defied all logic.

"Could the boy be wearing an electromagnetic shield even more advanced than ours?" Someone else ventured. The eerie green glow on the fallen comrades' belts revealed the failure or deactivation of their once invincible shields.

Fear hung heavy in the air, laced with the acrid stink of burned metal and ozone. Three soldiers who survived stood rooted, knees knocking rhythmically against each other.

"Supernatural?" one gasped, eyes wide with a terror that transcended mortal comprehension.

"Advanced tech?" another choked out, voice barely a whisper.

"Wizardry?" the third rasped, his hands trembling so violently they resembled fluttering leaves.

Suddenly, a booming voice shattered the eerie stillness. **"No. It's a man!"**

Two soldiers whipped around, eyes falling upon me. From their perspective, I wasn't just a lanky individual in aviator glasses and tattered clothes; I was a force of nature, an untamed predator with a feral smirk promising pain. My eyes, blazing with unyielding resolve, reflected the flames that danced across the pieces of Midas's body.

"A monster," the soldier in the middle croaked, his gaze unable to escape the chilling abyss of my irises.

I reached out, and with a flick of my wrist, grabbed his shoulders which snapped his electromagnetic shield with an ease that bordered on the supernatural. The red light on his belt blinked mockingly turning green, his heart pounding a frantic tattoo against his ribs.

"Mercy," he rasped, his eyes on the ground, unable to bear the weight of my icy gaze.

Violence didn't define me. Compassion was my compass, the guiding star that steered me through the treacherous landscapes of life.

Despite belonging to the race of the most superior beings, I refrained from using my power and suppressed it all the time. But before people who sought to disrupt my purpose, who harmed the small group I care for – **mercy took a backseat.**

My head crackled the smirk of a venomous serpent coiling around my lips. I gripped the soldier's shoulder with enough force to pulverize the fragile bones within till the spine, the sickening crunch swallowed by his agonizing scream. He crumpled into a whimpering heap, unconscious and broken.

The remaining soldiers, guns trembling in their hands, could only watch in petrified silence. They aimed, fingers white-knuckled on the triggers, but their fear was a tangible cage, paralyzing them with its icy grip before an unarmed man.

I ignored their silent pleas, my focus solely on the enigmatic figure of Aryan Aracari. Unlike the trembling pawns around him, he stood unfazed, a pillar of stoicism amidst the pandemonium.

"He's no human," I stated, my voice devoid of emotion but heavy with unspoken power. Though the bullets I'd redirected at him in a lightning-fast display had been effortlessly blocked, I sensed a keen intellect lurking beneath his calm exterior.

While the other soldiers perceived me as a blur when their bullets magically deflected, Aryan Aracari, it seemed, could precisely follow my movements.

Aryan met my gaze, a flicker of surprise flitting across his face. "An Asparian," he mused, his voice carrying the weight of a seasoned hunter appraising his prey. "A fascinating specimen indeed. A boss-level threat."

Aryan's hand erupted into a blazing geyser of flame, aiming it directly at me. In a desperate reflex, I flung the soldier caught in my grapple toward the fiery torrent. His scream tore through the fog as the inferno met the soldier's force field, deflecting the flames and clearing a path toward Aryan. The soldier crumpled to the ground, unharmed but shaken.

Taking advantage of Aryan's exposed hand, I lunged, aiming a vicious kick at his chest.

With reflexes honed like a predator, he snagged my leg, halting my attack. Undeterred, I sprang into the air, still trapped in his grasp, and hammered my other knee into his chest. His force field absorbed the blow, yet a flicker of surprise crossed his face.

He released my leg with a brutal twist, sending a searing pain through my ankle.

This momentary lapse was all he needed. Another scorching inferno surged toward me. In a split second, I reacted, grabbing and deflecting his arm upwards.

The flames skyrocketed, an ephemeral fountain swallowed by the fog. My right fist, poised for a counterattack, found itself met by a brutal head-butt, sending my vision reeling. This was the first time I had been genuinely wounded, the first time I felt even remotely outmatched.

The air crackled with anticipation as I wiped up the blood flowing down my nose. We were locked in a desperate dance of fury, a whirlwind of fists and feet meeting an impenetrablc wall of shields.

My blows, a flurry of punches, kicks, and karate chops, were met with unwavering defense. His fists blocked my knuckles, his knees deflected my kicks. This wasn't just a fight; it was a study in controlled violence, a testament to honed reflexes and raw power.

In the blink of an eye, I saw my chance. With a blur of speed, I snatched a knife from his uniform pocket, its glint cutting through the fog. My hand was mere inches from his eyes when the world turned dark.

A monstrous hand clamped around my throat, lifting me off the ground like a ragdoll, the knife fell from my hand. The steel of his glove, getting warmer, burning against my skin, promising a horrifying demise.

My mind raced. Escape seemed impossible, my overconfidence a bitter pill to swallow. I had underestimated him, foolishly believing a swift victory was within reach.

Now, with Charlie cornered by the remaining soldier, my options dwindled to a single bleak choice. Raising my hand in surrender, I met Aryan's steely gaze.

He wasn't a man who reveled in the kill, but in the subjugation of his opponent. A cold smile stretched across his face as he slammed me to the ground, the victor basking in the chilling silence of a battle hard-won.

The Lumberjack's Mansion, Axe Room, 12:00 A.M.

Midnight found us weary and interrogated, stripped bare of our intentions in this desolate land. It was time to be presented before the true master of this country. Aryan Aracari, merely a commander, was a shadow compared to the true power behind him.

Propelled by Aryan's watchful eye, I stepped into the owner's domain. Relief, a fleeting visitor, washed over me at the sight of Charlie, hands restrained but alive. Midas, his head severed yet immortal, rested within a platinum birdcage on a wooden stool beside him.

The room, a macabre museum, showcased an unsettling predilection for axes. Each wall boasted trophies of destruction: axes rusty and ancient, axes glinting with diamonds, axes dwarfing men in size.

The air crackled as the owner, a spiky-haired enigma, finished polishing a behemoth iron ax and hung it with practiced ease. His yellow eyes sparked like lightning; his brow furrowed in a permanent scowl. A black-green checkered kimono draped his lean, muscled frame as he pocketed a silver-splitting maul the size of a normal hammer.

"Ion Whisper," the name rolled off his tongue with an unsettling melody, "No, call me *The Lumberjack*." His voice, calm beneath the veneer of malice, sent shivers down my spine.

The Lumberjack. The name fit like a shroud in this chamber of blades.

Charlie, cuffed and captive; Midas, a gilded head in a silver cage; and me, the harbinger of death for 47 of his men. Yet, I sat unchained, a mockery of freedom. His presence, a thick ironwood forest, held me prisoner within its oppressive aura. It was as if he knew I was no threat to him.

A stark poster pasted on the door shrieked its edict: "Speak without leave, meet death without warning." My lips pursed into a resolute line, mirroring the silence of my companions. Here, the Lumberjack held the sole right to orchestrate the macabre symphony of words.

The Lumberjack reclined on the ground, his legs crossed as he addressed us. "I've heard your story of why you came to Asparia. And that you killed most of my men. But before I punish you for what you have done, I want to share with you what I do."

His expression shifted to one of apparent delight as he looked at me. "Asparians, wonderful creatures. Everything about them was fascinating; too bad the race became extinct. Only a few Asparians are left now. But their country, Asparia, is the greatest wonder on this planet." Standing up, he strolled through the room. "Every bit of Asparia is filled with energy—the rocks, the crust," he picked up a silver ax and hurled it against the wall, cracking it, "the trees I cut myself—all of it contains energy so pure and precious, more valuable than a hundred countries made of gold."

The Lumberjack approached my face, and with a gentle touch, he removed the blue glasses shielding my eyes. Panic coiled in my gut, replaced by a strange warmth as he murmured, "These glasses, an alloy of Asparian and Crux steel," he murmured while I forced my eyes closed. "These glasses help you control the energy that's overflowing in your eyes. A power so immense, it threatens to unravel the world you see, hence the lid you keep. That's why you are closing your eyes now, right?" He placed the glasses back on my face.

Hesitantly, I nodded, the truth prickling like a whisper against my skin.

"Even Asparians," he continued, leaning closer, "are vessels of this raw energy, a potent cocktail of instinct and vulnerability.

It's so strong and destructive, so valuable and useful. Yet, you fell to Aryan, a scion of the Aracari race, hunters of your kind. Their hulking frames and uncanny knack for reading movements—a legacy honed against your ancestors. Mainly, the alphas of the Aracari race have this ability to predict the opponent's move, eyeing a single movement." The Lumberjack spoke with enthusiasm.

"It has been 11 years since my men and I claimed this country from the control of Casa. I have personally fought various battles with Casa, but in the end, we came to an understanding. Now, we extract the energy from Asparia, create Span Doorways, and sell them to Casa at half the usual rate. This is all to maintain peace, as Casa can't afford battles with us without bloodshed."

He took a seat, and Aryan presented him with a curious horn-like device, wires snaking like metallic nerves. "Killing you," he began, a wry smile playing on his lips, "offers no solutions. Instead, your arrival gifts an opportunity." He raised the machine, glinting in the flickering firelight. "You came here to get a Span Doorway in exchange for your energy? Well, all you need is this machine. The process is simple: the Asparian extracts his energy inside it on a monthly basis, and after about 6 months, when enough energy is extracted, it will produce a tiny blue ball."

He showed us a sample of the blue ball, hardly a centimeter in size, and explained, "This ball is the essence of the Span Doorway. Just put it inside the location pistol and shoot it toward a door; a shimmering waterfall blooms, a portal to your desired destination. This waterfall is the Span Doorway; it's a portal that can take you to any place that you set on the location pistol."

He took out 3 differently colored balls from his pocket, each one between the gaps of his fingers when he showed us. "The color of the balls tells how far the portal will connect. The blue balls are for traveling through the planets, the light blue ones for traveling to any place on the planet, and lastly, the white ones for traveling anywhere in a small city."

The Lumberjack deftly showcased the versatility of the white spheres, demonstrating their ability to create portals without the need for a location pistol.

With a calculated throw, he projected a white ball at the window, envisioning the door in his mind. Instantaneously, a cascading portal materialized on the window's surface, connecting seamlessly to a corresponding opening on the door.

The Lumberjack, with a flourish, inserted one of his axes through the window, and it emerged from the door on the other side. He elucidated that when these white spheres burst, they assumed the form of the object into which they exploded, maintaining their ephemeral existence for a span of 5 to 8 minutes.

The Lumberjack's loomed closer, his grin stretching wide. "Now," he boomed, his voice echoing through the cavernous museum, "you might be wondering what comes of all this exposition. Well, consider it your reprieve." He tossed the horn-like, metallic device toward me, its surface glinting in the dim light. "As a punitive measure, I'll let you all go home. Your task? Craft the blue spheres and dispatch them to me biannually for the next 2 years. Although your friend won't return to Earth, at least you'll linger in the realm of the living. Just 2 years, and freedom shall be yours."

The echo of the Lumberjack's words brought a modicum of relief. Despite our failed mission, the prospect of returning home cast a glimmer of solace. Yet, shadows swiftly darkened the horizon.

"However," the Lumberjack interjected with a malevolent smirk, "there's a minor complication. I cannot overlook the deaths of my 47 men, so I've decided: **I'll kill just one of you.**"

Terror choked my throat. The relief of a moment ago curdled into a bone-deep dread. My gaze darted between Charlie and Midas, their faces mirroring the horror that gripped my own.

"Reconsider this, brute!" Midas' disembodied voice rasped, a note of defiance cutting through the suffocating silence.

The Lumberjack's response was swift and ruthless. A blur of motion, and Midas's platinum birdcage met the keen edge of a random ax. Forehead and cage shattered in tandem, cascading to the ground in a grotesque ballet of dismemberment.

"Silence is golden," the lumberjack growled, his eyes burning with fury, "especially for severed heads."

Midas' voice, though weakened, remained firm. "Violence won't solve this. You cannot kill me, not truly."

The Lumberjack scoffed, a hint of amusement playing on his lips. "Curious, isn't it? A head without a body, yet your consciousness persists. I thought severing your link to the brain would be the end, just like those mindless undead you call zombies."

Midas' spectral eyes narrowed. "Even I don't understand it," he admitted, a note of melancholy creeping into his voice. "Centuries I have spent yearning for oblivion, yet it eludes me."

The Lumberjack's voice dripped with a caustic mix of amusement and contempt. "Aren't you all a delightful collection of curiosities?" he drawled, his gaze lingering on Midas's gleaming head. "A mythical figure plucked straight from legend."

He swiveled to me, his smile sharpening like a chipped blade. "And you, a descendant of the first human. Quite the pedigree, wouldn't you say?"

Then, his eyes flicked to Charlie, a sneer twisting his lips. "And as for you," he paused, drawing out the agony, "a common-or-garden human. Utterly useless. Perhaps that's why they plucked you from the tapestry of time – a blank slate, easily manipulated, easily discarded."

Charlie flinched a visible tremor wracking his body. The word "useless" hung in the air, a poisonous dart that found its mark with unerring accuracy. Shame and anger warred in his eyes, his fists clenching and unclenching as he fought the sting of the lumberjack's barb.

I felt a surge of protectiveness, the need to shield Charlie from this verbal onslaught. My gut clenched with guilt; A gloom as I look at my own failures, yet there I stood, powerless to erase the cruel truth etched onto his face. The air crackled with tension so thick it felt like a living entity, suffocating us with its invisible grip.

The Lumberjack, basking in his cruelty, let out a guttural chuckle. "Aw, so sad for being called useless," the Lumberjack continued to mock Charlie, his tone dripping with condescension. "Oh, don't fret, little hero, you all serve your purpose, even the dull blades like you. Alright, let's give the 'useless' guy a task. If this human completes the challenge, all 3 of you will go home. But if he fails, only 2 of you will."

The Lumberjack, a cruel smirk twisting his features, gestured toward Charlie with a gnarled thumb. "Entertainment, wouldn't you say, Aryan?"

Aryan, ever stoic, merely nodded. The Lumberjack's gaze then fell on me, his smile sharpening into something predatory. "Let's play a little game. Pick a number between one and five hundred."

Uncertainty gnawed at me. Randomly, I blurted, "257."

"Ah, I see," the Lumberjack responded with a sinister smile and turned back to Charlie. "So, two hundred fifty-seven push-ups it is."

The daunting challenge hung in the air, and the room was thick with tension. Even a seasoned athlete would struggle with that, let alone Charlie.

My heart raced faster than a bullet train, not because I doubted Charlie, but because I knew he wasn't known for his physical prowess. I could hardly believe he had ever performed a proper push-up in his life.

Charlie swallowed, his face etched with a mix of resignation and defiance. He knew this wasn't just a push-up challenge; it was a test of his will, a gauntlet thrown at his very existence. Charlie assumed the push-up position, gravity becoming his greatest adversary.

"One, 4, 8," As Aryan's monotonous count echoed through the room, each number felt like a hammer blow to my heart. Meanwhile, the Lumberjack sat comfortably entertained by the life-and-death game unfolding before him.

Six minutes stretched into an eternity. "Fifty-," Aryan continued the count. Charlie's breathing grew ragged; his muscles screamed in protest, yet he pushed on.

His form faltered, and his knees threatened to buckle, but he fought gravity with every ounce of his being. He had surpassed his own limits long ago at 16, fueled by a desperate hope and the flicker of rebellion in his eyes.

Sixty-five. Charlie's vision blurred, sweat stinging his eyes. His chest heaved; each rise was a monumental effort.

Then, The lumberjack's mocking voice cut through the tension. "Wrong posture!" He shouted, noticing Charlie's fatigue-induced change in push-up form. "Aryan, start again from 60."

I averted my eyes, unable to witness the torment, feeling utterly helpless. "Sixty-eight," Charlie heard Aryan's voice, mustering the strength to complete at least 70. Deep down, he knew the number was beyond his reach. His physical power had abandoned him, and only sheer mental strength kept him going. But it wasn't enough.

The cruelty of it all stung like a fresh wound. Charlie slumped to the floor, his body utterly spent. He was a warrior stripped of his weapons, his spirit bruised but not broken. The Lumberjack's taunts echoed in the room, a poisonous chorus celebrating Charlie's "failure."

"Once a useless, always a useless," the Lumberjack remarked, observing Charlie's plight. "So, I gave you a chance, and you blew it. Now, whom should I kill? I'm so confused."

He approached Midas, saying, "Killing the cursed king would be a big feat; too bad he's immortal."

Then he turned to me, "Killing an Asparian would be an even bigger feat, but without him, the plan to make the blue balls wouldn't work."

Finally, he sat beside Charlie, who lay motionless on the floor, "Well, killing a pathetic human like you wouldn't be a feat at all."

He stood up and turned away, "Ah! Guess I'll let you all go." He announced.

Was it all over? Was it genuine? A trick? My mind reeled with questions, replaying the volatile dance of the past minutes.

He strolled away, hands seemingly nonchalant in his pockets. But then, a tremor of manic energy seized him. He pivoted, his voice tight with an unsettling obsession, **"Hold on, I just remembered the perfect feat!"**

Before we could register his shift, he whipped out a chillingly small maul from his pocket. In a blink, the brutal truth of his freedom offer became crystal clear. It was never about liberty; it was about satiating his warped sense of achievement.

With inhuman force, he slammed the maul between Midas's golden brow, completing his twisted declaration, **"KILLING AN IMMORTAL!"**

Midas's once-radiant features contorted in silent agony. **His once-golden head started rusting and eventually turned black… as the life in his eyes faded away.**

CHAPTER EIGHT

WARM WATER

Alist (Diary)

Toronto Replica, Random Street, 9:53 P.M.

Gasping streetlights flickered like dying breaths, casting shadows that writhed in the wind's cold caress. My boots left hollow echoes on the deserted, asphalt veins of replica Canada.

How long had I wandered these lifeless arteries since dawn bled into this endless night? I couldn't remember. There were no cars, no whispers of life, only the sorrowful symphony of rain; each dropped an icy needle on my skin.

Exhaustion, a leaden weight in my limbs, forced me to a halt in the middle of the road. A hacking cough ripped from my throat, scraping like bone on stone.

Clearing the acrid taste, I exhaled, a plume of white fog betraying the frigid air that bit at my flesh. It gnawed at me, but not as fiercely as the guilt that twisted in my gut, a venomous serpent coiling tighter with each passing hour.

The waning crescent moon, a ghostly sliver amidst the thunderous tapestry of clouds, offered a cold comfort as I slumped onto the wet ground, head cradled in my arms.

Two days. Two days since the Lumberjack had tossed us, Charlie and I, back into this hollow shell of our hometown. Two days of drowning in an ocean of self-recrimination, each wave whispering of that helpless time.

(2 days ago)

Lumberjack's Mansion, Ax room, 12:28 P.M.

That moment, that horrifying spectacle, replayed on a loop in my mind - the sickening crunch of flesh against bone, the rust blooming across Midas's once-golden skin as the Lumberjack's maul tore through him like a ravenous beast.

Midas, the friend I'd dreamed of sharing countless times with, ripped away in an instant. Barely knew him, the thought tore at me. Yet now, the future stretched before me, barren and empty, regretting I couldn't save him.

I could close my eyes and conjure visions of him woven into our ragtag band of friends, his booming stories filling the tavern, his nimble fingers coaxing melodies from his lute. A new life stretched before him, freedom at last after centuries trapped in a gilded cage.

Immortal, he claimed, always mending, reforming, defying death's icy touch. Even that severed brow hadn't stopped him. But the Lumberjack's maul, spitting sparks and leaving wounds that bled rust and ash, had.

How? The question gnawed at me, an unanswered riddle etched in the bedrock of my despair. Was it the Lumberjack's inhuman strength or some infernal magic bound to that accursed maul?

"The debt is paid," the Lumberjack had declared, his voice tinged with amusement that curdled into unease as he met my gaze.

A burning flicker of fury mingled with my grief, fists clenching around nothingness. I couldn't cry, my Asparian physiology denying me even that solace. Yet, a drop of blood, a crimson testament to my anguish, traced a silent path down my cheek.

Toronto Replica, Random Street, 10:13 P.M.

"You should come home, dinner's ready." My eyes rolled on the back, hearing Alma's words from behind.

How did she even find me? How didn't I sense her before?

She stood before me, a shivering silhouette in her rain-soaked coat, an umbrella clutched like a fragile hope in her hand. Her hair, normally a cascade of raven wings, clung damply to her forehead, framing a face flushed not just with the cold but with a quiet determination that mirrored the stormy clouds above.

"You see," I rasped, my voice as empty as the deserted streets, "if you're carrying an umbrella, you might as well..."

"Open it? Maybe I will," she interrupted her voice barely above a whisper. "But only if you come with me. Everyone's worried sick; you've been gone for hours."

My resolve, already brittle as ice, threatened to shatter under the weight of her concern. "I just need some time alone," I croaked, the words heavy in my throat. "Go back, Alma. I'll be fine."

But her eyes, reflecting the moonlight's struggle against the storm, held a stubborn echo of my own grief. "No," she said, her voice firm despite the tremor in her chin. "Why are you even hurting yourself?"

With a quiet gesture, she tossed the umbrella aside, mimicking my earlier defiance. Then, in a silent act of solidarity, she removed her soaked coat, laying it on the set ground like a shield against the rain and the cold. Finally, she sat beside me, a silent promise of shared solitude amidst the storm.

A gust of wind whipped Alma's wet hair across her face as she met my gaze, defiance sparkling in her eyes.

"That's a brave side I'm seeing of you," I remarked. "Don't be stubborn, you'll be sick."

"So will you. You're more susceptible to the cold than I am," Alma expressed with concern. Her hair, body, and clothes were all soaked. "It's up to you whether you want both of us to endure the risk of pneumonia."

Couldn't argue with that.

Apartment 4H, 10:40 P.M.

The apartment floor became a muddy canvas beneath our dripping boots. Shivering like castaways clinging to a raft, Alma and I stumbled through the doorway. Regret hung heavy in the air, thicker than the steam rising from our damp clothes.

"Jerry," Bill started, his voice rough with remorse as he reached for my shoulder. "I… I can't even express how sorry I am, dude. I met Albert quite years ago – imagining him dead, seeing Asparia under new control - it never crossed my mind. I thought it was a perfect plan, but… I'm sorry, your friend –."

I felt the sting of anger rise, but it was swallowed by the icy grip of grief. My response was a silent shake of the head, and a cold shoulder turned toward him.

Tanya emerged from the kitchen, her eyes widening at the sight of us. "Oh, you 2 look like drowned rats!" she exclaimed, but her voice quickly softened with concern. "Jerry, a hot bath is waiting for you. Strip off those wet clothes and hop in. Alma, you go after that."

The warmth of the suggestion battled the chill in my bones. "Go ahead, Alma," I mumbled, sinking onto the sodden bed cushion. My teeth chattered a counterpoint to Tanya's gentle ministrations.

"No, you should go first," Alma insisted, her gaze full of worry. "You're freezing."

Frustration bubbled up, but I recognized the futility of arguing. "Let's not play this 'no, after you dance," I snapped harshly, coughing between words. "My lungs feel like sandpaper, and I'm one sneeze away from an avalanche. Just get in there, dry off, and let me have some peace."

My harsh words lingered in the air, echoing back in the subsequent silence. Shame burned in my gut as I saw Alma's eyes welling up with tears.

With a quiet sniff, she hurried toward the bathroom, leaving me alone with my gnawing guilt and the rhythmic patter of dripping water from my trousers.

Regret clawed at me as I bowed my head, rubbing my thighs. Tanya, like an elder sister, sat behind me, untying my man bun, and drying my hair. My eyes closed tightly as I cleared the mist from my fogged-up aviator glasses.

Rain-slicked and grim, Charlie stomped into the apartment, a stark contrast to my own soggy misery. He was completely dry, for unlike some other people I was familiar with, he actually knew how to use an umbrella.

He found me fumbling with my glasses, the world still a blurry watercolor.

"We've had enough," his voice cut through the steam like a knife, hand landing heavy on my shoulder. "My damn Earth fixation snagged us in real trouble this time. No more. No more begging, no more portals. No more going back to Earth. I won't gamble with our lives again." His words crackled with guilt like embers of a dying fire. "Just… rest, Jerry. You need it."

I listened in silence, my mind adrift in a sea of thoughts that suddenly snapped into focus when it was my turn to bathe.

The hot water was a siren song, beckoning me away from the storm in my head.

I sank into the steaming tub, letting the warmth leech away the chill and the weight of Charlie's pronouncement. My eyes fluttered closed, drowning in the abyss of comfort, the scalding water slowly pushing reason back to the surface.

Apartment 4H, 1:00 A.M.

Tanya and Alma finally retreated to their caravan while Bill and Charlie snored softly in their makeshift beds. Leaving the tub after an hour-long soak, I emerged like a ghost, a bathrobe clinging to my damp frame, long hair unbound like a waterfall down my shoulders.

My fingers drummed an absent rhythm on Charlie's desk, my gaze snagged on the vibrant mosaic of photos plastered across its surface. A collage of memories, each snapshot capturing a stolen moment from our adventures.

Yet, among the grinning faces and joyful embraces, one glaring absence gnawed at me – Alma. Where was she, the quiet storm of our ragtag group?

"Next time," I muttered to myself, the words carving a promise into the air. "Next time, I'll convince her to be in a group photo." Unlike other girls, drawn to the allure of the lens, Alma was as elusive as a wisp of moonlight, forever flitting just beyond the frame. No flashbulb could capture the depths of her spirit; she hated to be photographed.

I scrawled a reminder across my palm with a black pen, a lifeline against the tide of forgetfulness: "Picture with Alma." The thought echoed a silent oath, a pact with tomorrow.

My hand drifted toward the pen, returning it to its resting place beside Charlie's diary. Not a diary in the conventional sense, but a chronicle of his life in Alistia, his adopted home. His ink bleeding onto the pages in tales of a new life woven with threads of friendship and wonder.

I cracked open the worn leather cover, a wave of nostalgia washing over me as I delved into the past. Each line was a brushstroke, painting moments into my mind: The day Charlie met me for the first time, the day Tanya confessed to him, the day we all had our first dinner as friends.

But then, there it was, a photograph tucked amidst the pages. A younger Charlie, barely 10, beaming amidst his smiling parents. Below, a stark inscription in his neat handwriting: "Miss you!" The words struck me like a physical blow, the weight of their unspoken grief anchoring me to the present.

As I turned the pages of Charlie's diary, my eyes snagged on a captivating entry nestled amidst the familiar ink. It wasn't merely a chronicle of his journey; it was a whispered riddle, a tantalizing glimpse into the mystery of the train we took to Asparia.

Charlie's insatiable curiosity had led him to uncover the intricacies of this enigmatic locomotive, a train woven into the fabric of Alistian history.

Driven by a relentless thirst for knowledge, Charlie had delved into the internet, devoured dusty tomes, and even gleaned whispers of myth. Combining these fragments with his own experience, he'd pieced together a breathtaking story.

According to his findings, the train had its roots in the bygone land of the Magus. Once a haven for a mere 679 wizards, renowned for their nobility and power.

However, a twist of fate unfolded when the lords of 3 hundred nations sought to forge alliances with these powerful beings. Despite their small population, half of the wizards attended the alliance ceremony, only to find themselves imprisoned for life by the very nations they had hoped to call allies.

With a mere 340 wizards remaining, Magus dwindled. Facing annihilation, they channeled their defiance and the memory of their trapped kin into a marvel of steel and magic – the Magus Train.

Each year, it embarked on a symbolic quest, not for gold or glory, but for something far deeper - the universal human yearning for home. It traversed the labyrinthine pathways of memory, a metallic heart pulsing with the promise of belonging. **Like a multidimensional vehicle to… home.**

Charlie's words danced across the page, painting a picture of this ethereal vessel. He described 26 carriages, each a portal inscribed with a letter, shimmering keys to forgotten homelands. A person's very name, the key that unlocked their destiny, determined the portal that would return them to their roots. The last carriage, denoted by the letter 'A,' while the first carriage, marked 'Z.'

A person could return to their place of origin by opening the carriage corresponding to the initial letter of their real name. For instance, if a person whose real name starts with 'Y' opens the door of the second carriage when the train stops, he will reach his place of origin.

Bill's cryptic instruction to open the final carriage, the portal marked with 'A' – it all made sense now. My name, Alist, resonated with the very essence of Asparia. In Charlie's case, with a name commencing with 'C,' peering through the window of the third-last carriage showed a glimpse of the familiar railway station of his hometown, Canada, on Earth.

My mind reeled with the implications. If Charlie's research held true, a path back to Earth, independent of the perilous Span

Doorway, lay within reach. All it required was patience – waiting until the Magus Train's annual voyage, 10 months away.

General Anmolbir's Bungalow, Living Hall, 2:02 A.M.

The phone's shrill chirping shattered the night's stillness, a jarring contrast to the peaceful slumber I'd just slipped into. It was an unknown number, and an unsettling pang of apprehension tightened my chest.

Who could be calling at this ungodly hour? Unless, of course, there was an emergency. Hesitantly, I answered the call, bracing myself for whatever news awaited.

Little did I know that single decision would plunge me into the heart of a whirlwind, face-to-face with General Anmolbir in his secluded bungalow.

I sat across from him, my head throbbing from sleep deprivation, nervously twisting the cord of my phone.

"So, you planned to whisk your dear friend back to his own time," General Anmolbir's voice was a smooth, sardonic drawl, echoing the confession I'd just offered. "A clandestine trip through a smuggled Span Doorway from Asparia, erasing his memories like dust motes, returning him after a mere Alistian week…while 3 years slipped by back on Earth."

I could only murmur a sheepish confirmation, biting my lip as the weight of my actions sunk in. His words hung heavy in the air, tinged with a sardonic amusement that grated on my already raw nerves.

"And you and your cohorts," he continued, settling back in his plush recliner with a flourish, "apparently believed the Casa board to be a gaggle of fools. Did you truly think we wouldn't notice your absence from Casa classes for 2 months, your complete disappearance from the replica country's records?"

His gaze met mine, a sharp glint in his eyes, "Also, you broke another cardinal rule – leaving the country."

My throat grew dry as I stammered, "So… are we to be hanged at dawn?"

General Anmolbir chuckled, a low, rumbling sound. "If a commoner had committed such transgressions, death would indeed be a grim reality. But you, my friend, are no ordinary individual, are you, Jerry?"

He sipped his authentic Indian tea, the aroma of cardamom and ginger wafting across the room. "The Casa cares only for the preservation of the timeline. And since your plan wouldn't create temporal paradoxes, thanks to your… memory-wiping scheme, I believe an oversight can be… tolerated."

Relief washed over me, momentarily eclipsing the gnawing anxieties that still lingered. But then, another wave of worry replaced it.

"General," I began, the words tumbling out in a rush, "Our initial plan… it went futile. Charlie said he'd accepted it and was staying here. But I read his diary… deep down, he wants to go back. And he can! But he needs us, my help and Alma's, to board the Magus Train."

General Anmolbir raised an eyebrow. "So, what's the dilemma, Jerry? Wouldn't you do anything for your friend?"

"It's not that simple," I sighed, the burden of this impossible choice weighing heavily on me. "Charlie wouldn't ask for help anymore. He doesn't want to cause more trouble. And if I never mention it, maybe… maybe he'll stay. Forever. But sending him on that train… It's goodbye, truly goodbye. Even if I try to bring him back later, a year in Alistia could be centuries on Earth. I can't bear the thought of losing him, but neither can I trap him here against his will. It appears I am caught in some crossroads."

Anmolbir handed me a cup of tea, mirroring his own, as we delved into the complexity of my predicament.

"Just holding the cup warms my hands, a simple joy I wish could last forever. Today, the hot water bath provided a similar joy – a sensation I crave, just like I desire the perpetual company of all my friends," I confessed, seeking solace in the comforting heat of the tea.

"The allure of warm water is undeniable, especially in those icy winter baths. Yet, it's ephemeral. Sooner or later, the warmth dissipates, leaving you with nothing but cold water," General Anmolbir philosophized.

"Picture this, General. If I'm wealthy, I'd have an array of geysers to bask in an endless supply of warm water." I remarked.

"A tempting dream, Jerry. But then what? Wouldn't you grow numb to the luxury, the heat becoming a mere background hum? The more you indulge, the more the precious warmth loses its edge, eventually scalding you. No matter if you have limited or limitless things, in the end, you'll either crave them or hate them," General Anmolbir cautioned, his words leaving a lingering resonance.

He set down his own cup, the tea now tepid, a symbol of time's relentless march, as he posed a final choice, "So, it's up to you now. Do you want to crave your friend or hate him? Spend the next 10 months in joy, bidding him farewell on a happy note. Or let him be, potentially spending a lifetime with him, or perhaps parting ways long before that."

My intentions crystallized as I listened to him speak. "I have a dream, a vision for my life. I see myself playing the guitar in the company of all the friends I've made throughout my entire existence. I want Charlie to be a part of that circle," I whispered, stretching my hands in a gesture of determination. "But I've lost one already, Midas. I won't lose another, so maybe I need to become stronger."

"That's the fascinating part— you're already strong. You, Jerry," he declared, his voice a velvet-lined trap, "Are the very reason I graced this replica country as a teacher despite being one of Casa's elite 21 soldiers, warriors exceedingly even formidable Asparians like Demy."

General Anmolbir strolled toward a massive, artistically crafted wooden wardrobe; he extracted an object from within, its purpose veiled in shadow.

"Asparians are born masters of the 5 senses— sight, sound, smell, taste, touch. The resilience in harnessing them to their utmost potential unlocks an inhuman level of speed, senses, and instincts."

He paused, savoring the weight of his words. Then, with a flourish, he flung a bullet from the concealed drawer. It streaked across the room, propelled by his fingers with the force of a pistol shot, embedding itself in the wall with a shuddering crack.

"For men like me, it takes a lifetime of grueling discipline and effort to achieve this feast, to master the 5 senses," he elaborated, his gaze fixed on the lodged bullet. "But for you, Jerry, a gem even among Asparians, you were born with not 5 but 6 senses – sight, sound, smell, taste, touch and aura. An asset beyond measure, the very reason I watched over you, preparing you for the Casa citizenship test. Pass it, and a meeting with the architect of Casa awaits."

"The architect of Casa? The man who built the whole country? He wants to meet with me? I didn't know I was so precious," I mused, approaching him. "Even though I've been activating my powers since the age of 8, I don't fully comprehend them. I've never undergone any training, so my abilities aren't skill-based, nor are they akin to the more general powers like invisibility, super-speed, or super-strength," I explained, maintaining eye contact.

"To illustrate," General Anmolbir, a sphinx wrapped in human skin, chuckled. In a blink, his fist, capable of pulverizing boulders, hurtled toward me.

But fear was a stranger in my world. Without a flinch or diverting my gaze from his face, my pinky, a wisp against his granite-hard hand, halted the blow. A gust of air whipped our faces, a testament to the clash unseen.

"Instincts," the General declared, amusement dancing in his eyes. "That's your crown jewel, Jerry. An inbuilt radar, a sixth sense whispering the secrets of attack and defense before your conscious mind even comprehends them. It's the core essence of your abilities; It's like an inherent reflex, which is why you didn't need formal training," he clarified.

His hand withdrew, mine mirroring the gesture. "Yes, your repertoire might lack flashy tricks like cloaking, blitzing, or superhuman strength. But yours, friend, is the power that surpasses all. You can see the invisible, stop the speedster, and slice through the toughest," he emphasized, his fingertip grazing the cerulean frames of my aviator glasses.

"Then there are your eyes," he continued, his voice tinged with awe. "Those pools of cerulean, your Asparian birthright. Your sight pierces farther than mortal eyes can dream. Science tells us it's your irises crafted to magnify tenfold. But they hold secrets far beyond simple magnification."

Intrigued, I pressed, "Such as?"

A mischievous glint sparked in the General's eyes. From his drawer, he produced another bullet, this one shimmering with an otherworldly sheen.

"These bullets are crafted from lead, copper, and a pigment extracted from the irises of deceased Asparians," he elaborated, eyes gleaming with excitement.

With the same deadly grace, he launched the bullet toward its predecessor lodged in the cracked wall. But this time, it didn't simply embed itself. It tore through the wall, leaving a gaping hole, its momentum carrying it into the next room.

"The iris pigment," he explained, savoring the impact, "not only grants enhanced vision, but when harnessed properly, it can even imbue projectiles with tenfold force, speed, and impact. Hence the name of such projectiles, impact bullets."

"Wow," I breathed, still reeling from the revelation of my own power and how it could be used.

Stepping outside the replica country had shown me just how formidable the world was, with beings like the Lumberjack and Aryan Aracari leaving. Yet, with General Anmolbir's assurance of my own latent strength, a burning question remained: how could I unlock it and push myself beyond what I knew?

"To increase one's strength," the General stated, stretching into a statuesque kung-fu stance, "One must first fully understand the strength one already possesses."

He exuded an aura of confidence, having mastered every style of kung-fu known to man. "This," he gestured to his pose, the iconic praying mantis stance, "Takes most years to learn, but for me, it took barely a month."

His words were a challenge, a gauntlet thrown down. "Try to keep up, but here's the catch: you can only protect and attack using the same style I'll be using — I don't care that you'll be seeing it for the first time."

"Okay," I replied awkwardly, tensely replicating his stance.

He wasted no time, launching into a flurry of strikes that caught me by surprise. Blows landed on my stomach and neck before I could react, my initial awkwardness a stark contrast to his practiced grace.

It took me a few moments before I could barely block his moves in the mantis pose. Something clicked. In the whirlwind of his attacks, I began to anticipate, to mimic. It was as if his movements left echoes in the air, whispers I could grasp after a beat. His mantis jabs, so swift and precise, became mine, albeit clumsier, more hesitant.

"It takes one minute for you to learn a move," General Anmolbir uttered, eyes gleaming with amusement, observing me replicate the technique I saw for the first time.

The tension crackled around us as we danced, shadows twisting on the walls. My blocks grew sharper, my counters bolder, mirroring his every technique mere moment after witnessing it.

He planned a quick victory, aiming at my face, but I blocked it and countered by landing a blow to his face, which he also intercepted. I was no longer on the defensive; we fought like equals.

"Another minute," he boomed, "And you've mastered it!"

The General rained blows upon me, but now, they felt sluggish, predictable. With a flick of my wrist, I deflected his hand, planting a precise hit on his torso that sent him reeling. He rubbed the spot, a playful grimace replacing his usual stoicism.

"Finally," he chuckled, "The third minute, and you've already transcended the technique!"

My chest thrummed with the thrill of victory, of discovering this hidden wellspring of potential within me.

"That was incredible," I exclaimed, my body buzzing from the intense exchange. "Now, teach me everything you know. All the styles, all the stances."

The General laughed, a deep, rich sound that echoed through the room. "All of them? Boy, there are over a thousand!"

Undeterred, I countered with a grin. "So, 3000 minutes of your time, then. Fifty hours, barely 3 days!"

"Don't be so full of yourself, brat," The General giggled. But his laugh morphed into a playful cackle as he launched a surprise attack. With a swift flick of his wrist, he hurled the massive wooden drawer from his wardrobe at me.

My reflexes kicked in, my left hand catching the projectile with ease. It was a distraction, though, a calculated move.

Before throwing it, General Anmolbir had taken out the impact bullets. As I focused on the drawer, 3 projectiles, gleaming bullets infused with power, shot from his fingertips. They tore through the air and also through the drawer, aimed to pierce my flesh.

Panic surged, but instinct prevailed. In a blink, I abandoned the drawer, my fingers blurring out, catching each bullet mid-flight, nullifying their deadly momentum. The spent shells clattered to the floor, silent testaments to my impossible feat.

Unfazed, the General pushed the attack, raining a downpour of everyday objects at me: a glass table, a porcelain teacup, a gilded lamp, a plush recliner. Each projectile hurled with superhuman speed became a blur in the air as he simultaneously charged close to me.

Yet, I met them all, not just catching them, but organizing them in a whirlwind of controlled chaos. The table found its place on the floor, the recliner beside it, lamp and cup resting gracefully on the tabletop.

General Anmolbir, inches from my face, hurled a translucent orb swirling with miniature galaxies. Asparians like me – reflex marvels – usually excel in such situations. Today, not so much. He knew our one vulnerability: a momentary sensory overload when confronting the universe's vastness.

My reflex? Fixating on the orb. My instincts? Gone.

Blank eyes, frozen body – an open invitation for the General to turn the tide. With a cruel grin, he clamped his iron grip on my head and slammed me into the glass table. My skull thudded, shards rained down in slow motion, carving red lines across my face.

I scrambled to my feet, fueled by pain and defiance. But Anmolbir unleashed a fury I couldn't match, elevating the stakes by taking the friendly fight to an even harsher level.

My attack, sluggish from the blow, met only empty air. He countered – With the impact bullets held between his fingers, he struck me on the side of my abdomen, propelling me into a mid-air roll.

The impact was so forceful that I crashed through the wall and into the adjacent room. The intensity of General Anmolbir's punch, combined with the enhanced force of the impact bullets… **was inhuman.**

Forty broken ribs screamed within me, yet through gritted teeth, I lied, "Perfectly fine." My legs betrayed me, collapsing halfway onto a chair. "Didn't feel a thing," I croaked, fooling nobody. "Or maybe I'm...fractured!"

Anmolbir, relishing his dominance, settled back in his recliner. "That blow should've knocked you out cold. Hell, a normal human would be a bloody crater. Guess your physiology echoes Surapsa."

"Surapsa? The first human?" I inquired, wincing with each word due to the pain radiating from my ribs.

"Yes, Surapsa—the first human to ever exist. The one who was granted superior abilities of instincts by God himself."

"Surapsa is the ancestor of all Asparians. So, what do you mean by my body matching his physiology?" I queried, my curiosity overcoming the physical discomfort. "Don't all Asparians have physiology like Surapsa's?"

"Their physiology is similar but not the same—more like a cheap copy," General Anmolbir revealed with a hint of disdain. "The descendants of Surapsa didn't even possess a fraction of his power. Surapsa was truly a God in a mortal body. **He defeated the deadliest of beasts with a flick of his eye; explosions merely tickled him. He waved off tsunamis with just the sheer force of his fists—the second strongest Asparian in history.**"

"Wait," I exclaimed, my voice strained as I struggled to maintain an upright position. **"You said Surapsa could wave off tsunamis with the sheer force of his fists, yet he is JUST the second strongest?** I can't help but wonder, what feats did THE STRONGEST one accomplish and... **who he was?"**

CHAPTER NINE

FROM BOOKS TO BONDS

Alist (Diary)

Apartment 4H, 9:07 A.M.

Stacks of books teetered precariously, threatening to avalanche at any moment. Excitement battled fatigue as I combed through my book collection on the trail of a long-lost treasure.

"Am I handsome?" I blurted, the words catching in my throat like forgotten plotlines. A genuine question slipped from my lips as I turned to Tanya, who was helping me with the chaotic task.

Tanya, wearing a mischievous smile, countered with a teasing tone, "Why do you ask? Is it about a girl?" Her laughter danced in the air, taking on an almost mocking cadence. "Don't tell me you're about to transform into a whole new person, flexing and delving into the lovey-dovey stuff."

My cheeks burned under her gaze. "Just... hypothetically," I mumbled, stacking a battered Tolkien on top of a chipped self-help manual, "If, say, I mustered the courage to, you know, talk to someone... do you think they'd... accept the invitation? Am I generally considered attractive among girls?"

Her laughter softened, laced with a hint of surprise. "Jerry," she said, leaning forward, her voice dropping to a conspiratorial whisper, "haven't you noticed the shy glances, the barely muffled giggles that follow you down the institute halls? You're like a walking oblivion charm, leaving a trail of broken hearts in your wake. Have you never noticed the attention?"

"Never in my life," I breathed, the word tumbling out in a single, disbelieving gust.

"You heartbreaker," Tanya chuckled, her gaze fixated on the balancing act of my loaded hands. "I bet you could trip over a love confession and still miss it."

An awkward blend of a look and a laugh crossed my face as I got out of the apartment. The elevator bell's chime cut through the moment, jarring the awkward tension. Juggling my literary bounty and a mini smart TV like a circus performer, I fumbled for the button.

"Here, let me get that," Tanya offered, reaching for the lift panel.

But my pride, or perhaps a misplaced sense of balance, intervened. Pivoting on one foot, I transferred the TV to my toes, a precarious perch balanced by the master of the 6 senses. With a flourish, I jabbed the button, then caught the falling TV in my free hand just as the elevator doors slid open.

"You could have just asked me, Jerry. I would have pushed the button for you," Tanya murmured as we stepped into the lift, the mini television back in my left hand. "Or you could have showcased your impressive flexibility pushing the button with your feet."

With an air of nonchalance, I adopted a more confident tone, "Well, turns out, I am just practicing to flex." The elevator doors closed, leaving Tanya amused by the unexpected reveal.

Alma's Caravan, 9:20 A.M.

"Novels, mangas, comics, T.V. shows, movies," I declared with a flourish, plugging the mini television into Alma's caravan's power outlet. "Warriors against boredom, all of them!"

The dusty stack of books threatened to topple like a bibliophile domino rally. Alma, perched hesitantly on her bunk bed, eyed the colorful paper mountains with a mix of amusement and apprehension.

"So many!" she murmured, her voice barely above a whisper.

"Not many, just 64!" I insisted, injecting charm into my voice. "Once the habit takes root, they'll feel like secrets in the night." I winked, hoping to dispel the shadows in her eyes. "And this television, this little magic box here? Pure entertainment gold: also, I've got you a subscription to an app where you can watch anything for free."

Alma traced a worn manga spine with a hesitant finger. "But... I don't really watch anything," she stammered. "And all this... you shouldn't have spent so much."

"Nonsense!" I scoffed, kneeling beside her. "Half these veterans are from my Captain Demy days. The rest? A mere cost compared to a friend's smile." I squeezed her hands, the fabric worn soft from her constant fidgeting. "Besides, where else would my salary go? Survival needs are met, so bringing joy to my friends becomes goal number one. And you are definitely on that list, Alma."

The flicker of pain in her eyes tugged at my heartstrings. "it's... it's not my hobby; I don't have hobbies," she whispered, her voice laced with a shadow of past disappointments.

My grip tightened. "That's why you feel lonely, and that's what I'm here to fix," I declared with a smile. "Sure, you have us now, but what if... Well, let's just say things go south. You deserve a backup plan, something to keep you occupied."

Alma's eyes widened at the word 'south.' Though silent, her gaze clearly communicated, "Don't you dare say another word about that, Jerry!"

"Free day!" I announced, bursting with enthusiasm. "Let's finally nurture that elusive hobby of yours. Don't worry; if something doesn't spark joy, we'll switch it up. I'm here for the long haul, a hundred stories if needed, until you find something that clicks."

A mischievous glint lit up Alma's face. "A hundred stories, huh?" she chuckled, a sly smile playing on her lips.

"A hundred, definitely!" I confirmed, brimming with excitement.

The rickety ladder of the bunk bed creaked like a rusty lullaby as Alma ascended, her bare feet whispering against the worn wood.

Reaching the top, she settled onto the thin mattress, a fortress of blankets built around her. I, propped against the wall below, the words of my favorite book poised on my tongue, awaited her signal.

Morning turned to evening. The caravan, bathed in the golden glow of the setting sun, became our stage. I, the tireless bard, wove tales of fantastical worlds and brave heroes, while Alma, my reluctant audience, found herself drawn into the flickering realms beyond the page. Each "no" was a whispered clue, leading us closer to the hidden door of her passions.

Seven novels, 3 mangas, and 4 comics later, the windows blurred with the mist of dusk, and the silence had deepened. My patience remained steadfast, fueled by the thrill of rediscovering my old favorites even while searching for Alma's spark.

But there was something else. In the stolen glances between page turns, in the way her lips twitched at a funny line, I noticed a different kind of story unfolding. A story written not in words but in the soft curve of her smile as she listened to me read.

Then we switched to the television. Show after show, movie after movie, I paraded past her indifferent eyes. Titanic's epic romance met only a yawn. A hilarious comedy elicited a polite laugh, gone quicker than a butterfly's flight.

Was she playing me? Or was there something beneath her serene façade, a hidden depth defying my attempts to reach it? **All that time, I looked at the screen changing movies, while all that time, she kept looking at... me.**

Alma's Caravan, 11:40 P.M.

The caravan door swung open with a flourish, and Bill barreled in, arms straining under the weight of a bulky contraption. His booming voice filled the small space, shattering the gentle hum of the movie I'd paused.

"Here you are!" he announced, setting the machine that the Lumberjack gave us down with a thud that sent dust motes dancing in the dim light.

"I thought you were at the construction site," I replied, my brows furrowed.

Bill snorted, a sardonic smile twisting his lips. "The day has ended, dear; it's about midnight. By the way, Charlie called, sounding more lost than a kitten in a labyrinth. Apparently, some people have a peculiar appreciation for procrastination. It's been a month. Didn't you need to pour your Asparian energy into this machine? Remember, you and Charlie are to supply the Lumberjack with the Span Doorway spheres."

"Ah, that's a pain," I muttered, grabbing the machine with a touch of weariness and frustration, memories of the incident in Asparia resurfacing.

"So, what's going on here? You 2 are locked in a battle of wills with this pile of scrap?" Bill inquired, surveying the scene as I connected the machine's wires to my arm. Alma remained silent, a picture of stoicism.

"Just trying, for hours on end, to find a story that sparks Alma's interest. So far, nothing's doing," I explained, discreetly hiding the injection site on my arm.

A soft voice, barely audible, cut through the silence. "Well, Jerry," Alma started, "how about you tell a story that captivates me? Ouch!" she exclaimed with a startled cry, having bumped her head on the ceiling as she repositioned herself on the bunk.

Bill's eyes widened in surprise; his initial assumption shattered – Alma wasn't mute.

"Jerry, you always harp on about wanting your friends surrounding you in your final moments," Alma continued, her voice polite yet firm. "It's like making your friends happy is your sole purpose. Why this specific goal? What shaped you? Who made you the person you are? That's the story I want to hear."

A smile tugged at my lips as warm memories surfaced. "Then perhaps the question shouldn't be 'what,' but 'who.' Without him, I wouldn't be here."

"Sounds intriguing," Bill chimed in, sliding onto a chair in the mini kitchen. "I'm all ears for a good story."

"Okay, if you both insist," I said, turning off the television. "It all goes back to 3 years ago when I first met... Charlie."

CHAPTER TEN

THIS TIME... I'LL ROLL THE DICE

Alist (Diary)

(Three years ago)

My residence was a modest town in replica Canada, primarily inhabited by military personnel. Back then, I was barely a sprout, much shorter than I am now. And forget flowing locks; my only claim to fame was a wild crop of long fringes.

My Thirteen had just etched itself onto my calendar when Captain Demy, my unwavering guardian, bid farewell, urging me to embark on a new journey in a bustling city.

The preceding 5 years were spent under Captain Demy's tutelage, homeschooled, and surrounded by a tinge of solitude.

During this time, Captain Demy forbade me from contacting my old school friends. To fill the void, I delved into reading and followed weekly shows and movies. My afternoons were hymns whispered to the strings of my guitar, each notes a yearning for connection, a melody longing for an audience.

And in the quiet hush of twilight, I chased after nascent dreams of becoming a songwriter, first stumbling through sonnets in a tattered poetry book, then weaving them into tapestries of song.

Captain Demy's departure ripped open the cocoon, leaving me with a newfound freedom that was both intoxicated and terrified. His parting words, a cryptic plea to limit my contact with others, still echoed in my mind.

Yet, the embers of childhood friendship burned bright, their warmth refusing to be extinguished. With trembling fingers, I unearthed a sheet of paper – a lifeline to the past, a constellation of phone numbers leading back to kindergarten.

Franco, Tony, Mark, and around 40 others – I couldn't wait to ask about their current lives. Excitement pulsated within me as I anticipated reconnecting with them.

My heart drummed a nervous rhythm as I dialed Tony's number, eager to rekindle the forgotten spark of camaraderie. But the news that greeted me was a sledgehammer blow, shattering the fragile hope with chilling finality.

My breath hitched in my throat as my mind grappled with the inconceivable. I then dialed Mark. Once again, I was met with the distressing news that hit me even harder. Fingers trembling, I hurriedly called another number, and the pattern persisted—a cascade of shocking revelations.

Call by call, answer by answer, a shiver ran down my spine, each answer a chilling refrain. Forty-three names were etched in ink but carved in ice. Each of them—dead!

Each met their demise before the age of 12, scattered across different places, times, and causes. Some by accidents, others succumbed to diseases, a few took their own lives, and some met tragic ends.

A tide of tears, long absent, surged down my cheeks. Their salty warmth mingled with the bitter embers of despair, a desolate cocktail on my skin. Captain Demy's cryptic words echoed in the hollow halls of my mind, a haunting melody alongside the chilling tapestry of their demise.

Was this the reason he'd cloaked me in solitude? Was the world beyond the town walls a graveyard of friends, a silent testament to a truth too terrifying to confront? How was this even possible in the first place?

And there I was, convinced to follow Captain Demy's words. The dusty town road snaked behind me, a fading memory in the rearview mirror.

My escape bag bulged with relics of friendships buried by the cruel scythe of time: Captain Demy's Asparian cape, salvaged from the bin like a tattered dream; the blood-stained essay sheet, a testament to sacrifices never acknowledged; a contact list filled with names etched in ice. Each, a whispered echo of laughter lost, dreams unfulfilled.

Toronto Replica, 12:46 P.M.

Stepping into the bustling city, I inhaled the vibrant chaos, a stark counterpoint to the cloistered solitude of the past years. In this concrete jungle, anonymity promised a fresh start.

My new apartment, spartan and sterile, awaited its baptism of laughter and tears. My roommate stood awkwardly in the doorway, his youthful face etched with lines older than his years.

"Myself, Jerry," I blurted, unable to contain the excitement of human connection after an eternity of isolation. "New guy, nice to meet you! Where are you from? You look… familiar, somehow. Any other friends around? Or maybe…" I hesitated, the words tumbling over each other in my eagerness, "maybe I could be your first?"

"Charlie," he responded, his expression a tad reserved compared to my previous chitter-chatter.

His gaze swept over me, lingering for a beat. I felt a prickle of self-consciousness under his scrutiny. My attire, clearly out of place, screamed summer's neglect: a gray suit pant clinging stubbornly to my form despite the heat, and blue aviator glasses

perched on my nose, far from their natural habitat of sun-drenched skies.

"Likewise," he replied, a smile pulling at his lips that didn't quite reach his eyes. The warmth in his voice was genuine, but a low hum of sadness resonated beneath it.

"Is something wrong?" I inquired Charlie, sensing his unease.

"Everything is!" He spat out, the pain raw and visceral. "One minute, you're playing Snakes and ladders with your family; the next, you're dumped on this alien planet. I'm an earthling, by the way," he added with a ghost of a chuckle, the humor failing to reach his eyes.

Despite hailing from a quaint small town, I was well-versed in the Casa system, whispering promises of second chances for plucked-from-Earthlings.

The entire population, both in Casa and the replica countries, comprised Earthlings plucked from specific points in time. While most saw it as a glorious rewind, a fresh start after a botched first draft, Charlie viewed it as a cruel abduction.

Casa Institute, Seminar Hall, 2:00 P.M.

The next day, Charlie found himself squeezed into the orientation seminar, an initial baptism into the mysteries of their relocation. The reason, it turned out, was morbidly pragmatic: saving them from "uneventful fates."

As the seminar emptied, 3 towering figures, bulges threatening to burst from their ill-fitting clothes, leaned against the doorway. Classic bullies, their sneers honed years before arriving in Alistia, probably alumni of the citizenship test prep classes.

"Useless number one, useless number 2," their voices dripped with venomous mockery, trailing after each exiting seminar attendee. When Charlie emerged, a bony hand hovered over his head, the middle bully drawing, "Useless number 16."

Bullies transcend time and space, fueled by the intoxicating fumes of perceived superiority. The truth about Alistia's inhabitants hung heavy: their mockery embodied the discrimination between the 2 categories. Those brought from the end of their lives carried a sense of pride, having lived a past life with purpose and influence. Conversely, those brought back due to their perceived lack of impact were considered inferior and branded as "useless."

"Useless" echoed through the halls, branding him with a scarlet letter before he'd even begun his new life. Despite the sting, Charlie, physically frail and harboring a healthy dose of cowardice, couldn't muster a retort. He swallowed the insult and slunk away, the weight of his absent family settling like a leaden cloak on his shoulders.

That's when I saw him. His hunched frame, the defeated slump of his shoulders. On a whim, I decided to offer solace, a spark of human connection in a landscape of cold stares.

"What business do you have here?" Charlie mumbled, eyeing me warily from a nearby bench.

"Just wanted to make you feel accompanied," I said, offering a genuine smile. Starting anew without the anchor of the family left one adrift, and I vowed to be his life raft. My mission, absurd as it might seem, was simple: to become his friend. This lonely figure, ostracized by fate and circumstance, deserved a hand to hold, a voice to cut through the deafening silence. And so, with the zeal of a newly minted knight, I embarked on my quest to befriend the boy branded "useless."

From that day forward, I shadowed Charlie like an inseparable companion, my presence accompanying him everywhere, with the notable exception of the bathroom – even shadows have their limits.

I delved into the intricacies of his life, unraveling the details of his hobbies, which, to my amusement, were starkly contrasting to my own. While he found solace in the pages of science fiction books, a genre I deemed somewhat uninteresting, he harbored a disdain for music, television, and any activity that exuded a sense of enjoyment.

Toronto Replica, Gaming Parlor, 4:09 P.M.

Faced with this chasm of incompatible hobbies, I proposed the universal language of games – surely even the nerdiest of souls appreciated a good battle of wits or brawn. We started with the outdoor arena, a symphony of flying feathers and soaring balls.

Football? He barely saw the blur as I one-kicked it into the goal. Badminton? My shuttlecock was a phantom, leaving him chasing empty air. Baseball? Every swing met the sweet spot, every ball an arc sailing over the fence. Chambira? Let's just say gravity seemed to have a special fondness for Charlie's ankles.

The truth was, it wasn't just my will to dominate. Something felt different. Back in my old town, with my old friends, I was just decent, not a prodigy – I had fun playing all the time. Maybe it was the awakening of my Asparian powers, my senses hyper-amplified, and reflexes bordering on the supernatural.

Charlie, catching on to the lopsided slaughter, suggested retreating indoors. He explored the realm of billiards, foosball, table tennis, and more, hoping for a change in fortunes. He became highly competitive, hoping to take revenge for the lost games.

He'd strategize and plot his moves, yet every attempt was met with an effortless counter. Unfortunately for him, the outcome remained consistent – a series of resounding defeats.

Some games are intricate dances of skill, others are a test of sheer strength, but all require reflexes. And there I was, master of the 6 senses, reflexes etched into my very being.

Charlie's shoulders slumped, the inflatable billiard stick falling limply from his hand. "Point made," he muttered, his defiance melting into resignation. The last embers of competitive fire flickered and died, replaced by a bitter ash of frustration. This wasn't a game; it was a demolition derby, and he was the crumpled sedan at the finish line.

I winced, the echo of his words stinging like salt in a fresh wound. "Look, I..." I began, the apology stuck in my throat. What could I say?

"Let's just forget the games," Charlie interrupted, his voice laced with a quiet hurt. "Maybe… maybe we're just too different."

"Let's just play one more." I began to speak.

"It's pointless to play when the other party is so overpowered!" Charlie declared frustration etched across his face.

"I could... hold back a bit," I offered tentatively, picking up on his evident irritation.

"It's equally pointless when the other party holds back," Charlie retorted in annoyance. "Even if you win that way, there's no sense of victory."

His words resonated with the dissatisfaction of a competition devoid of challenge, a sentiment that rendered triumph hollow and unfulfilling.

The atmosphere in the gaming parlor was heavy with the weight of Charlie's words, and a palpable discomfort lingered between us. The gaming outing had ended in an unexpected turn, leaving me grappling with a sense of sadness and an uncertainty about how to bridge the growing gap between us. I didn't know any other way to bond with him.

Then, from across the chasm of distance, Charlie's voice cracked the tension. "Snakes and ladders," he said, his words hesitant, unsure, yet tinged with a faint spark of curiosity. "It's a mere game of chance, but... there's something personal about it for me. My Sundays used to be filled with laughter and the click of dice, climbing ladders with my parents."

Hope, a flickering candle in the wind, danced within me. "Sure," I responded, a smile stretching my lips like a bridge across the void. Perhaps, in this simple game, we could find a flicker of connection.

Across the worn Snakes and ladders board, Charlie's voice held a hint of nostalgia as he spoke of well-worn dice and familiar squares. "A game of luck, yes, but experience counts for something. I'll beat you 10 times over; mark my words. Your reflexes won't stand a chance against my seasoned skills."

The game began with a dance of fate on a cardboard stage. Charlie's token landed on 4, a tentative first step. My turn yielded a 3, then a ladder, propelling me skyward to 86. Surprise flickered across Charlie's face, a momentary shadow eclipsing his confidence.

Still, a smirk lingered on his lips. He had the dreaded 99 in his sights, the monstrous snake promising a dramatic descent. His turn again, a 6 propelled him forward, then another – a 2. My turn. Six.

Charlie chuckled; the tension masked by a nervous giggle. "What are the odds?" he muttered; eyes narrowed.

My token danced across the board, landing triumphantly on 92. Another roll, another 6 -- Ninety-four. Ninety-six. Ninety-eight.

Charlie's sweat glistened, but the looming serpent at 99 seemed to offer solace. One more roll, a 2... Ninety-nine, and then, a hundred. Victory.

Charlie stared, dumbfounded. The sequence of sixes defied probability, defied everything he knew about the game. He insisted on another round. However, the subsequent games unfolded much like the first, with me winning decisively in 3 turns and then in 2 turns. Charlie's frustration boiled over.

"SOMETHING'S OFF!" he shouted, unable to comprehend the sequence of wins. Desperation crept into his voice as he demanded, "One more."

Even in the third game, I emerged victorious in 2 turns. "Something's fishy," he finally croaked, his voice tinged with disbelief. "How the hell did you manage that, Jerry?"

"Funny thing," I replied, a nervous laugh escaping my lips, "It's part of my instincts, part of the 6 senses I own. I can precisely roll the dice in a way that lands the number I want."

His face contorted in a blend of frustration and disappointment. "What?! Not fair!" he roared, slamming his palm on the board. "That was the one game I wanted you to play normally. The one with a personal connection, remember?"

"It's just that I can control the dice," I spoke hesitantly in fear of his harsh reaction.

I wasn't a sailor of emotions, ill-equipped to navigate the turbulent depths of Charlie's sorrow. His fury wasn't just from losing. It was a bitter cocktail of bitterness - the sting of every overturned game, the gnawing ache of my power oozing into something as simple as a childhood board game.

The raw pain of his own perceived uselessness reflected in my supposed victory. The pain reminded him of being away from his parents, with whom he actually enjoyed playing this game.

His annoyance heightened, "It doesn't mean if you can, you should. I wanted you to play fairly, or it would take the meaning out of the game!"

Fear pricked at me. "It's a reflex, Charlie," I stammered, trying to explain. "Even if I don't want to, it just happens."

"AHH!" he shouted, throwing his hands up in exasperation. "Then we can never play! Done with you, done with this," he snarled, and with that, he stormed out of my sight, leaving me alone with the echo of his accusations and the silent snakes and ladders board, a stark reminder of the chasm that had widened between us.

Apartment 4H, 10:30 A.M.

The week that stretched before us felt more like an awkward ballet of 2 roommates sharing a confined stage than a blossoming friendship.

Each morning, my voice tinged with growing desperation, I'd ask, "Will you read and review my poetry book now?" Each time, Charlie would respond with a dismissive "tomorrow." Today marked the third "tomorrow," and the air between us crackled with unspoken tension.

Charlie, hunched over the table, was scribbling furiously on a letter to the Casa board. The sudden, jarring scrape of his pen crossing out a word echoed like a thunderclap. He looked up, eyes flashing with frustration.

"Listen," he said, his voice tight, "I don't like poetry. I don't get it. It's not my thing. Leave me out of it." His pen met the paper again, but the letter ripped under his angry stroke. "I don't like when you follow me everywhere. I have a lot going on, and I don't like to be accompanied by another… problem."

My stomach hollowed. "Oh," I managed, my voice choking with hurt. He didn't just dislike my work; he dismissed the very heart of my being.

To an artist, a creation isn't merely words on a page; it's a piece of their soul laid bare. His rejection felt like a slap, leaving my eyes stinging with unshed tears.

Toronto Replica, Talent hunt contest, 9:00 A.M.

This morning marked Charlie's last day attending the seminar. This time, I broke from my routine of accompanying him. Instead, I ventured out alone, drawn by the flicker of excitement surrounding an open talent contest.

Age was no barrier; any skill was welcome. It held the promise of validation, perhaps even an escape from the gnawing loneliness.

Little did I anticipate that the contest wasn't about talent; it was designed to test one's confidence and mental fortitude in challenging situations.

On that stage, bathed in harsh lights, I poured my heart into one of my best poems. "I see you in the stars," I began, aiming the words at the panel of 3 judges shrouded in authority.

But what unfolded wasn't applause but chilling mockery. A judge's cackle pierced the air. "You see the person in the stars? Who's that, your dead grandmother?"

My breath hitched, the needle of ridicule twisting in my chest. "Oh, I... I have another poem," I stammered, offering a different verse as flimsy armor against the onslaught.

"Before that," another voice sneered, "explain the fashion disaster. Shades indoors? You're the walking definition of 'quirky.'"

Heat crawled up my neck, sweat beading on my forehead. "I prefer it this way," I mumbled, the words hollow.

"Prefer freakish, you mean?" the third judge interjected, triggering a cacophony of laughter. My vision blurred, tears threatening to spill.

"Go on," the mocking voice grated, and I recited, desperately clinging to the rhythm of my words. But halfway through, another blow landed. "The most boring drivel I've ever heard," the woman yawned, boredom etched on her face.

That was the breaking point. I should have bowed, mumbled a "thank you," and retreated, leaving them to their cruel amusement. But instead, the tears that had been held hostage streamed down my face, blurring the stage lights as I turned and fled. Their laughter pursued me, echoing in the hollow cavern of my despair.

That day, the stage wasn't about talent or applause. It was a gauntlet, a test of resilience I, a barely formed soul, was ill-equipped to face.

And in that flight, in the sting of tears and the echo of scorn, I tasted the bitter dregs of humiliation, a lesson in vulnerability etched forever in my young heart. The realization dawned on me, a bitter clarity piercing my fog of hurt.

The stage hadn't been a platform for talent, but a crucible for resilience. The judges, in their cruel jest, weren't testing my poetry, but my ability to stand unbent in the face of ridicule. It was a twisted game for the shameless or the unshakably confident, a world away from the validation I'd naively sought.

Apartment 4H, 6:00 P.M.

The click of the deadbolt echoed like a tomb closing after I slammed the apartment door shut and locked it. I sank onto the couch, the plush cushions doing little to soften the blow to my spirit.

My limbs felt brittle, like porcelain on the verge of shattering. "Maybe I was too easy to break," I thought, the echo of the judges' taunts still ringing in my ears. Did their words have to be so cruel? What purpose did it serve to humiliate me like that?

Suddenly, a muffled voice broke through the fog of self-pity. "Why are you crying?" Charlie mumbled, materializing on the opposite couch, mirroring my slump like a spectral reflection.

"I was bullied," I choked out, wiping a trail of tears that had escaped unnoticed. "And why are you crying, Charlie?" My voice was thick with a maelstrom of emotions I couldn't quite untangle.

Charlie lifted his head, his eyes mirroring my own, red-rimmed with misery. "I was bullied too," he whispered, the single word laden with a world of sorrow.

My head snapped up. "Bullied? You?" The switch to anger, sharp and sudden, surprised him. "Those 3 boys from before?"

Charlie nodded, his eyes flitting away to the ceiling like he couldn't face the accusation in my voice. "They said..." His voice trailed off, swallowed by another wave of tears.

He blinked, only to see that I... was gone. The couch beside him, where I had been a heartbeat ago, was empty. My presence, as tangible as sunlight moments before, had vanished as if I were a phantom, dissolved into the air.

Panic gnawed at him, icy and relentless. Every other detail of the room remained stubbornly in place: the cushions slumped in my wake, the forgotten mug on the coffee table, the dog-eared book by the lamp – everything except the apartment door.

It stood open, an accusatory maw in the gathering dusk, the wind whispering through it like a taunting laugh.

Charlie's hand hovered over the knob, his mind still caught in the whirlwind of my abrupt departure. Then, a glint of blue against the faded wood snagged his attention. My poetry book lay sprawled open on the threshold, pages ruffled by the afternoon breeze.

As he picked it up, his gaze fixed upon a page that had randomly unfolded. A poem, scrawled in my hand, leaped out at him. The ink seemed charged with raw emotion, each word echoing a loneliness that mirrored his own:

ALONE… ALONE… ALONE,

Small seed like me is sown.

I'm craving for an enemy,

No friend can I see.

ALONE… ALONE… ALONE,

In silence, I'm grown,

Where beginnings are the dead ends,

And ruins are my friends.

As he devoured the poem, Charlie stumbled upon a truth he hadn't dared to acknowledge – a flicker of hope amidst the ashes of grief.

If I, with my stoic veneer, could harbor such vulnerability, then perhaps happiness wasn't as unattainable as he'd believed. Perhaps, even in the wreckage of our shared realities, we could find solace in each other's company.

He yearned to delve deeper into my poetic musings, recognizing that he wasn't the sole bearer of loss; I, too, had weathered my own storms. Charlie had misjudged me, misread the mask I wore. He understood that happiness could still be found, even in a world devoid of our original families.

A slow smile curved Charlie's lips, chasing away the shadows that had clung to him for far too long – For he had finally found a common ground between us.

Toronto Replica, Random corner, 8:26 P.M.

Meanwhile, where was I? On a hunt – a pursuit to confront the trio responsible for tormenting Charlie.

"Seems like you don't have any other job to do?" I quipped sarcastically, spotting the 3 boys in their usual bullying corner, their sinister activities halted by my arrival.

The night air was heavy, its coolness barely cutting through the burning rage that coursed through me. As they turned toward me, abandoning their latest victim, I couldn't help but relish the ominous delight reflected in my eyes. This wasn't the version of me that usually surfaced.

"This town is expansive, and even with my heightened Asparian vision and aura-sensing abilities, it took me 40 minutes of barefoot running across the city to find you," I said, my aura exerting an overwhelming presence despite my diminutive stature.

"What business do you have here, kid?" the tallest boy sneered, amusement evident in his eyes as he sized up my 1.55-meter frame.

"Last week," I growled, my voice laced with steel, "you called my friend 'useless.' I let it slide. But like an unruly insect, you keep biting, don't you?" My vision pulsed with clarity, their raw emotions a toxic buffet. "We swat a gnat once, twice, but when it becomes a persistent pest, there's only one solution: crushing it."

A nervous chuckle rippled through them. The smallest, probably the ringleader's shadow in the flesh, sidled closer, a sneer twisting his features. "What're you going to do, little man?" he spat, but the bravado lacked its usual bite.

My smile, if you could call it that, was a chilling harbinger of what was to come. "A little lesson in humility," I purred, the aura tightening its grip, their cocky swagger wilting under its weight.

"Two fractured fingers for you, shrimp." I then pointed to the leftmost one, his bravado replaced by a tremor, "a shattered leg for your cowardly silence."

Finally, my gaze met their ringleader's, his eyes wide with a dawning dread. "And for you, a reminder that true strength isn't measured in inches – A few broken ribs, just to even the playing field – Just a little punch in your chest."

A handkerchief materialized from my pocket, a blindfold woven from defiance. "And I'll do it all," I declared, voice resonating with cold fury, "with one hand tied behind my back, on one leg, blindfolded. Just to show you how utterly USELESS you all are."

The boy in front of me attempted to slap me. His misguided swing met an iron wall at my wrist. With a swift twist, I disarmed him, the sickening crack of his fingers echoing through the night.

"Four fractured fingers for disobedience," I said, my voice devoid of emotion, eyes sealed by the blindfold. His screams were a guttural chorus of regret, each whimper a verse in the unfolding symphony of consequence.

The second boy, fueled by fear, tried to flee. A blur of controlled fury intercepted him, a whisper of my leg sending him sprawling onto the hard Earth, his leg twisted at an unnatural angle.

"Running only prolongs the inevitable, friend," I murmured, my words laced with a chilling calm.

But instead of the expected brutality, I leaned in, my voice taking on a deceptively gentle tone. "You see, I'm a genuinely amiable person. You can beat me all you want—land punches, slaps, kicks. I don't experience pain from human attacks. Even if you inflict harm or mock me, it's fine. I'll merely shed a few tears in solitude and carry that suffering with me for the rest of my life. BUT…"

My words hung heavy in the air, punctuated by the ragged gasps of my victims. Then, I shifted, my remaining hand bound behind my back, a testament to my self-imposed limitations. My gaze fell upon the ringleader, the one who orchestrated this pathetic dance of cruelty. He cowered, his bravado a deflated balloon in the face of my measured, chilling calm.

"It's okay," I reassured him. "Five years ago, 8 Casa soldiers took away everyone I held dear—my parents and the entire military squad that were my friends. That was the day I first activated my Asparian powers. I might call it a reflex that I eliminated all 8 soldiers, cutting through their diamond-hard force shields with a mere SHEET OF PAPER! But deep down, I know it wasn't just a reflex."

His eyes widened, reflecting a dawning horror. I felt him shrink under the weight of my unvarnished pain. I stepped closer, like a one-legged horse. His breath hitched, sweat beading on his brow.

"And since that day," I whispered, unleashing a controlled storm in the form of a single punch that connected with a sickening crunch, his ribs protesting the symphony of pain I conducted. "I've PERSONAL GRUDGES against those who hurt what I love!"

Apartment 4H, 9:45 P.M.

As I made my way back home, regret gnawed at my insides, a relentless beast with teeth like broken promises. My actions, fueled by an unholy trinity of panic, anger, and self-loathing, left a bitter aftertaste in my mouth.

Was it panic, or had I failed in fulfilling my purpose of making, helping, and maintaining friends? These questions haunted my thoughts.

Since leaving Demy's gruff tutelage, my world had tilted on its axis, spinning into a dizzying blur of darkness. The news of my friends' demise hit me like a sucker punch, leaving a gaping hole in my already threadbare existence.

Humiliation at the competition, pointless brawls with nameless faces – it all felt like a perverse confirmation of Demy's warnings. Even Charlie, the closest I'd come to friendship, remained just out of reach, a flickering candle in the storm.

Captain Demy's words haunted me, a grim melody looping in the hollow chambers of my skull. "Bonding," he'd rasped, "a cruel dance of joy, heartbreak, and regret." Was the old man right? Was chasing connections a fool's errand, destined to end in tears and shattered trust?

In the solitude of my apartment, I contemplated whether living a lonely life might be a better choice. The bitterness of recent experiences left me disillusioned, and I resolved to change my purpose and change myself.

Was it all for nothing? The dream of a million friendships, once a blazing sun in my sky, now flickered like a dying ember in a downpour. Maybe there were no good people left in the world.

"Maybe solitude is its own kind of sanctuary," I muttered, shoving open the door to my apartment. The thought was a bitter pill, a grim acceptance of my self-imposed exile.

But just as I was about to retreat into the familiar numbness, a voice broke through the fog.

"Hey, Jerry! You got the makings of a real Robert Frost in you." Charlie's voice, a warm hand on my shoulder, was a ray of sunshine piercing the gloom.

"You read my book?" My voice, rusty from disuse, held a mix of surprise and tentative hope.

"Every page!" Charlie's enthusiasm was infectious, a balm to my bruised soul. "Your words gave me courage and touched my heart. Especially the one titled, *Alone*."

"Yeah," a smile, fragile at first, bloomed on my face, tears threatening to spill. "Poured my guts into that one. Two stanzas for now, but I'll add more."

Charlie held out the book, his eyes sparkling with genuine awe. "But the thing is, Jerry, you won't need to add any more stanzas to that poem – Because from now on, you'll never be alone."

Hope, a flickering ember, roared back to life. The carefully constructed walls of self-isolation crumbled at the mention of "never alone." Maybe Demy wasn't entirely right. Maybe a million friends was a fool's dream, but starting with one, with Charlie, was a purpose worth embracing.

"Snakes and ladders?" Charlie's playful challenge hung in the air, breaking the tension.

Words were unnecessary. My smile, brighter than the dying afternoon sun, spoke volumes. The dice tumbled in Charlie's palm, not just markers of a game, but symbols of a newfound connection, a fragile pact against the loneliness that threatened to engulf us both.

"But you'll just move your tokens, because," he continued, grabbing 2 dice in his fist, "this time... I'll roll the dice!"

CHAPTER ELEVEN

"HELLO, CHARLIE"

Alist (Diary)

Flicking off the switch, I burrowed deeper into the covers, the warmth cocooning me in a blissful silence. Ten months. Ten entire months had vanished like a firefly extinguished mid-flight.

My gaze drifted upwards, tracing the familiar patterns on the ceiling, each line etched with memories of my recent life that felt both distant and achingly real.

Days melted into a montage of bustling classrooms, the comforting rhythm of my part-time job, and the contagious laughter echoing during late-night movie marathons with Alma.

Tanya, with her infectious enthusiasm, was always an eager third wheel, ensuring our movie nights were never predictable. Weekends were escapes filled with the shared glee of rollercoasters at amusement parks, the hushed awe in museums, and the quiet companionship amidst dusty library stacks.

We were a merry band, Charlie, Alma, Tanya, and me, exploring the city with wide-eyed wonder. Bill, ever the elusive one, remained on the periphery, lost in his gym and his "work," or perhaps excuses that masked something deeper.

Even amidst our carefree days, we had our responsibilities. We would diligently supply the Span Doorway spheres to the Hovershell goons, ensuring a smooth relationship with the Lumberjack. It was a necessary task, one that kept us out of trouble and allowed us to maintain our idyllic existence.

This, perhaps, was the life I'd been searching for, the purpose that had eluded me for so long. If only time could stand still, freeze-framing this scene of normalcy and belonging.

Maybe, just maybe, if things never changed, if we could all continue living happily and safely, perhaps I wouldn't need to send Charlie back to Earth. Maybe we could continue this life in Casa, for tomorrow, we will hold the farewell of the Casa Citizenship Classes.

Sleep eluded me. Yet, beneath the excitement, a tremor of fear pulsed, for I didn't want this dream to end, whether my eyes were opened or closed.

Casa Institute Hall, First floor, 11:47 a.m.

Tanya, adorned in an aquamarine tiara atop a stunning two-piece outfit, glanced at me quizzically amid the bustling crowd of students gathered for the citizenship test results.

The hall buzzed with excitement as everyone donned their unique cosplay costumes, anticipating the impending celebration. The Casa classes were already over and the individuals who cleared the citizenship exam would be receiving their visas in less than a week.

Today marked a farewell party, to be precise, a costume farewell party personally organized by General Anmolbir Singh.

"Weren't you supposed to cosplay?" Tanya inquired, her ensemble exuding an air of elegance and whimsy.

I chuckled, adjusting my blue aviator glasses. "Technically, I am. For today, I'm Captain Demy."

Tanya raised an eyebrow, skepticism etched on her face. She scrutinized my attire, her gaze sweeping from my royal blue suit to my black tie and white shirt. "You do look suspiciously... normal," her tone tinged with curiosity.

"Long story," I muttered, grabbing a glass of fruit punch from a passing waiter." My initial plan was to go full-blown Captain Demy. It turns out, his authentic Asparian armor costs more than 13 months of our rent, and that's just the replica! The real one...let's not even go there. So, I settled for his cape, but the cold weather had other plans, forcing me to layer under a blazer. Hence, the hidden cape. Got it, Tanya?"

Tanya, ever the understanding friend, nodded slowly. "Fair enough. Emoung," she added with a mischievous grin, "well, call me Princess Jasmine." She struck a graceful pose, the tiara sparkling under the festive lights.

"Jasmine, huh?" I mused, finishing my fruit punch in one smooth gulp. "Disney princesses... no matter the hardships, they always believed in happy endings, right?" I winked, tossing the empty glass with practiced ease. It landed perfectly on a waiter's tray, eliciting a surprised blink from the unsuspecting man.

"And here's the tiara of our happy endings. For tomorrow lies a great future for us," Tanya announced.

Alma finally squeezed through the throng of costumed revelers, joining our group with a shy smile.

I observed her attire with a keen eye, taking in every detail without making it seem awkward. Her Eevee ensemble was impeccably crafted, from the meticulously styled hair to the matching brown boots.

While Eevee never ranked high on my personal Pokémon favorites, Alma had somehow elevated it to an entirely new level of adorable.

"Hey guys, do I look alright?" she asked, adjusting the furry brown tail of her costume.

Before I could offer a compliment, Charlie, sporting a classic Mario get-up complete with a fake mustache, piped up. "Bill already left."

"Classic Bill, never able to spare a moment for us." A hint of sarcasm laced my voice. "In that case, Charlie, perhaps you could do us a favor and retrieve his coat? He might have left it in the library."

Charlie raised an eyebrow. "And how do you know that?"

"Elementary, my dear Watson," I chuckled, gesturing dramatically. "See the partially open curtain through the window? If you glance downstairs at the library window, you'll notice a mirror reflecting a chair, upon which rests Bill's precious coat."

"Not everyone has binoculars for eyeballs, Jerry," Charlie retorted dryly. "Besides, I can only see the window from here. And why should I be the one fetching it?"

The playful smirk I'd worn faltered slightly. "Look, that coat is practically glued to Bill's side. Besides, he hardly seems to care about any of us these days. So, do the heroic deed and fetch it while Tanya and I contemplate whether Bill deserves a spot on our 'friend' list any longer."

With a resigned sigh, Charlie embarked on his monumental quest to the library.

Just then, Tanya's phone buzzed. Glancing at the message, she shot Alma a mock glare.

"Seriously, Alma, I'll kill you," she said, a playful lilt in her voice, "we've been living together for a year! Do you really need to text me to ask if you want to see cool stuff in the art gallery?"

Alma's cheeks flushed a delightful shade of pink as she bit her lip sheepishly. Tanya, ever the forgiving friend, simply nudged her affectionately and led her toward the gallery.

Art Gallery, Second floor, 12:03 p.m.

The air crackled with anticipation, buzzing not just from the vibrant costume party but also from the newly opened art gallery.

General Anmolbir, the charismatic host, held court, showcasing Casa's artistic treasures to a diverse crowd. Tourists, visa applicants, and even costumed revelers mingled, their eyes drawn to a gleaming shotgun embedded in an authentic glass frame.

"This, my friends," General Anmolbir declared, his voice booming, "is a replica of the very shotgun used by the architect of Casa himself!"

Cameras flashed, capturing the historical artifact as both tourists and costumed figures, including Tanya and Alma, marveled at the display.

But the serene atmosphere was shattered by an unexpected sound – the gushing roar of a waterfall.

A hush fell over the crowd as a hulking figure, 8 feet tall and radiating menace, materialized from the newly formed waterfall on the wall, a Span Doorway. He pointed his pistol, aiming directly at General Anmolbir's emerald turban.

"Crab Aracari," someone in the crowd gasped, recognizing the inscription on the man's weapon. "A Hovershell militant!"

Panic rippled through the room. Memories of the Hovershell's ruthless invasion, led by Crab Aracari, 3 years ago, surfaced, chilling the air. A woman's voice trembled, "He... he used the Span Doorways to attack the Chairmen's building... killed everyone..."

Even Tanya and Alma, usually fearless, felt a tremor of fear run down their spines. The only question in their minds is, why has he come here?

General Anmolbir remained unfazed. He fixed Crab Aracari with a calm gaze, his voice steady despite the gun pointed at him.

"This frame, my friend," he said, tapping the bulletproof glass, "is crafted from the finest materials. Even the strongest pistol wouldn't scratch it."

Crab Aracari, towering over the General, seemed intrigued by this unflinching display of courage from a man half his size. A strange smile played on his lips.

General Anmolbir, his eyes locked on Crab Aracari's, slowly turned his head, and raised an eyebrow. "Nice replica, wouldn't you agree?" he said, his voice laced with a hint of mockery, his fingers tightening around the shotgun inside the frame.

The tension was palpable; the room transformed into a scene of a high-stakes standoff. The pressure from General Anmolbir's grip intensified, and the bulletproof glass, once impenetrable, began to crack.

With a deafening shatter, the glass exploded, showering the floor with shards. Undeterred, General Anmolbir held the shotgun aloft, his voice ringing with inhuman strength, "Too bad it isn't a replica!"

Library, Ground floor, 11:53 a.m.

Charlie tiptoed into the library, the hush of the place amplifying his own awkwardness. Libraries were supposed to be quiet, but this silence felt...charged.

He couldn't quite put his finger on it. As he scanned the room, his gaze fell on Bill's coat hanging carelessly over a chair. Bill, notorious for losing things, had somehow managed to leave his most prized possession behind – and in a library, no less!

As he picked up the coat, he accidentally caused a cascade of letters to spill out onto the floor. Draping the coat over his shoulders, he instinctively gathered the fallen letters.

A mischievous glint sparked in his eyes as he reached for the coat. Morals whispered at him, reminding him about the sanctity of someone's privacy and respecting unshared words.

But here he was, alone in the library, and temptation played its devilish tune. Curiosity, that insatiable beast, clawed at him.

He flipped open the first letter, his heart stuttering at the name scrawled at the top – Griffin Wander. A name he vaguely recognized, a name Jerry had mentioned in hushed tones.

Memories of Jerry mentioning a certain Griffin Wander flooded back; apparently, Griffin had written letters to Alma, influencing her to follow Jerry.

The letter, dated a day before Bill's first arrival, sent a jolt through Charlie. It addressed Bill directly, the words crisp and clear:

"Dear Bill, Tomorrow, you'll meet a boy in blue aviator glasses waiting by the elevator at precisely 8:27 AM. That's Jerry. He and his 2 friends, Charlie and Tanya, will be leaving for the Casa Institute at 10:04 AM. But remember, Bill, you mustn't join them."

A cold memory pricked Charlie's mind: Bill refusing to join them at the institute, citing a gym session. Now, with a suspicious letter clutched in his clammy hand, Charlie swallowed hard, unease gnawing at his insides.

Something was terribly wrong. He placed the first letter on top of the stack, each one dated further back in time, each syllable laced with chilling revelations.

Letter 2 (Dated one week before Charlie's Earth plea denial)

Dearest Bill,

Remember convincing Charlie that you could get him back to Earth? Now's the time. Weave a tapestry of lies, fabricate a grand plan for your own escape, and whisper sweet nothings about Span Doorways. His trust is your key; use it wisely.

Yours truly,

(Griffin Wander)

Letter 3 (Dated 4 days before me and Charlie boarded the Magus Train)

Bill, my friend,

Two Magus Train tickets have found their way to you. Convince Charlie, Jerry, whoever — to board that train. I know the price is steep, Midas' life hangs in the balance, but think of the grander scheme!

Remember, secrecy is paramount.

Your unseen companion,

(Griffin Wander)

Letter 4 (Dated yesterday)

Bill,

Those Span Doorway spheres Jerry and his cohorts plan to deliver next week? Destroy them. Vanish them. And let the Lumberjack know, loud and clear, that defiance is in the air. Consequences be damned.

Until next time,

(Griffin Wander)

"Destroyed!?" Charlie shrieked, the word echoing in the room like a death knell. The Lumberjack wouldn't hesitate to paint the town red if they failed to deliver the spheres.

Sweat beaded on his forehead, conjuring the unsettling memory of their last encounter with the ruthless leader. The realization slammed into him with the force of a meteor: Bill, a spy? A puppet dancing to the tune of an unseen puppeteer who knew their every move?

His fingers trembled as he tore open the next letter, bracing himself for the secrets it held.

Letter 5 (Dated Today)

My precious Bill,

An attack is coming. Leave the institute, but not before leaving your coat in the library on the chair beside the grand mirror. Charlie will fetch it.

Remember to brush your teeth,

(Griffin Wander)

His gaze snapped to Bill's coat, which he had fetched. Each letter, a brick in the dam of his understanding, had revealed Bill's actions, but the bigger picture remained shrouded in mist.

With trembling fingers, he reached for another letter, drawn to the 2 words emblazoned upon it like a chilling invitation: **"Hello, Charlie."**

Art Gallery, Second floor, 12:08 p.m.

A deafening CRACK echoed through the art gallery, followed by a spray of metal shards. Anmolbir's shotgun blast, aimed at the bullet hole of Crab Aracari's pistol, not only shattered the incoming bullet but also pulverized the gun itself, sending 3 of Crab's fingers flying and his left hand erupting in a geyser of crimson.

The crowd, already panicked by Crab's arrival, erupted into chaos, their terrified screams mingling with the metallic clang of the broken pistol.

Amidst the pandemonium, the crowd scurried for safety, their fleeing forms a living tide flooding down the stairs. Only Anmolbir and the wounded Crab Aracari remained, locked in a deadly ballet of violence.

"Costume party, General?" Crab sneered, his voice laced with venom. His gaze settled on Anmolbir's attire – the emerald turban, the black suit pants, and the single rose adorning his chest pocket. "Shouldn't you be playing dress-up as your favorite character?"

Anmolbir's reply was a mocking smirk as he twirled his handlebar mustache. **"My favorite character," he drawled, "is ME!"**

With a roar, he charged, aiming to blow Crab's head off with the remaining shotgun blast. Crab Aracari's hand, clumsy with adrenaline, fumbled, sending the weapon clattering away.

Unfazed, he launched a flying kick, aiming for Crab's legs. But the hulking Hovershell militant remained unmoved, his legs as sturdy as ancient redwood trees.

Capitalizing on Anmolbir's misstep, Crab lunged with his massive hands. With lightning reflexes, Anmolbir whipped out a bolt pen from his pocket and launched it like a projectile.

It struck Crab's neck, delivering a sharp sting. But the Aracari's physiology proved too resilient; the pen glued harmlessly struck the tough bone beneath his skin.

Three failed attempts fueled Crab's fury. He seized Anmolbir, his monstrous hands wrapping around the General's torso like iron bands. Ripping pressure tore at Anmolbir's suit, his skin beneath stained crimson as blood welled from unseen wounds.

"This will hurt a lot," Crab growled, tightening his grip, intent on crushing Anmolbir like a brittle twig.

Though pain stole Anmolbir's voice, it couldn't touch his spirit. He met Crab's gaze with a defiant quirk of his lips, his voice a rasp but laced with pride. "You're right; it will hurt. A lot."

With lightning reflexes, General Anmolbir's leg shot upward like a thunderclap, delivering a powerful kick to the bolt pen lodged in Crab Aracari's neck.

The force of the blow triggered a surge of electricity that coursed through Crab's body with an intensity capable of staggering even the mightiest of creatures.

Propelled by the shock, Crab's iron grip loosened, allowing Anmolbir to fall free. But the General wasn't done.

Clutching the pen lodged in his neck, he used its momentum to slam himself down onto Crab's chest. The pen, already embedded, pierced further, delivering another agonizing shock as Anmolbir landed with the full force of gravity.

Anmolbir, despite his own blood loss, followed up with a brutal kick to Crab's leg. Crab Aracari, overwhelmed by the dual assault of pain – the searing agony of the electricity and the gaping wound in his chest, followed by the kick – writhed on the ground, his fingers spasming, his vision dimming.

Shivering from the shock, Crab's eyes fluttered closed, the light fading fast.

Anmolbir himself was barely clinging to consciousness, his knees buckling under the relentless blood loss. He struggled to crawl, then to stand, fueled by a flicker of defiance, an ember of his indomitable spirit.

From the depths of his agony, Crab roared, a primal sound of fury and pain. His hand, guided by instinct rather than control, swept across the floor.

Anmolbir, with the last vestige of strength, mirrored the roar, unleashing a final blow. His fist slammed down on the pen protruding from his own stomach, driving it deeper.

The metal conducted the remaining charge, a final burst of electricity frying the nerves within him, a fatal jolt that stole his life in an instant.

Anmolbir, the pain a vise around his body, could only reach out for the shotgun on the floor. But darkness claimed him before he could touch it.

As his vision swam and faded, the final image seared into his mind was Aryan Aracari and his soldiers, weapons glinting, pouring through the newly formed doorways, promising a terrible new chapter in the unfolding chaos.

CHAPTER TWELVE

THE DICTATOR OF DESTINIES

Alist (Diary)

Casa Institute Hall, First Floor, 12:01 p.m.

The festive buzz of the Casa Institute Hall evaporated instantly as the doors slammed shut with a chilling thud. 114 individuals, their costumes a jarring reminder of the joyous occasion just moments ago, now huddled together, fear etched on their faces.

Two Hovershell goons, Silk and his unnamed partner, stood guard, rifles glinting ominously.

"All set," Phantom, a dark-skinned figure with an air of grim determination, announced, securing a bomb to the hallway wall outside.

Panic erupted. "What's happening? Why are you doing this?" the crowd demanded, voices overlapping in a desperate chorus.

One of the goons smirked, his tone devoid of empathy. "Simple. We don't waste bullets on a crowd. This place goes boom, and afterwards, we come back for the Asparian with aviator glasses. A little energy extraction from a dead body, you see."

A tremor of disbelief rippled through the crowd. An elderly woman, her eyes wide with horror, croaked, "But why kill us?"

Silk chuckled, a chilling sound in the tense silence. "Orders, Grandma. The Lumberjack only wants the Asparian and his friends. But hey, being here, might as well send a message to Casa. Tomorrow's news will be interesting."

A man's voice, tight with anger, cut through the despair. "You think we'll go down without a fight?"

Phantom stepped into the hall, his voice dripping with cruel authority. "We're leaving now. The button sets the bomb off. Try escaping; we're waiting outside. And inside? The bomb senses movement. Cut a wire, disarm it, boom anyway."

Hopelessness settled over the crowd. They were trapped, their colorful costumes now stark reminders of the impending darkness. The 16 goons' departing laughter echoed in the hall, a chilling prelude to the silence that followed, broken only by the ragged breaths of fear.

But just as despair began to suffocate them, a casual voice sliced through the tension.

"So, if this bomb detects motion, does that mean it blows up if I touch it, and we all die together?" My voice rang out, calm and measured, through the hallway.

Phantom, Silk, and their partners jerked in surprise. Phantom cautiously stepped outside, finding me standing just inches from the bomb, a dozen rifles aimed squarely at me.

"We didn't see him!" the goons outside exclaimed in unison, their voices tinged with shock and fear.

Silk's jaw dropped. "He was just in the hall! How did he get here?"

Phantom, eyes narrowing at my glasses, couldn't hide his surprise. "Move aside, Asparian," he growled, rifle unwavering. "Don't bluff; you wouldn't dare touch the bomb."

"Pointing a gun at someone while asking a favor? Uncivilized, wouldn't you say?" I countered, my voice calm despite the rifles trained on me. "Try *please.* "

With a casual flick of my wrist, I grasped the bomb, sending a collective gasp rippling through the room. Faces paled, the goons dropping their weapons in panicked disarray.

"This madman might just trigger the explosion!" The goons screamed.

"No! Stop!" they screamed, sweat beading on their foreheads. The crowd echoed their fear, whispers of "Are you crazy?" flying like panicked birds.

Even Phantom's voice cracked with genuine fear. "Careful! We can talk! Please remove your hand! I'll defuse it…"

"Defuse? Please? Nah," I chuckled mockingly. "I've got a better idea."

In a move defying logic, I ripped the bomb from the wall, my hand a blur of speed.

A collective gasp escaped the room as hearts pounded like war drums. "FOOL!" The crowd and the goons exclaimed collectively.

Phantom, his hands raised in surrender, pleaded, "Forgive me, please, just--"

Ignoring his pleas, I turned around, everyone holding their breath, anticipating my next move. They all believed I was about to do something recklessly foolish.

And I didn't disappoint them.

With a powerful throw, the bomb sailed through the window, its trajectory aimed not at the ground but at the distant sky.

A tense silence stretched as they watched it arc upwards, "Now," I uttered, pointing at the sky and then...BOOM! A brilliant flash erupted among the clouds, far from their trembling forms.

Silence, then pandemonium. Phantom collapsed to the ground, stunned by what he had just witnessed.

"He tossed the bomb in a way that it was in motion and, at the same time, in a way that the motion detectors didn't register any motion for a specific amount of time. That's...that's the power of an Asparian! – such precision," he murmured in disbelief.

"So, the Lumberjack sent you?" I choired. Still reeling from the bomb's disposal, my sudden appearance startled Phantom – his pistol snapped up, aiming straight at my head.

"Calm, are you?" he rasped, desperation lacing his voice. "Weapons. Again. A bomb just filled the room, and you...don't even flinch?"

I chuckled, holding his pistol effortlessly. "Panic's my usual routine, believe me. But today? No pressure." My voice turned cold. "Because there wasn't any."

He frowned, eyes darting between me and his fifteen-armed men. "No pressure? What are you talking about?"

"Power," I smirked, raising my pinky finger right in front of his eyes. "Do you know what that is?"

He hesitated, eyeing his backup for some reassurance. "Numbers," he finally declared, his voice betraying a sliver of doubt.

"Think you can overpower me with sheer numbers?" I challenged, my smirk widening.

He swallowed, his confidence wavering. "Yes," he muttered, the word barely audible.

My pinky danced away from his eyes, then snapped back. In a blur of motion, his own reflection replaced it, and then... darkness.

"Power is when they think they can defeat you, and right then, you crush their cerebrums out," I uttered, standing tall among the 16 hardly beaten Hovershell goons. "Ahh, even mosquitos last longer than them."

"Perhaps you all should...leave," I suggested to the awestruck crowd.

Silence, then thunderous applause. Some cheered, others gaped, all speechless after witnessing my lightning-fast victory.

The elderly woman finally piped up, a smile dancing on her lips as she turned to leave, "Not all heroes wear capes,"

"Oh, I do wear a cape," I corrected, awkwardly pulling out Captain Demy's blue Asparian cape from behind my coat. "Um, it's just lurking behind my coat."

The departing crowd's cheers faded into the background as a prickling sensation alerted me to a different kind of presence.

Turning, I met the familiar gaze of Aryan Aracari, the man who introduced me to the harsh realities of my powers in our first encounter. With unsettling calmness, he was gathering the bodies of his fallen comrades, depositing them gently inside the hall.

"Another unfortunate encounter, wouldn't you say?" Aryan's voice was deep, smooth as polished obsidian, but held no trace of emotion. **"What's with you always beating my men?"**

Library, Ground floor, 12:08 p.m.

The weight of Charlie's revelation hung heavy in the air.

"Bill?" Tanya gasped, her voice trembling. "He... he was working with them all along? And he wrote to The lumberjack about the damn spheres?" Her gaze darted between Charlie and Alma, seeking solace in their shared disbelief.

Charlie nodded, his face grim. "It seems Griffin Wander had him wrapped around his finger. This changes everything."

His voice softened as he turned to Alma, who stood frozen beside the dusty shelves, her face pale and eyes downcast. "Alma, you used to receive letters from a man named Griffin Wander, right? You never really told Jerry or me much about him. Do you think there's any connection between those letters and these ones? Is there something you're not telling us?"

Alma felt a surge of panic rise within her, her heart pounding in her chest as she struggled to find the right words. She glanced at Charlie, her eyes pleading for understanding, but her mouth refused to form a coherent response.

Seeing the turmoil in her eyes, Charlie softened his tone. "Hey, it's okay," he said gently. Taking a deep breath, Charlie tore open the seal of the second-to-last letter addressed to him; determination etched on his face as he prepared to unravel more of the mystery.

Letter 6

Poor Charlie,

There are 2 things, "what should happen" and "what is going to happen." My role, you see, is to bridge that gap. Fate is rarely carved in stone, my friend. While some events may seem predetermined, there's always a chance to alter the course.

Right now, a grim melody plays. What is going to happen is you hear a gunshot outside the library as soon as you finish reading. And then 6 minutes later, sharply at 12:17, you and Tanya lay dead on the ground.

But a different score awaits, one where you hold the pen, composing a future filled with promise. The final letter in your left hand holds the key. It's a compass guiding you toward a path free from this preordained tragedy. Take it, Charlie. Embrace the power to change your fate.

The choice, as always, is yours.

Sincerely,

(Griffin Wander)

Each word in the letter resonated with a suspenseful harmony. As Charlie finished reading, the sound of a gunshot pierced the air from outside, precisely as described in the letter, startling all 3 of them.

"This Griffin Wander can see the future?" Tanya shrieked, her voice laced with terror.

Charlie, however, remained composed, a furrow etching itself onto his brow. "No, that's not possible," he murmured thoughtfully. "Only the Casa board can see the future, and even their power is limited by the Green Sphere. This planet, thankfully, is free from the paradoxes of time travel. Their visions are restricted to other worlds."

"That doesn't hold true for Griffin Wander," a sudden, unexpected voice broke the silence. Alma, her gaze unwavering, met Charlie's eyes. "He's beyond the Green Sphere. He possesses the ability to see all possible futures, to mold every destiny. We are in the presence of *The dictator of destinies.*"

Casa Institute Hallway, First Floor, 12:10 p.m.

The weight of guilt pressed heavily upon me as I confessed to Aryan, "The moment I witnessed the Lumberjack's brutal slaying of Midas and accepted his deceitful offer of peace, a dark burden settled upon my soul."

We were disposing of the bodies under the cloak of darkness, using a discreet side exit. "The thought of ending the Lumberjack's reign of terror and taking matters into my own hands has haunted me ever since. Your sudden arrival seals my resolve," I admitted, a resolute smirk playing on my lips. "And I couldn't be more grateful."

Aryan, unfazed by my bravado, launched into a historical narrative. "On Alistia," he began, his voice measured, "the first human Surapsa, empowered by the God Asparus, rose from a common beta to the most formidable being, the purest Asparian. This power birthed a race unlike any other, the strongest Alistia had ever known."

He paused, securing the hall door with a decisive click. "My people, the Aracari, were once the rulers of these rulers. We reigned supreme, our raw power allowing us to tear through mammoths with our bare hands. We were the apex predators in a world teeming with prey. But then came the Asparians; their crusade for 'wildlife preservation' was a mere mask for their true agenda: our annihilation. We were the dominant force, yet they were the true barbarians!"

His voice hardened. "A single Asparian could decimate a hundred Aracari. Their reflexes, honed by divine power, far surpassed our own. Though we outnumbered them, they drove us to the brink. Survival demanded adaptation. We developed a technique honed over generations to predict all physical movements to counter their unmatched reflexes. Over centuries, we honed this skill, passing it down through generations until it became ingrained in our very nature – for as we evolved, it became our own, REFLEX!"

My fist clenched in response, my gaze drawn to the metal glove encasing his right hand, a silent promise of a fiery reckoning. "So, your kind barely survived ours," I taunted, reveling in his discomfort. "Seems you miss your precious force field belts. Considering that, wouldn't you say your odds against me are slim to none?"

Aryan's jaw tightened. "Discarding the shield was a deliberate act," he stated icily. "Using one against an Asparian would be a disgrace to my people."

"Fair play, then," I conceded. "Thanks to your machine that siphoned my Asparian energy for those Span Doorway spheres, I'm back to operating at a fraction of my power, much like last time. However, before we get down to business, indulge me with a personal story. I've had enough of your glorified race history."

Aryan averted his gaze, his eyes lingering on his right arm as if haunted by unspoken memories. "I... I'd rather not," he mumbled, his voice tight.

"So, you want to die like a less-developed character?" I scoffed, theatrically giving him a double thumb-up. "Fine by me!"

Aryan's face hardened, his outstretched hand pointing at me with murderous intent. The tranquil hallway shattered as a torrent of inferno erupted from his metal glove. The narrow confines offered a scant escape.

I launched myself toward him, my body a blur as I instinctively dodged the searing wave of flames. My momentum propelled me onto the wall, defying gravity as I ran vertically.

His hand, wreathed in fire, reached out in a futile attempt to ensnare me, but I barely eluded his grasp. With a deft shift, I transitioned from the wall to the ceiling and then to the opposite wall in a seamless display of agility.

In a blur of motion, I closed the distance between us, the intense speed of my approach merging seamlessly with the flames that sought to consume me.

The sheer force of my arrival, coupled with the residual heat from the flames, created a localized effect that momentarily nullified the inferno, allowing me to cut through it with my body.

My plan was audacious. With a surge of adrenaline, I lunged forward, both hands clamping down on the searing metal of his outstretched gauntlet. The world blurred as Aryan retaliated with a bone-crushing punch that landed squarely on my face.

The impact sent a jolt through my skull, stars exploding in my vision as a crimson stream erupted from my nose, staining the floor. Yet, through the haze of pain, my grip on the gauntlet only intensified. I knew that monstrosity housed his most lethal weapon - the flamethrower.

Fueled by desperation, I wrenched my hands apart, tearing the metal casing with a sickening screech. Sparks flew as mangled fragments clattered to the ground in slow motion. My palms, exposed to the inferno's lingering heat, were seared a mosaic of red and black.

But Aryan was relentless, his onslaught unyielding. With a cunning maneuver, he feigned a strike with his right hand, only to unleash a punishing blow from his left, mirrored the first blow, connecting with my jaw with a sickening crunch.

Staggering back, I instinctively used the momentum to propel myself upwards, launching a flurry of kicks at his legs while simultaneously using his body as leverage to climb. In a seamless maneuver, I executed a backflip, landing directly in front of him, and unleashed a powerful kick aimed at his face.

He had no choice but to block. His left hand grasped my right foot, but I countered with a swift kick from my left.

He attempted to disarm me by wrapping his right arm around my leg, his outstretched hand mirroring the stance he used to unleash the flames before.

Time seemed to distort around us. A desperate gamble flickered in my mind. "He's bluffing," I thought, a flicker of hope battling the rising tide of fear. "The glove is gone. There's no way he can…"

My thoughts were cut short as the skin on his outstretched hand began to blister and char. A plume of steam erupted from his arm, the reflection of his fiery red nerves starkly visible in my mirrored aviator glasses.

His hand continued to heat, morphing into a grotesque amalgamation of bone and blue flame. The uniform fabric from his shoulder to his wrist disintegrated, revealing a horrifying spectacle – a skeletal arm wreathed in vibrant blue flames with fiery red arteries.

A chilling realization dawned on me. The flamethrower wasn't within the gauntlet; it was his hand! I had fallen for his elaborate ruse, and now I was trapped. My legs were immobilized, my hands too far away to reach him, and the precious seconds ticking by offered no solace.

In a desperate act of defiance, I cracked my knuckles, the sound echoing hollowly in the tense silence. My mind raced, searching for any sliver of hope, any escape from the fiery oblivion that awaited.

A tingling sensation on the periphery of my vision drew my gaze to the left. My body moved on autopilot, my hands falling limp in a gesture of surrender. I could have fought, I could have tried to escape, but the sight that met my eyes irrevocably altered the course of the battle.

The inferno erupted from his hand, engulfing me in a searing wave of heat that propelled me through the air with unimaginable force. I slammed against the opposite wall, the impact so powerful that the entire structure crumbled, leaving no trace of me in its wake…

Library, Ground floor, 12:13 p.m.

Letter 7

Charlie,

At precisely 12:14, you and Alma must stand close to the library door while letting Tanya stand in the middle of the library. You mustn't go outside until 12:15, or else you'll get caught. Alma must hold the doorknob; Tanya must look straight at you. And you must keep your eyes on the letter even after finishing reading it.

A better destiny awaits,

(Griffin Wander)

The clock ticked ominously, each second echoing in the tense silence of the library. Charlie's heart hammered against his ribs, mirroring the frantic rhythm of Tanya's trembling breath. Alma, her knuckles white around the doorknob, seemed carved from stone, her eyes reflecting a terror that mirrored his own.

Charlie's gaze darted between the letter clutched in his hand and the 2 girls beside him, their faces etched with a mixture of fear and hope.

"We'll be alright, right Charlie?" Tanya's voice shattered the silence. Her question hung in the air, unanswered, a stark reminder of the precariousness of their situation.

Charlie swallowed hard, forcing a smile that felt brittle and unconvincing. "Hopefully," he murmured, his voice betraying the gnawing doubt that gnawed at him. "Perhaps Jerry will find us in time."

Even as he spoke, his eyes caught a glint of white on the letter, a hidden message obscured by a cleverly placed sticker. With trembling fingers, he peeled it away, his breath catching in his throat as the horrifying truth unfolded before him.

The words, stark and unforgiving, revealed a chilling reality: Griffin Wander's "better destiny" wasn't about saving lives. It was a cruel manipulation, a twisted game where the players were mere pawns in his grand scheme.

A surge of primal terror coursed through Charlie. He flung the letter aside, the flimsy paper fluttering to the ground like a fallen leaf. His eyes locked on Tanya; his voice laced with urgency.

But it was too late.

Without warning, a deafening crash shattered the tense silence. A monstrous vehicle, emblazoned with the insignia of the Hovershell, materialized through a newly created portal of the Span Doorway, its occupants emerging with weapons drawn.

Tanya, caught in the crossfire, let out a scream that ripped through the air. The sickening sound of metal meeting flesh filled the air as blood sprayed, staining her Princess Jasmine costume crimson.

In an instant, her body slumped lifelessly to the ground **as the tiara of happy endings broke on her crushed head.**

The fallen letter lay on the ground, a grim marker of the tragedy that had just unfolded. Its final words burned into Charlie's mind, a chilling reminder of the danger they now faced:

"TANYA IS DEAD… Now RUN!"

CHAPTER THIRTEEN

PERSONAL GRUDGES

Alist (Diary)

My perception surpassed that of any ordinary individual, transcending even the heightened senses of a typical Asparian. My eyes, in particular, held an extraordinary power, brimming with energy so potent that it granted me the ability to see for kilometers on end.

Not only could I observe distant scenes with unparalleled clarity, but I could also discern multiple occurrences simultaneously within a vast radius of 10 kilometers.

In a critical moment, as the searing flames of the Aryan Aracari threatened to consume me, my senses flared, alerting me to a danger lurking nearby.

My head snapped to the left, and even through the blinding light filtering through the keyhole of the locked hallway door, I saw it. I peered through the slender aperture of the closed hall door, my vision piercing through the darkness to the window beyond. And there, in that fleeting picture, my body froze.

I beheld the scene unfolding in the library, and my body tensed as I bore witness to the tragedy befalling Tanya. A shockwave pulsed through me as the realization dawned – a car hurtling toward her, sealing her fate before my very eyes.

The world seemed to slow down, the heat emanating from Aryan's glove a distant hum compared to the thunderous silence that had engulfed me.

Casa Institute Main Hall, Ground Floor, 12:21 p.m.

The chaos around the institute grew even larger as the spherical Span Doorways materialized around Casa Institute. Their operation was elegantly simple: upon collision with an object, the Span Doorway sphere bursts, unleashing a cascade of water in the exact shape of the collided object.

This watery manifestation can cover an area of up to 9 by 6 feet. Picture this: if the sphere collides with a Rubik's Cube, the cube transforms into a flowing square of water. Attempts to touch the cube would result in your fingers passing through, emerging from wherever the cube is now connected.

Usually used on walls, these volatile portals, conduits for instantaneous travel, pulsed with an otherworldly hum. But their arrival wasn't a peaceful one. Emerging from these portals were the Hovershell goons, effectively barricading any escape routes.

With the outside now overrun, the people trapped inside were forced to take refuge within the main hall, the once peaceful seminar hall, now a temporary hideout, awaiting a climax.

Alma and Charlie, their breath ragged from narrowly escaping the clutches of the menacing goons that prowled the library, stumbled into the hall, a scene of sheer terror unfolding before them.

The air was thick with the stench of fear and despair, punctuated by the cries of the wounded who, like them, had barely evaded the hail of bullets. Limbs trembling, hearts heavy, they bore witness to the agony of their fellow survivors – some wounded, others weeping for lost friends – some still more resigned to the grim reality of their impending demise.

Sweeping across the hall, Alma's gaze fell upon the faces of those around her, mirroring the hollowness gnawing at her own heart. Tanya. Her cheerful roommate, finally a confidante, her constant source of laughter and encouragement, was gone.

Overcome with the gravity of her loss, tears cascading down her cheeks in a torrent of grief—the first time she allowed herself the vulnerability of open weeping.

Charlie, usually the beacon of strength in times of crisis, stood by her side, his own anguish palpable in the heavy silence that enveloped them. With a solemn gesture, he removed his Mario mustache, his gaze drawn to a gaping hole in the ceiling – the gateway through which tragedy had descended upon them.

Amidst the rubble lay a figure, broken and battered. Dust swirled around him, trapped beneath the debris, a stark reminder of their precarious situation, a testament to the violence that had shattered their sanctuary.

A voice broke the silence, heavy with sorrow. "Amazing boy he was," the man rasped, gesturing toward the figure. "An Asparian, they called him. Saved us on the first floor, fought them all off single-handedly. There was a fierce battle raging above, then a deafening blast... and he came crashing down, breaking this very spot."

Charlie's breath hitched. "Jerry?" he choked out, the name a whisper lost in the tense atmosphere.

"Gone, kid," the man replied solemnly. "Even with the fall, his hand twitched under the rubble. But just for a fleeting moment. His face was caked in black dust, likely from the blasts, and blood oozed from his tightly shut eyes. Didn't respond to my calls. Even if the fall hadn't done him in, his insides are probably crushed."

Disbelief contorted Charlie's face as he crumpled to the floor and dragged himself toward my aviator glasses. The blast, muffled by the distance, had seemingly left them unscathed, lying near the pile of rubble that held me.

A sickening crack, like a bone snapping in half, tore through the hallway. The heavy oak door, a desperate shield against the encroaching nightmare, shattered inwards.

Shrieks and gasps erupted from the huddled crowd as Aryan Aracari, a monstrous silhouette, filled the doorway. A primal terror, thick and suffocating, squeezed the air from their lungs. But it was the sight in his hand that sent a fresh wave of horror crashing over them.

The frail form of the old woman, the one I'd helped escape the chaos below, dangled in his grip. Her head, once crowned with silver hair, was now a grotesque mask of crimson. Blood, dripping from his fist, stained the floor in a macabre pattern.

Aryan's voice, dripping with a chilling authority, boomed across the room breaking the stunned silence. "Convenient, finding you all gathered," he declared. "This expedition has cost us dearly. Noam," he addressed his right hand man who had just entered, "form them into a line. I haven't got the time for pleasantries."

Chaos erupted. The survivors, their faces contorted in a mixture of terror and despair, surged forward in a desperate attempt to escape. Screams ripped through the air as they clambered over one another, a frantic scramble for the nonexistent exits.

"Futile," Aryan roared, his voice silencing the crowd with a deafening force. He tightened his grip on the old lady's head, his cruelty a perverse performance. "It's cold out there," he mocked, his voice laced with sadistic amusement. "Wouldn't you all like some warmth?"

His right hand began to glow with an ominous blue light. The heat emanating from it was palpable, even from a distance. The survivors, knowing what was to come, squeezed their eyes shut, unable to bear witness to the barbarity about to unfold.

A bloodcurdling scream, the last of the old woman's defiance, pierced the silence. Her eyes bulged from their sockets, her entire body contorting in an agonizing spasm.

The inhuman heat from Aryan's hand melted her flesh, the stench of burning flesh filling the air. Her limbs twitched involuntarily, a grotesque puppet dance in the face of her demise.

Aryan didn't relent until all that remained was a skeletal skull, the skin on the head reduced to a pool of molten flesh on the floor.

The survivors, eyes still tightly shut, could only hear the sickening sizzle and smell the acrid smoke; the horrific image burned into their minds forever.

The crowd recoiled like a frightened wave as Noam advanced, his voice dripping with twisted amusement. "Come on, guys, join the line! It's no fun this way," he chuckled, the sound grating against the tense silence.

Grief had anchored Alma to the ground, her knees buckling beneath its weight. But amidst the crushing sorrow, a flicker of defiance sparked in her eyes as they locked onto Noam's.

He was the one behind the wheel, the embodiment of the nightmare that had claimed Tanya. Her hatred for him burned bright, a stark contrast to the chilling fear gripping everyone else.

Noam, relishing her vulnerability, sauntered over and settled beside her. "Let's start with you, shall we?" He purred his voice, a sickening contrast to the solemnity of the scene. "Step forward and lead the line. The others will follow shortly."

Alma remained a statue, her face a canvas of conflicting emotions: fear battling with a burgeoning rage. She yearned for vengeance, but her body felt leaden, shackled by the sheer enormity of their predicament.

Noam's amusement twisted into a snarl at her defiance. "Fine then," he spat, his voice laced with venom. "I'll do things the old-fashioned way."

He raised his pistol, the cold metal glinting under the harsh overhead lights. It hovered menacingly just in front of Alma's face.

Instead of flinching, her green eyes flared open wider, their depths burning with an unyielding fire. The other survivors squeezed their eyes shut, bracing for the inevitable.

Some even cupped their ears, unable to bear the thought of another life becoming extinct. Noam's finger tightened on the trigger, slowly squeezing halfway down.

The silence in the room was deafening, every breath held in anticipation of the gunshot that never came. Instead, a sharp sound cut through the air.

Whack!!!

The noise echoed like a thunderclap, but not the one everyone dreaded. Confusion rippled through the crowd, mirroring the bewilderment etched on Alma's face, Aryan's stoic façade and even Noam's eyes, which now stared vacantly ahead like those of a lifeless doll.

In the blink of an eye, the world had shifted. The wooden chair behind Noam was gone, replaced by a swirling vortex of water.

From its depths, a hand materialized, its form as solid as rock, its color a stark, unsettling gray. With a swift, silent motion, it pierced through Noam's chest, emerging in the center with the man's stolen heart held aloft.

Blood trickled from Noam's slack mouth, painting a grotesque picture against his pale skin. The rock hand, now slick with blood, showcased the heart before Alma's face, pulsating faintly in its unnatural grip.

The hand clenched into a fist, squeezing Noam's heart. No blood touched her skin, forming a disturbing halo around the gruesome display.

A primal instinct surged through Alma. This hand, radiating a warmth, ignited a flicker of recognition within her. With trembling hands, she reached out and grasped it, a strange comfort washing over her in the face of the macabre scene before her.

Noam's blood stained her fingertips, the raging nerves a stark contrast to the unnatural warmth emanating from the hand.

The scene remained frozen, a tableau of horror and a twisted sense of satisfaction warring within Alma. The arm protruded from Noam's chest, a grim reminder of his demise, yet the tension had shifted, replaced by a chilling uncertainty. Where did this hand come from? Who, or what, wielded it?

Charlie's mind raced; the only one in the room seemingly holding the key. "The weight-crushing Jerry wasn't the rubble," he realized, his gaze fixed on me as I effortlessly levitated the heavy rocks overhead.

With a smooth motion, I withdrew my hand from the Span Doorway I'd created on the ground. Simultaneously, the arm plunged into Noam's chest, retracted, and vanished into the back of the chair (now back in normal state) on the opposite side of the hall.

"The dried bloodstains on his cheeks weren't from wounds; he was crying!" Charlie's internal monologue continued.

The afternoon sun streaming through the hole in the ceiling cast a spotlight on me, transforming me into a figure of stark contrast against the dusty backdrop. My features seemed almost monstrous, yet a sense of purpose emanated from me as I raised my head.

With a stretch of my shoulders, I moved with unnatural grace, causing the dust from the blast to effortlessly dance off my body, revealing unblemished alabaster skin beneath.

A startling realization dawned on Charlie as he witnessed my effortless actions. "He saw Tanya die," Charlie concluded silently. "His injuries from the blast... healed? Or were they ever there in the first place? He wasn't trapped, unconscious under debris... he was simply... grieving?"

Every eye in the room, including Aryan Aracari's, was glued to me. My naked form rose from the ground, the blast having stripped my clothes to wisps. Rage thrummed through me, manifesting in the pulsing veins across my chiseled chest.

My clenched fists, the arteries starkly visible, told a tale of simmering fury. Veins throbbed with rage beneath my chest muscles, my six-pack abs taut with tension. I held Captain Demy's blue Asparian cape, the sole survivor of the blast's wrath, and draped it around my lower half and molded the remaining into a kimono, providing a semblance of modesty.

With rock-hard biceps straining, I gathered my long, black hair into a ponytail atop my head. Blood streamed down from my eyes, forced closed, mingling with the dried crimson already staining my cheeks. My aviator glasses lay forgotten on the floor, lost in the chaos.

A palpable shift occurred. The chaotic energy of a hundred and 60 individuals evaporated, replaced by a tense standoff between 2 overwhelming presences. Aryan's confidence wavered. His initial fury at my survival morphed into a chilling apprehension as he sensed the raw power emanating from my form. My hand shot out, accusingly pointed at him, a silent challenge in my gaze. A mix of grief and a manic smirk contorted my face.

"You little bastard," Aryan Aracari hissed, his shock punctuated by the sight of numerous Span Doorway spheres nestled in the spaces between my fingers.

He darted a glance down at his belt, where the small bag holding his own spheres had inexplicably vanished.

"He managed to pilfer them during our skirmish above, just before the assault?" Aryan mused incredulously, his mind racing to comprehend the unforeseen turn of events.

My voice, barely a rasp, held the weight of simmering grief. "First, Midas," I muttered, the name laced with pain. "Then Tanya!" My voice escalated, and my teeth gritted in barely contained fury. "I have the Span Doorway spheres. I just want to escape. My power stands at a meager one percent. My mental state is weary. My body depleted."

I exhaled deeply, my voice cracking. "Yet," the word echoed in the stunned silence, "something compels me! It whispers that destroying every foe within these walls would bring solace."

My voice sharpened, a transformation taking place, turning me into a merciless entity. "Because, Aryan, I harbor a deep aversion toward you. **Because I've personal grudges against those who hurt what I love!**"

By the very fabric of the cosmos, Asparian!" Aryan Aracari boomed, his voice echoing through the chamber like a malfunctioning ventilation system. His fist, a beacon of

malevolent cerulean light, pulsed with an otherworldly energy. "How would you fight me? Aren't you out of juice?"

"Well," A grin, feral and unnerving, stretched across my face. **"It's time to give my heart... a WORKOUT!"**

I bellowed back, my eyes snapping open and locking onto his. The overwhelming aura of my blue iris intensified, engulfing my entire irises in a celestial blue glow. This colossal surge of energy shattered the nearby rubble, causing the fragments to levitate and swirl around me in slow motion.

Aryan's hair whipped back, and the force of my aura rippled through the hall. The white cement walls crackled.

"Not only is his aura formidable, but he's also wielding the force with precision!" Charlie exclaimed in awe, witnessing the words that materialized on the cracked walls: *"You"*, *"Are"*, *"Dead."*

With fiery fury burning hotter than the flames he commanded, Aryan Aracari prepared to unleash his wrath upon me. His colossal arm, charged with malevolent energy, aimed to strike me down. But in a split second, I vanished.

All that remained was the Span Doorway, a testament to my swift evasion and the initiation of my own counterattack.

In a display of agility defying his bulky frame, Aryan contorted his body to an impossible degree. His maneuver was impressive, but my reflexes were lightning-fast.

I had materialized beside him, a blur of motion. My right foot launched into a mid-air kick aimed at his back, narrowly missing its mark as he contorted his body.

As he straightened, a glint of steel flashed as Aryan drew his thin metal blade, lunging at me. His attack was predictable, his blade tracing an arc toward my chest.

My reaction was instantaneous. My hand shot up, not to block, but to slip between the gap of my middle and ring finger.

The blade, seemingly slicing through an ethereal plane, passed through the Span Doorway sphere I had held in the gap. It transformed into a liquid portal, passing harmlessly through my chest like a phantom.

Without missing a beat, my other hand surged forward like a meteoric punch, the thin sword turned portal slipped from Aryan's grasp as he attempted to parry my blow.

My speed was a cheat code. My fist slipped through the gaps in his fingers like a phantom, transforming into a karate chop mid-air. It slammed into his chest with a thunderous crack that echoed through the hall. Aryan, a mountain of a man, grunted, his face contorted in agony.

Panic flickered in his eyes as he unleashed the full fury of his blue inferno, aiming the superheated blast directly at me.

I reacted instinctively, raising my leg to meet the fiery assault. The impact, akin to a miniature explosion, reverberated through the hall.

Despite the searing heat, my body remained impervious. My toes, gripping his burning fingers like a vise, redirected the inferno toward the ground. The floor erupted in a geyser of blue flames, fragments of floor tiles raining down in slow motion.

Aryan, immune to his own power, watched in bewilderment as I stood amidst the inferno, untouched. My blue eyes, ablaze with power, locked onto his flabbergasted face.

He attempted a final, furious attack, drawing 2 daggers from his belt. But even this movement couldn't escape my vigilance.

With outstretched hands, I seized the swirling tile pieces above us, each palm housing a Span Doorway sphere. With a burst of energy, the portals transformed the tiles into conduits, and my hands emerged near Aryan's head in a swift, precise motion.

With surgical precision, my palms struck both sides of his face, the force of the impact rupturing his eardrums and leaving him momentarily stunned. Caught off guard, his dagger strike fell short, unable to reach me as I maintained a safe distance.

"He's anticipating my counter-anticipation," Aryan Aracari surmised, his voice tinged with grudging respect, "blending his strikes with the Span Doorways, creating combos even I struggle to predict."

In a blur of motion, he lunged, the blades flashing upwards, aiming to cleave my arms from my body. I vanished, my hands dissolving into swirling blue portals as blades sliced through empty air.

As he lunged toward me, I feigned a defensive posture, only to pivot and strike at his hands with lightning speed, disarming him in a whirl of motion. Superheated steam erupted as his fiery right hand collided with my bare palm.

"That's some God-level battle IQ," Charlie murmured in awe, his eyes fixed on the intense exchange unfolding before him.

Our clash descended into brutal hand-to-hand combat, each blow resonating with bone-crushing force. His fist blurred through the Span Doorway portals I conjured on my palm, swallowing his attack whole.

The fist reappeared, erupting from the opposite palm and slamming into his own face with a sickening crunch.

Catching him off guard, I unleashed a barrage of strikes, each one landing with precision. But Aryan's monstrous physique proved resilient, absorbing blow after blow without faltering.

Our duel became a blur of motion, a lightning-fast exchange of blows that left onlookers struggling to keep pace. Blue flames and glowing eyes were the only visible markers in the whirlwind of combat as our clash reached a fever pitch.

Aryan, though skilled, relied on predicting my moves based on a single observation. But my repertoire was vast, a flowing stream of techniques: karate chops, boxing jabs, feints, kung-fu strikes, and even elements of sumo and other martial arts.

I used every weapon at my disposal: backs of hands for offense, palms for defense, deflecting his attacks and turning them against him.

Aryan's face contorted in pain, a crimson cascade spilling down his cheek from a fresh wound. His Hovershell uniform hung in tatters, his ribs cracking under the onslaught. His internal organs screamed in protest from the hundred blows he'd taken.

Desperation tinged his eyes. He unleashed the full fury of his inferno, a superheated blast aimed directly at my chest. But I was ready, the Span Doorway on my palm absorbing the searing heat.

With a surge of power, I redirected the inferno back at him, coupling it with a forceful shove that sent Aryan hurtling out of the hall, crashing through the wall with bone-shattering force.

With a fierce blast of flames that scorched the ground, Aryan nullified the force pushing him. Battered and smoldering, he roared back to his feet, a primal defiance overriding the pain etched on his face.

Outside, his Hovershell-clad soldiers gasped in horror. Their invincible leader, now a battered husk. Driven to desperation, Aryan roared back to his feet, primal defiance overriding the agony etched on his face.

"This ends now!" he bellowed, coughing blood. "One final move, Jerry!"

Without hesitation, I shot out of the shattered hall, propelled by a wind of fury. Aryan's hand began to morph, his fiery fingers twisting and merging into a monstrous drill of flame aimed to pierce my very being. The spinning inferno, a whirlwind of heat and light, dwarfed any attack he'd unleashed before.

My left hand clamped down on his bicep like a vice while my right desperately met the fiery drill at the wrist, barely holding it back.

Time seemed to suspend; the world shrunk to the searing pain in my straining muscles, the deafening roar of the flames, and the glint of a chilling blade.

Aryan, it seemed, had anticipated this very move. A pocket knife, sharp and merciless, hovered a hair's breadth from my throat, wielded by his free hand.

He had played his final gambit perfectly, calculating that I wouldn't dare to release his arm to deflect the blade.

My life threatened to flicker out in an instant, the radiant blue energy of my eyes reflecting the terror and helplessness I felt.

A searing line blossomed across my neck, a crimson kiss from the blade's caress. The cold steel pressed against my throat, a chilling reminder of mortality. A single ruby tear escaped the wound, tracing a path down my skin before vanishing into the fabric of my clothes.

But then, something primal, something beyond me, surged through me. In that critical moment, something took over, moving faster than conscious thought. What followed was beyond the blur of motion, too swift for anyone to comprehend.

In a blink, I had twisted completely around the axis of the knife, wrenching Aryan's flaming arm from his grasp with my bare hands.

In a single, fluid motion, I circled him, his own fiery drill becoming the instrument of his demise. It ripped through his chest, exiting in a burst of infernal light from his back.

Aryan's eyes, wide with disbelief and betrayal, met mine for a final fleeting moment. Blood trickled from his lips as he attempted a futile gesture of surrender with his remaining hand. I met his hand with a firm grip.

"There's no pain," I whispered, my voice tinged with a strange sense of detachment. Then, with a roar that echoed across the battlefield, I slammed his hulking form, 6 and a half feet of unyielding muscle and fury, into the unforgiving ground.

CHAPTER FOURTEEN

HAPPY ENDINGS

Alist (Diary)

Alma's Caravan, 11:56 P.M.

"I said heart, don't pump feelings,

I said sleep, no more dreams,

I said mind, shut down all the thoughts,

I said mouth, no more screams,

Then all 4 said, just cry too hard,

The hurts would heal; we are a team.

Time is taking things too far,

Don't mind, I reach wherever,

All the plans are falling apart,

Don't mind, I do whatever.

I know there's only one end,

And happy endings are not forever."

The room pulsed with a heavy silence, the only light a solitary candle casting an amber glow on the worn wooden interior of Alma's caravan.

It felt like the air itself was thick with unspoken words, mirroring the weight in each of our hearts. I had just finished reading her a new verse from my poem collection, my voice echoing in the stillness.

My voice trailed off; the raw emotion etched into each syllable was palpable in the confined space. Outside, the world was cloaked in the inky darkness of a moonless night, a mirror to the desolation I felt within.

Time, once a relentless river, now seemed to stretch endlessly before me, each passing moment an eternity of pain.

Alma, her face etched with a matching sense of sorrow, climbed down from the bunk bed ladder, the creak of the wood a stark counterpoint to the suffocating silence. Her voice, when she spoke, was barely a whisper, heavy with unshed tears.

"You told me I should tell you everything about me if I trusted you," she said, her words breaking like waves against a desolate shore. "Jerry, I trust you the most in this whole world. I want to tell you all about Griffin Wander, about me, about my parents."

Sadly, I didn't hear her. My heart, numb with despair as vast and unyielding as the cosmos itself, couldn't bear the weight of another story.

Standing abruptly, I moved away from her, my face a mask devoid of any emotion. My voice, when I spoke, sounded hollow and detached, a stark contrast to the raw vulnerability she had just displayed.

"It's quieter than usual here," I said my words a deliberate deflection, a desperate attempt to change the subject. "Maybe it's because Tanya's not here."

My gaze swept around the familiar interior, searching for solace in the mundane. "I love coming to your caravan, talking to you. You're a good listener. It's peaceful here."

Alma's voice, laced with a hint of desperation, cut through my carefully constructed façade. "Jerry, I'm talking about something else," she began, only to be interrupted by the touch of my finger on her lips. The warmth of my touch felt incongruous with the coldness in my heart.

"There's something I've been meaning to tell you," I confessed, the weight of my revelation hanging heavy in the air between us. "Asparians, like myself, experience a momentary loss of power when they gaze upon the starry night sky or a picture of the cosmos. And when I look into your eyes, the same thing happens. Because, Alma, I see the Universe... **and I am not talking metaphorically, I literally see the entire universe.**"

As my gaze pierced the depths of Alma's iris, the familiar green melted away, replaced by a breathtaking vista. A million galaxies swirled into existence, expanding outwards to reveal the Milky Way, then our solar system, then Earth.

The descent continued, zooming in on a towering skyscraper before finally settling on a middle-aged man seated at a desk, visible through the building's window. The panoramic journey through the cosmos ended abruptly, with me standing inexplicably within the opulent mansion. Was this a waking dream?

The man, his presence commanding yet enigmatic, closed his diary. A jolt of shock ran through me as I recognized it as an identical replica of the one I used for my poems, even the handwriting mirroring mine perfectly.

The chair screeched as he spun around, revealing a face split between the rugged charm of a full beard and handlebar mustache and the cold efficiency of a cybernetic eye.

One eye, a steely blue, held my gaze with a lifetime of stories, while the other, a glowing blue orb encased in metal, seemed to pierce right through me.

"You harbor deep regret, don't you?" His voice was a mix of sympathy and knowing amusement. "Visions of Tanya flood your mind: her playful way of combing your hair, her snarky remarks, the irreplaceable void she leaves in your group, the loss of a good friend."

I stood frozen, speechless, as he delved into the depths of my soul, unraveling emotions I hadn't dared to confront.

"But your true regret lies not in what you've lost but in what you still have," he continued his words, revealing a stark revelation. "You fear losing Charlie, your anchor in a turbulent sea."

I swallowed hard, struggling to comprehend the uncanny accuracy of his insights. "Who are you?" I whispered, my voice barely audible above the tumult of my thoughts.

"Think of me as your inner voice, your conscience; perhaps I also could be your future self," he explained cryptically. "I am Alist."

"Tomorrow, the Magus Train departs," he said ominously. "You have a choice: to cling to what remains or to embrace what lies ahead."

His voice, laced with philosophical musings, laid bare the core of my conflict. "What truly haunts you, Jerry. What is the perceived lack that drives you to lose those you hold dear – the lack of strength?"

"Yes!" I finally managed to utter the word, bursting forth with raw conviction. "I'm not strong enough!"

"A notion I once held as well," Alist replied, his gaze lingering on the vast emptiness surrounding the mansion.

"And are you?" I swallowed hard; the question laced with desperation. "Are you strong?"

"Yes," he conceded, his voice devoid of pleasure. **"But does it matter? I have won countless battles in my life.**

Fights after fights, conflicts after conflicts. Each one I conquered, yet never once in my life... I've felt the sense of victory."

His chilling words sent shivers down my spine, the hollowness within him mirroring the emptiness I felt.

Driven by a desperate need for a tangible answer, I launched into a flurry of kicks, punches, and karate chops, each attack aimed at him with primal fury.

He sat unfazed, an immovable object in the face of my desperate assault. Nothing seemed to harm him or even push the wheels of his chair.

Frustration mounting, I lunged forward, grabbing his face in a vice-like grip. "Stop messing with my mind!" I roared, my voice hoarse with desperation.

His remaining blue eyes held my gaze through my aviator glasses. "Do what you're supposed to, Jerry," he stated, his voice calm despite the chaos around him. **"Before the warm water turns... cold."**

With a gentle push of his pinkie finger against my forehead, the world dissolved into a vortex of stars. I plummeted through the galaxies, the pain of the attacks I'd launched at him echoing in my bones. The mansion, the conversation, the man - all dissolving into the cosmic tapestry.

I jolted back to reality, disoriented and off balance, collapsing onto the caravan floor.

"Jerry!" Alma cried out, rushing to my side, her voice laced with concern. "What happened?"

"I... I think I hallucinated," I stammered, my heart pounding a frantic rhythm against my ribs.

"Hallucinated? But why is your nose bleeding?" she exclaimed, panic creeping into her voice.

My hand flew to my face, confirming her observation. A throbbing pain emanated from my chest, a testament to the physical manifestation of my internal struggle.

The lines between reality and the encounter with Alist blurred. Was it a glimpse into the future, a conversation with my subconscious, or something far more profound?

The night consumed me in its relentless grip, leaving me captive to my torment. The flames that consumed Tanya's body the next day devouring her mortal coil in the Indian tradition, cast grotesque shadows of despair onto my soul. We stood there in solemn silence, dressed in white, paying our final respects.

Amidst the somber atmosphere, my thoughts drifted to the Casa system and its unforgiving decree of fate. Had the Casa board brought Tanya here to escape an ill-fated death at 23, only for her life's tapestry to be cut short at 19? It was a bitter irony that gnawed at my soul, highlighting the cruel unpredictability of life.

The same gnawing fear gnawed at me for Charlie. His Earthly destiny promised 40 years, yet his very presence at my side felt like a ticking time bomb, a constant threat of defying fate and condemning him to a premature demise. The Lumberjack's wrath festered, a venomous serpent coiling around our necks, choking the hope of ever leading a normal life.

Apartment 4H, 10:36 P.M.

The flames went off; the ashes turned cold as the moonlight found its way to the land.

"Tomorrow, Jerry, the visas," Charlie's voice, heavy with exhaustion but laced with a hopeful veneer, pierced the silence of our shared apartment.

His eye patch lay discarded, a testament to the long night spent battling his own demons. "Maybe, just maybe, we can forget this madness and start anew. Tomorrow is one last game of Snakes and ladders before we step into Casa; what say you?"

A nostalgic smile stretched across my lips, a stark contrast to the storm raging within. "Indeed," I croaked the words, leaving a metallic tang in my mouth. "Though, since you began rolling dice for me, your reign has been legendary, leaving me trailing at 68 defeats to only 9 wins."

"Good night, Jerry," he said, his smile, genuine and warm, was the last image I held onto as he drifted off to sleep. "Jerry, apart from my parents, you're the best person I've ever met in my life," he mumbled, his voice thick with slumber.

Perhaps I should've slept through the night, attained visas the next day and then settled in Casa alongside Charlie and Alma. Sleep, however, remained a distant prospect.

At 3 AM, raw desperation fueled my steps as I stood before Alma's caravan, knocking with a trembling hand.

"I've a favor to ask," I uttered, my voice husky from the night's torment.

Railway Station, 4:30 A.M.

And so, I found myself on the platform, the rhythmic clatter of the train a metronome counting down the seconds of my self-inflicted heartbreak.

They say if you truly love someone, set them free even if it means a lifetime devoid of their presence, even if it means hurling them across the void of uncertainty, never to hear their voice again.

The sorrow mirrored on Alma's face was a punch to the gut. We were both etched with the same despair, a chilling testament to the sacrifice we'd made.

My hands, usually steady, trembled like fallen leaves as I deposited Charlie on the Magus Train, still nestled in the fabricated memories Alma had woven. Back to his Earthly life - parents, a familiar past, and a future far longer than what we could offer here.

As the Magus lurched forward, my knees buckled, and I crumpled onto the platform. The world blurred through a salty haze as tears, hot and unexpected, streamed down my face. My aviator glasses, usually a shield of cool, reflected the rapidly shrinking image of the train, a cruel echo of my choice.

"What have I done?" the question ripped through me, a desperate plea swallowed by the indifferent night. Tears, a torrent of grief threatening to drown me, poured down my face.

Alma, a comforting weight beside me, offered the only solace in this storm. My voice, raw with emotion, cracked between choked sobs. **"I just... I just wanted to play one last game of Snakes and ladders with him. Was that... too much?"**

BEYOND THE DIARY

Aamira

The biting wind clawed at my face, snowflakes swirling around me like a maelstrom of tiny white daggers.

It had been a marathon session with Mr. Alist's diary, starting at the witching hour and stretching into the unforgiving light of dawn.

My eyes felt like sandpaper, and a migraine throbbed behind them, a relentless drummer reminding me of my folly. As if the weather and self-inflicted torture weren't enough, a fresh challenge awaited me in the form of a six-foot-tall blanket of snow covering the world.

A persistent thought hammered through the haze: it couldn't be real. Alistia, Asparians, portals – these belonged to the realm of fantastical fiction, not the reserved Mr. Alist I knew.

The diary hadn't shed much light on his current self. The vibrant, passionate teenager Alist described seemed a world away from the quiet, introspective man I interacted with.

I craved answers. I needed a face-to-face conversation with Mr. Alist. I needed to know if the fantastical world within the diary pages was real or a figment of his imagination. And, of course, there was the small matter of apologizing for stealing his private thoughts.

I trudged through the pristine white landscape, every step a battle against the relentless cold. My only solace was the hope of a steaming cup of coffee – Mr. Alist, I knew from his meticulous pantry, had a bottomless supply of that one beverage.

My quest for caffeine was abruptly halted by the sight of a figure sprawled ungraciously on the snow. A crumpled ball of paper lay near their head like a discarded knight's helmet. A tall, fit man of indeterminate middle age, clad in pristine white athletic wear, lay unconscious.

His face, obscured by a pair of shades, was contorted in pain. But what truly snagged my attention was his right arm. The sleeve of his pristine white jacket hung limp, the fabric swaying gently in the breeze. Where a hand should have been, there was only a dark, prosthetic attachment tucked discreetly beneath the cloth.

"Hey, are you alright?" I knelt beside him, my voice laced with concern.

He blinked slowly, his hand instinctively flying to his nose, which was turning redder than Santa's cap. "Ugh, Jerry, you little rascal," he mumbled, his voice thick with sleep and pain.

A jolt of surprise shot through me. "You know Mr. Alist?" I blurted out, my mind racing.

He chuckled, a dry rasp escaping his reddened nose. "Know him? We practically shared the same breakfast cereal!"

"And here I thought you were just passed out drunk," I muttered, skepticism clinging to my voice like the snowflakes on my eyelashes. "But why were you lying unconscious on his doorstep?"

A mischievous glint twinkled in his black shades as he sat up, brushing the snow off his pristine white pants. "Well, let's just say I had a pressing matter to discuss with the good ol' doc, and he wasn't exactly keen on entertaining guests."

He puffed out his chest, a hint of pride in his voice. "So, I stood my ground, planted myself firmly in front of his door, daring him to make me move if he had the guts. You know, a good old-fashioned deadlock."

"And?" I prompted, my curiosity piqued.

"Turns out he had guts," he chuckled, his eyes twinkling with amusement. "The last thing I remember is this paper projectile hurtling toward my face, and then... darkness." He picked up the crumpled paper, his brow furrowing in mock thought. "Classic Jerry, always resorting to unorthodox methods."

I stared at the paper ball, then back at the man. "But that wouldn't knock someone unconscious," I said, my voice laced with confusion. "Let alone break their nose."

He shrugged, a playful smile dancing on his lips. "Well, I've seen Jerry do some pretty incredible things with paper, especially considering he's one of the most superior beings on the planet."

My jaw nearly hit the floor. Superior beings? Asparians? Was Mr. Alist's fantastical story actually true? A wave of awe and disbelief washed over me, momentarily erasing the throbbing ache in my head.

Before I could process this revelation further, the man extended a hand, his smile widening. "The name's Bill Blear, by the way."

The name sparked a primal fear within me. Bill Blear? The infamous traitor from Mr. Alist's diary, the one who had betrayed his trust and sided with Griffin Wander?

My initial awe curdled into a potent cocktail of anger and disbelief. I recoiled from his outstretched hand, my voice laced with icy fury.

"According to Mr. Alist's diary, you're the backstabbing scoundrel who…" My voice trailed off, searching for the right words. "You Bastard!"

Bill's smile faltered slightly, a flicker of sadness crossing his eyes. "Did he really use such harsh language for me in his diary?" he asked, his voice barely a whisper. "Did he call me a "Bastard ?"

"I might have embellished it a bit," I admitted, the anger dissipating slightly. "But the word suits you well!"

Unperturbed, Bill effortlessly wrested the diary from my grasp, flipping through its pages with casual indifference. "Ahh, I see. The story isn't over yet, my friend," he remarked, his gaze scanning the incomplete narrative. "Our tale of friendship has yet to unfold."

"Then why did Mr Alist deny you entry?" I demanded, my eyes narrowing with suspicion.

"Well, there were other reasons," he conceded, his tone tinged with secrecy. "But you see, this diary only chronicles his life up until the age of 17. Much has transpired since then."

"He was deeply resentful toward me during those tumultuous days," Bill reminisced, his voice tinged with nostalgia. "He even went so far as to apprehend me, bind me, and threaten my life. Beneath his gentle exterior lay a fierce and merciless persona, driven by regret."

"Regret?" I echoed, a pang of empathy seeping into my voice.

"He used to say," Bill continued, his voice dropping to a husky whisper, "that none of it would have happened. None of them would be gone if only he had been... THE STRONGEST BEING OF THE UNIVERSE!"

STRONGEST BEING OF THE UNIVERSE

Alist

Coincidences, as we perceive them, often transcend even the realm of the divine. Some occurrences possess odds so infinitesimally small, a mere one in infinity, that deeming them impossible would seem rational.

Yet, the gamble of such a minuscule chance looms large, for if it were to manifest, it held the potential to shatter the very fabric of reality as once known—a world once familiar.

Such was the case with Asparus, whose fateful discovery of the Crux—a substance wielding power to unravel matter, reducing beings of boundless omnipotence to nought but nothingness—altered the cosmos forever.

In a twist of fate, Asparus had used it to eradicate his brethren. By a sliver of chance, the death knell of a God species became the genesis of our mortal realm.

Haunted by his act, Asparus scoured the infinite expanse, a solitary sentinel in search of any lingering spark of the power he had extinguished. He knew his task, stark and absolute: to eradicate any trace of this godlike existence from the tapestry of reality.

Even a single survivor could unravel the fragile order he had unintentionally established, for Asparus understood the inherent danger of unchecked omnipotence. No cage, no law, no force could restrain a being unburdened by the shackles of mortality.

His mission was singular and unwavering: to unravel the very essence of existence itself. To achieve this, he assumed mortal guises, immersing himself in the lives of mortals to comprehend their struggles, aspirations, and the driving forces that propelled them forward.

"And yet," Asparus's voice, an echo of millennia in his mind, resonated with a tremor of disquiet, "it remains an enigma wrapped in a riddle." Eons had bled into eons since this world's first breath.

He'd worn countless skins – colossal giants bestriding planets, ephemeral insects, even the fleeting guise of self-proclaimed deities. He'd burrowed into the Earth as a microbe, felt the sun on his leaves as a plant, and experienced existence from its most rudimentary twitch to the dizzying heights of sentience.

Millennia bled into millennia, yet the answer remained stubbornly out of reach, particularly the enigmatic puzzle that was humanity.

Visions flickered through his consciousness - a kaleidoscope of mortal lives, each a temporary vessel for his immortal essence. "Despite inhabiting their flesh," he confessed, a sliver of something unfamiliar creeping into his voice, "I have remained a distant observer. No matter the physical torment – the searing agony of battlefields, the soul-crushing weight of captivity, and the sting of hurled insults – I have felt nothing. **No tear has mirrored a world in mourning; no sob echoed their sorrow.** "I have never..." His voice trailed off, a question hanging heavy in the silence, "...cried."

"Humans champion the cause of freedom, yet delight in visiting zoos," Asparus mused, embodying the plight of a lion confined from birth to demise within steel bars.

"They condemn hunters for the death of a mother elephant, yet heedlessly crush countless ants underfoot," Asparus pondered, experiencing life through the lens of a squashed ant, its journey to the hill abruptly halted.

"Their words flow with purity, yet their minds harbor venom," Asparus remarked, inhabiting the thoughts of a schoolchild, parsing the hidden motives of friends.

"A species capable of innovation beyond measure, yet blind to what they are doing," Asparus reflected, witnessing the forest's demise through the eyes of a towering tree, a silent observer of countless generations.

"But even as a God, who am I to pass judgment?" He wondered, the weight of his own actions heavy upon his conscience.

Asparus pondered, lost in a labyrinth of thoughts within the body of an American man, frozen mid-proposal to his fiancée, Maya. His thumb and index finger hovered over her ring finger, a vacant look clouding his eyes.

"Hey, snap out of it," Maya's voice pierced the veil of Asparus's reverie, her concern palpable as she gently urged him to continue.

He responded with a hollow whisper, his voice echoing from some distant realm, **"I'm not saying they are good or evil, or that any of us are,"** leaving Maya utterly bewildered.

"But if this world is merely a cosmic ballet of life and death," Asparus continued, his tone laden with solemnity, **"devoid of any deeper meaning, then its existence or absence should bear no consequence.** Perhaps creating it was a mistake."

A flicker of movement in his eyes sent a shiver down Maya's spine. And just like that... the world around them dissolved into its constituent atoms. The vibrant restaurant scene was replaced by the chilling emptiness of space. **The moon exploded in a blinding flash, the Earth disintegrated into dust, and the sun imploded like a punctured balloon as each star in space vanished.**

In an instant, Maya found herself adrift in the void, the remnants of her world a distant memory. The searing cold stole the warmth from her body, the lack of air, a tightening vice around her chest.

Panic clawed at her throat, a silent scream trapped behind nonexistent lips. She witnessed Asparus's true deity form, both humanoid and idealized, a sight both awe-inspiring and terrifying.

"Or perhaps I was too hasty," Asparus's voice resonated through the inky blackness, pulling Maya back from the brink of oblivion with a gentle tug on her finger. The world lurched back into existence, the familiar sights and sounds of the restaurant flooding back.

Maya gasped, a primal sound of relief and terror escaping her lips. Her heart hammered against her ribs, a frantic drumbeat against the sudden silence. The other patrons, oblivious to the apocalypse Maya had just witnessed, stared in confusion.

Across from her, Asparus sat with a nonchalant air, the diamond ring clutched in his hand. "Apologies for the dramatics, darling; I've recreated your entire universe." He said like it was no big deal, a mischievous glint in his eye. **"Though, I may have forgotten a galaxy or 2."**

And so, Asparus departed once more, slipping into the tapestry of existence to live yet another life. He held onto the belief that perhaps, in the course of this new journey, he might unearth the answers that had eluded him for eons, even if it took countless lifetimes. Fate, however, is curious and surprising even to the most ancient beings, **for even God can find solace in the promise of a new dawn.**

The biting Norwegian wind whipped at David's face, a stark contrast to the turmoil churning within him. Asparus, the ancient being trapped in this ordinary man's skin, stared out at the breathtaking beauty of the fjord, a landscape both serene and utterly foreign.

Here, in this remote corner of the world, David, a recent transplant from England, toiled away at a software company, a nine-to-five routine as predictable as the sunrise.

David's body wasn't an ideal one for Asparus, as he was well-versed in the skins of bodybuilders, athletes, and warriors. Just so you know he wasn't skinny, but years of hard labor in Norway had kept him trim.

His short, light brown hair, streaked with emerging gray, bore the marks of both the elements and inner anxieties. His face, etched with lines from years spent outdoors, held a hint of rugged handsomeness, accentuated by a neatly trimmed beard. His clothing, practical and functional, reflected his working-class background, yet held a subtle air of quiet respectability.

Life was far from easy. His parents' battled illness, the financial burden weighed heavily, and the loss of his wife to a tumor 2 years ago carved an ever-present ache in his heart.

Yet, amidst the trials, he found glimmers of warmth. The unconditional love of his parents and the innocent joy of his children – Avalon, his seven-year-old son, and Alma, his three-year-old daughter – were his anchors in the storm.

He sat before his computer screen, the weight of his responsibilities pressing down. "My life isn't perfect," he murmured, **"but for the first time in ever, it feels... real. It feels... loved."** He looked at his calloused hands, the very hands that soothed his ailing father, changed diapers, and built sandcastles with his children. Lines etched themselves deeper at the corners of his eyes, a testament to the silent battles he fought within.

He'd lived countless lives, witnessed the rise, and fall of empires, tasted the fleeting sweetness of love and the bitter tang of loss. Yet, this life, this seemingly ordinary existence with its undercurrent of quiet desperation, resonated with him in a way none other had.

His days were a symphony of ordinary moments – tending to his parents, working tirelessly for his family, and cherishing every second with his children. He wouldn't trade this life, not even for the promise of something extraordinary.

Every sunrise, every shared meal, every whispered bedtime story – these were the brushstrokes that painted the masterpiece of his existence.

"I've got problems and gifts," Asparus reflected. **"Yet, I find solace. Could it be... happiness?"**

Alma's fourth birthday brought a flurry of excitement. As he watched her shyly greet her classmates, a surge of protectiveness welled up within him. He had meticulously planned the party, wanting every detail to be perfect for his little girl.

Avalon, his spirited son, was a constant source of amusement and surprise. The boy's mischievous spark mirrored an eternal flame within Asparus.

They went swimming every weekend, their laughter echoing through the pool. In the evenings, Asparus's gifted hands danced over the piano keys, weaving melodies that soothed not only Alma but his own restless soul.

Gazing upon his children with a sense of wonder, Asparus marveled at the inherent beauty of existence. **"The fact that nothing ever makes sense, yet this life is so meaningful,"** he whispered, a smile tugging at his lips. **"Within its mysteries lie endless possibilities. One crafts one's own meaning."**

He no longer yearned for a grand cosmic purpose. He just wanted to live this life on a loop, living and dying, reincarnating and repeating...

Avalon burst into the room; his face flushed with excitement. "Dad, I got an 88 in social studies!" he declared, his voice bubbling with pride. "I know I promised a 90, but I understand now. I now know the correct way of learning. Soon I'll become a high-ranking social worker, and take you, Alma, grandma, grandpa, all of us on a world tour!"

Asparus met his son's enthusiasm with a warm smile. "What if you don't earn a ton' of money, genius?" he asked gently, his voice laced with a hint of amusement. "Would you still take all of us?"

Avalon paused, pondering the question for a moment. Then, a grin split his face. "Dad," he declared, his eyes sparkling with unwavering determination, **"then it'll be just the 2 of us — you and me, exploring the world."**

Asparus's heart swelled with pride and love. This simple, human exchange held more weight and beauty than the entirety of divine contemplation. He embraced his son, feeling the warmth of genuine connection. **In that moment, he realized that this life, with all its imperfections, was the greatest gift he could ever receive.**

He leaned down, resting his forehead against Avalon's, captivated by the boy's bright, hopeful eyes. But within those depths, something else flickered – a spark, a reflection that sent a jolt through Asparus's immortal core.

It was a mirror image, a miniature echo of his own vast power, swirling within Avalon like galaxies trapped in an infant's gaze.

A cold dread gripped him…

Coincidences, as we perceive them, often transcend even the realm of the divine. Some occurrences possess odds so infinitesimally small, a mere one in infinity, that deeming them impossible would seem rational.

Yet, the gamble of such a minuscule chance looms large, for if it were to manifest, it held the potential to shatter the very fabric of reality as once known—a world once familiar.

Asparus had never encountered such a phenomenon. His mortal son, this innocent child playing with a plastic truck, held within him the same omnipotent potential – a universal being trapped in a human form.

Avalon, innocent and unaware of his true nature, continued on blissfully, but Asparus couldn't shake off the sense of dread that gripped him. What would become of Avalon once he realized the extent of his abilities? He envisioned the potential of this boundless power, untamed and unguided, twisting reality into an unrecognizable kaleidoscope of chaos.

The weight of this realization pressed down upon him, his hands trembling uncontrollably. His face was etched with a tapestry of fear, regret, and a desperate, illogical hope that perhaps, just perhaps, he was wrong.

Time passed seamlessly....

Asparus, a shell of his former self, absented himself from work, haunted by the specter of his own creation. He had taken Avalon on a solitary trip to a remote mountaintop, a fleeting reward for the boy's academic achievement. Now, they sat in tense silence, bathed in the ethereal glow of the moon peeking through wispy clouds.

The air held a charged anticipation, as if nature itself held its breath. Avalon, normally fearless, clung tightly to his father, seeking solace in the familiar warmth. As the first snowflakes began to dance in the moonlight, the sky above them erupted in a breathtaking display of the aurora borealis—a maelstrom of shimmering light painting the inky canvas.

"His power is already blooming," Asparus whispered to himself, his voice laced with a chilling fear, his eyes never leaving Avalon.

"This was the best trip ever," Avalon said softly. "I love you, Dad."

"I love you too, son," he longed to reply, the words catching thick in his throat.

But the serenity shattered in a heartbeat. The world, once bathed in an ethereal glow, convulsed with a sudden, horrifying violence. A scream, raw and agonizing, ripped through the thin mountain air.

Avalon crumpled to the ground, his trusting eyes wide with betrayal as they stared at the knife protruding from his back. The Crux, forged from the essence of obliterated gods, gleamed accusingly in the moonlight.

Asparus stood frozen, his face contorted in a mask of unimaginable anguish, the weapon still clutched in his trembling hand. His eyes, heavy with sorrow, stared at his palms, roughened by years of hardship. The tips of his fingers, mirroring the desolate emptiness gripping his soul, reached for the inky black space – a void where stars dared not shine, where galaxies themselves seemed extinguished.

A single tear, the first to mar the eternal canvas of his existence, traced a warm path down his cheek. It was a foreign sensation, a testament to the depth of his grief. "So this is what it feels like," he choked out, his voice a rasp torn from his very core, "to cry."

He had been presented with an impossible choice – his purpose, the very reason for his being, or his son. He had chosen, and in that agonizing instant, he had lost both.

The auroras, once a breathtaking display of celestial fireworks, faded, replaced by an ominous gathering of storm clouds. The moon, like a beacon of hope extinguished, vanished, leaving Asparus shrouded in an endless, suffocating darkness.

He never returned home. Instead, he became a specter, a broken deity trapped in a tattered human shell. He wandered aimlessly, a desolate nomad traversing the barren landscape of his own despair. Hunger gnawed at his insides; a dull ache compared to the gaping maw of loss that threatened to consume him.

Weeks blurred into one another; his journey marked by the growing indifference in the eyes of strangers as he spent the nights lying on footpaths.

A weathered priest, his gaze a wellspring of compassion, spotted Asparus slumped by the roadside. The once-proud being resembled a discarded husk, his eyes hollow and reflecting the desolate emptiness above.

The priest, his own heart etched with the passage of time, knelt beside him, offering a canteen and a loaf of bread.

"This is a gift from the Lord, son," he spoke softly, his voice a balm against the harsh wind.

A raspy whisper, barely audible, escaped Asparus' lips. "No, I don't need sustenance," His attention, however, snagged on the faint hymns drifting from the nearby church.

A question, long buried, clawed its way to the surface. "Why," he rasped again, this time with a hint of genuine curiosity, "do you pray to... God?"

"For he made us, for he is the supreme," The priest replied gently, **"for he knows all the right answers."**

Asparus threw back his head and let out a laugh, a harsh, ragged sound that echoed through the emptiness. It was the hardest, the loudest laugh he had ever uttered, laced with a chilling mix of despair and defiance.

Asparus' face hardened, and a bitter silence descended. He stared deep into the priest's eyes, a lifetime of existential questions swirling within them. Then, with a humorless scoff, he clenched his fist and roared, **"RIGHT ANSWERS HUH… EVEN THE GOD DOESN'T KNOW!"**